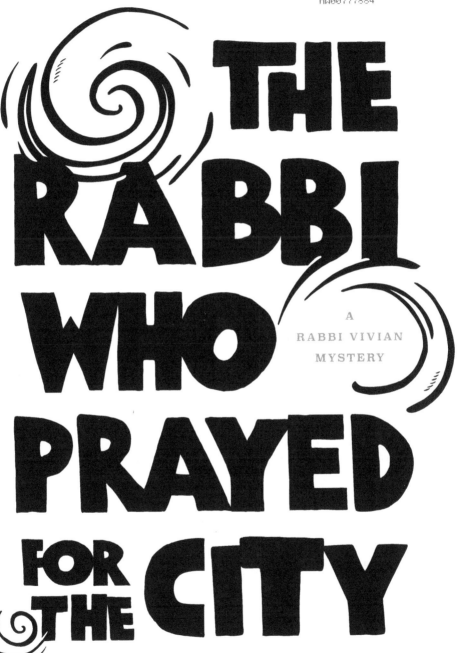

THE RABBI WHO PRAYED FOR THE CITY

A RABBI VIVIAN MYSTERY

RACHEL SHARONA LEWIS

Rachel Sharona Lewis
Watertown, MA
rachelsharonalewis@gmail.com

ISBN: 979-8-218-23113-2
Ebook ISBN: 979-8-218-23114-9

Book design and composition by Brian Phillips Design
Cover design by Brian Phillips Design
Edited by Anna Schnur-Fishman

First Edition

Printed in the United States of America

for Liz and Raya

CHAPTER ONE

"WHO KNEW THAT rabbis could be so good at karaoke?" said a voice behind Rabbi Vivian Green. She turned to see who it was. The darkness, cut by a neon strobe light hovering above, made it difficult to identify the speaker at first. But once the light rotated, Vivian noticed an older man who looked familiar standing close to her in the crowd. She grasped for his name but couldn't remember it.

Vivian was in upstate New York, along with a hundred or so other rabbis, attending the annual pre-High Holiday retreat hosted by Tekiyah: The Justice League of Rabbis. Most of the time, the organization trained rabbis to engage in social justice campaigns, but tonight was the final night of the gathering, and the organizers were definitely convinced that rabbis could—and *would*—flourish in the art of karaoke. Indeed, many of the participants braved the makeshift stage in the retreat center's dining hall and sang nineties pop hits and a few surprising contemporary songs to boot.

Vivian sloshed her drink around. "Why would any rabbi think that other rabbis couldn't do karaoke?" she asked, leaning closer to her friend and mentor, Mimi Geller. "It's not like we're monks."

"Hey!" Mimi said. "Monks can probably do karaoke just as well as the rest of us." She sipped her drink as a Reform rabbi from Arizona fell spectacularly short of the high note in a pop ballad. "And just as badly," she added, wincing.

Vivian raised her glass in Mimi's direction. "You make a very well-reasoned point. As usual." Mimi smiled, nodding in agreement. She had been Vivian's rabbi in college and, over the years, had made the shift to trusted colleague.

"So," Mimi said loudly, since she was competing with the instrumental intro of a Lady Gaga song. "How are you feeling about your decision to stay at Beth Abraham?"

Vivian sighed. "Good, I guess." She popped a potato chip into her mouth. "You know, fine," she said, crunching with perhaps a little more force than was necessary. "It's all well and good. It's—" She snapped up another chip. "It's okay, you know? The pay increase is nice. And that extra Friday night off each month...."

Mimi laughed in her characteristic mouth-wide-open fashion. It had been way too long since Vivian had gotten to hear that ridiculously loud laugh in person. At the comforting sound, her words began to rush out.

"You have to put in so much time wherever you are in order

to do the things that you really want to do, and even when you get to that point, it's not perfect, and so this seems like the right thing. The *good enough* right thing."

"That makes sense, I guess," Mimi responded, "even if you don't sound quite sure of it yourself." She was intimately familiar with the twists and turns of Vivian's rabbinate, and had had her own fair share as a congregational rabbi, though she had left the pulpit a few years earlier to take a job with Tekiyah. "But I wonder," Mimi continued, "if you could dream up your perfect job, would it be so different?"

Vivian closed her eyes, attempting to focus despite the prison chaplain belting out the chorus of "Born This Way" and dozens of rabbis either singing along or murmuring in side conversations all around her, ice rustling in their plastic cups.

She thought back to the morning's panel about different ways that congregations had worked with local allies to support their broader communities. Vivian had been one of the participants, sharing about how she helped organize Beth Abraham to build affordable housing on a piece of vacant land they owned. A rabbi from the Midwest described how her synagogue and several churches were working together to fill gaps in abortion care impacting their region. And a group of rabbis from California recounted how they had established an accompaniment network to welcome hundreds of Central Americans seeking asylum at the southern border.

"When I spoke on that panel today, everyone was so complimentary about our housing effort, and as soon as I walked off the stage, I felt like...maybe I'm fooling myself that I can do more there. Like, what if that's the only big win I ever have at Beth

Abraham? What if that was the only half-court shot I make, and the rest are just airballs?"

"Hairballs…for the rest of your career? That *would* be bad," Mimi said, leaning in closer, bellowing above the music. "But, as a cat lesbian, I appreciate you speaking my language." Vivian rolled her eyes. Sometimes a cat lesbian and a sports lesbian could barely communicate.

Yet Vivian *was* proud of Congregation Beth Abraham, and of her leadership there. And now that the senior rabbi, Joseph Glass, was finally retiring after years of hinting at it, and that she had officially been offered and accepted his position, she could have more of an impact, perhaps even avoid more *hairballs*. Indeed, the possibility of becoming the senior rabbi was part of why she had spent seven years in an associate position that most rabbis would have kept for only half the time.

But still…she wondered. What about always needing to be the one to initiate social justice projects and conversations, while knowing that to some congregants, she was just a young bleeding heart (and worse, occasionally wondering if they were right)? What about the inevitable board meeting, after any incident of antisemitic violence somewhere in the country, in which members voted to ramp up police presence, backtracking on past commitments to reduce it? What about the board president's cheery pitch to buy Israel Bonds every Rosh Hashanah, when she wondered if she was the only one worried that investing in Israel in that way meant investing in the state's endless occupation and persecution of Palestinians and increasing erosion of democracy?

Maybe there was a different congregation, a different job,

where things wouldn't be so…what was the word? *Incoherent*, she thought, and then realized she had said it aloud.

Mimi looked at her and seemed to decide that she could guess Vivian's train of thought well enough. "From what you've told me, Beth Abraham has actually been quite open to change," she said. "And, anyway, I think that you naturally gravitate toward people and communities that you can lovingly push, Viv. You may never have the perfect job, or the most *coherent* one, but it's clear that you have power there."

Vivian rolled her eyes again.

"I'm serious!" Mimi shouted over a Nirvana riff. "Your community *chose* you; they chose your vision. Now is the time to act, to work for the changes you want." Mimi paused, sipping her drink. "And maybe for a rabbinic partner who can hold that vision with you so you don't feel so alone."

"Hmm." Vivian tried to picture it. A broader swath of community members, not just the usual suspects, taking on roles in Beth Abraham's justice work. An associate rabbi who would be a true teammate, who she would strategize *with* instead of *around*.

Suddenly, a jaunty guitar hook filled the room, a refrain that Vivian would have recognized anywhere. She looked at the stage and saw two rabbis bouncing to the beat. One was an old friend from rabbinical school, Phil Schulman, who was gesturing to the rest of the room to clap along. Vivian laughed. It was very like Phil Schulman for his karaoke song to be an Indigo Girls hit.

The chorus of "Closer to Fine" soon filled the room. Vivian, Mimi, and many others picked it up right away. Swaying together, they shouted out the lyrics. "I went to the doctor, I went to the mountains / ....And the less I seek my source for some definitive / Closer I am to—" The whole room erupted in "fiiiiiiiine, yeah."

"You can always count on Rav Emily and Rav Amy to speak the truths we need to hear," Mimi said. Vivian listened closely to the verses, willing the words to settle into her mind.

Her eyes wandered back to Phil. *Hmm*, she thought. *Handsome...but not too handsome.* He led davening beautifully, as she had been reminded over the course of the retreat. His kids probably belted out classic feminist anthems and led Shabbat morning prayers well, too....

"Mimi!" Vivian shouted, leaning toward her. "Should Karla and I ask Phil Schulman to be our sperm donor?"

Phil was back on the chorus and dozens of singing rabbis surrounded them. Mimi shook her head and pointed at her ear.

"I SAID," Vivian repeated, "SHOULD KARLA AND I ASK—" It occurred to her that it might be good to cup her hands around Mimi's ear to finish the question.

Mimi let out her fantastic laugh. "Sorry about that. You're hard to keep up with, Vivian Green." Mimi kept dancing, but her eyes focused in on Phil as he serenaded the roomful of rabbis. "Maybe you should," she continued. "As long as you're okay with the potential offspring having a genetic predisposition to becoming a rabbi."

Vivian considered Mimi's point. An immediate, visceral reaction indicated that she did not at all want that for her child. But she was not sure that put Phil out of the running. She was probably not going to get everything she wanted when it came to a sperm donor.

Or a job. But she resolved to try.

Vivian smiled, feeling satisfied enough with her options, as she and Mimi danced harder when Whitney Houston's "I Wanna Dance with Somebody" began blasting through the room.

CHAPTER TWO

K̲ARLA DIXON LISTENED TO the hum of the printer as pages upon pages whirred past her, full of graphs and tables. She maneuvered a series of sheets out of the stack and stapled them together: "The Predicted Impact of Climate Change on Hurricanes in the New England Region: 2026–2036."

Flipping through the report's pages, Karla stopped at a graph that caught her eye. It showed the steadily increasing number of damaging storms that could come Providence's way as warming temperatures continued to shift weather patterns. She grabbed the full pile, which felt much heavier than a stack of paper should be, and set out for her department's meeting room down the hall.

Karla was a veteran of the administration of Mayor Margaret

Heath, who was now in her second term. After earning a master's in urban planning while working full-time at City Hall, Karla had risen in the ranks of Providence's Executive Office of Climate Adaptation and Resiliency, now headed by Winona MacLean.

MacLean, known to her colleagues as Nona, was widely respected for decades of work in disaster preparedness and response. For much of her career, she had worked for a variety of municipal governments in Virginia, but a few years earlier, she had accepted this position and moved to town. She told her colleagues that, as a member of the Narragansett nation, she appreciated the opportunity to return to Rhode Island, where her ancestors had lived and stewarded the land for tens of thousands of years.

She was a good boss, whip-smart, and she granted a great deal of autonomy to her staff...though Karla wished that Nona believed in the whole positive-feedback-in-the-workplace thing. She figured, though, that being the city's "chief catastrophist," as Nona referred to herself, made that difficult.

Karla walked into the meeting room and plopped down the armful of packets in front of her boss and several coworkers. They all sat silently, poring over the charts, until Nona spoke.

"There's no way to sugarcoat these figures. The projections continue to get worse. But I hear from our contacts in Washington that the feds are going to direct billions of dollars to municipalities in light of the new predictions."

"That's a relief," Karla said, flipping a page. "Though we can guarantee it won't be enough." She felt continuously surprised at how easy she now found it to state these apocalyptic realities out loud. Working in *this* office, for *this* boss, had forced her and her colleagues to become more acquainted with the truth. That, and the once-in-a-hundred-year storms that kept coming every few years. To Texas. To Florida. New York. The Carolinas. It was only a matter of time.

"It's something, and for now, it's what we've got," MacLean said. "Let's revisit the resiliency plan and figure out where the additional funds will most help our preparations." She paused to sip tea from a glittery silver travel mug that never seemed to leave her side. "And we'll need to communicate early and often with the budget office. These collaborations will be key to our survival."

Karla thought back to a prayer that she had heard her wife reviewing the previous week, a Rosh Hashanah classic listing the ways people might perish in the coming year. *Who by fire and who by water? Who by hunger and who by thirst? Who by earthquake and who by plague?* Though the prayer offered strategies for people to disrupt these decrees, the lack of political analysis, the lack of identifying who and what was responsible for these disasters, always made her blood boil.

Now that Karla had been with Vivian for six years, these mental jumps to prayers and biblical verses happened more and more. At first, it had felt like a complete stranger was inhabiting her brain. But a few years in, she had begun to play with these floating bits of text, even edit them when necessary. *Who by unjust resource distribution and who by government negligence?*

"Let's meet with Secretary Fox's team as soon as we can," MacLean said. "Karla, set that up, would you?"

"On it," she said.

The team discussed a few other pressing topics and then ended the meeting. As they walked out of the room alongside each other, Karla turned toward MacLean.

"Got any plans tonight?" she asked hopefully.

Every now and then, Karla tried to connect more with her boss, but in the years they had worked together, she had not made much progress. Outside of her official bio, Karla still had only a handful of clues that hinted at who Winona MacLean was.

She had one picture framed on her wall, a quote from Chief Joseph Nez Perce. *It does not require many words to tell the truth.* Occasionally Karla caught sight of a tennis racket in the corner of Nona's office, or at least a case shaped like one. There had also been one vague mention of a daughter; Karla imagined an adult, but didn't know for sure.

"I'll probably be curling up with a cup of tea and this report," MacLean replied. "Imagining what we might need to prevent total doom."

"That, um…sounds about right," Karla said, nodding, as though that was exactly what she had meant by "plans." She knew not to expect her boss to reciprocate the ask, but she still held out hope for a moment. Someday it could happen.

. . .

Karla had made quite a few plans—which, by the way, she would have been happy to share with her boss—in order to keep herself occupied while Vivian was away at the Tekiyah retreat. She'd been determined to get a lot of work done *and* to catch up with some friends she hadn't seen in a while, and tonight she would be meeting her buddy Freddy Fuentes at the new local brewery.

Unfortunately, Vivian did not appreciate a quality craft brew. She preferred hard cider, and in fact only tolerated beers that tasted, in her words, "fruity," which inspired a good deal of teasing. Karla, on the other hand, had practically counted down the days until LadiesLadies Brewery opened. She had sold Vivian on the narrative—a brewery in a refurbished barn fifteen minutes outside of Providence, run by two middle-aged lesbians who, by the looks of it on Instagram, were also the proud parents of three adorable beagles—and Vivian was open to it, but something always came up. And thus, scheduling this outing with Freddy had been at the top of Karla's list as soon as Vivian announced that she would be out of town.

When she had finished all sixty-seven pages of the new report, Karla made her way there, leaving City Hall just in time to arrive at LadiesLadies a few minutes before eight p.m. She parked in a gravel lot in front of the maroon barn. It was a hot night, cut by a gentle late-summer breeze, but the warmth was to be expected these days. Every September was hotter than the last.

The open barn doors revealed coils of tiny lights strung around vertical and horizontal wooden beams, and plaid everywhere: the tablecloths, the bar, the clothing of the other patrons. Karla found Freddy fast, even though he too was dressed in the uniform, blending easily into the background.

"You didn't get the memo?" Freddy said, scanning Karla's outfit: navy suit pants and a collarless green blouse.

"I guess I got too distracted by the cute puppies on the website to notice the dress code," Karla said. "Plus, I came straight from work. I hope they let me stay."

They found an open spot toward the back of the bar. From a nearby table, a plaid-clad waiter clearing dishes waved hello.

Karla and Freddy had been friends ever since they lived on

the same floor their first year of college. They had bonded over lesser-known indie rock bands, queerness, and their mutual love for a quirky economics professor who wove radical politics into her teaching. Freddy, along with his partner, Camille, had moved to Providence a few years earlier when he got a job at Leviathan Labs, a robotics company that had come to town not long before that.

"It's nice to be somewhere new for once," Freddy noted, scanning the drink list.

"Tell me about it," Karla said. "And I don't even have the excuse of being cooped up with a toddler. Speaking of which, how's Xo? Any new party tricks?"

"Of course!" Freddy said, sipping from a glass of water adorned with a thick wedge of lemon. "She's saying what seem like new words every day. But I can't always tell what they are. We were walking past a garden a few days ago and we heard her say something that sounded like, 'Eat flower.' But Camille was convinced that Xo said, 'Fight power.'"

Karla laughed. "Either way, it won't be too long before she's fighting the good fight."

"That's the hope," Freddy said. "As long as she is obedient to her parents."

"Hmm." Karla lifted an eyebrow. "I wonder if you can have it both ways."

"I'll report back on that experiment," Freddy said, looking back at the menu. "But first, let's get drinks."

They approached the counter and ordered from another employee decked out in plaid—some hoppy beers that Vivian definitely would not like, nachos, and a serving of fried pickles that the menu had been pushing hard with larger print. They retrieved their beers and a number stand and headed back toward their table.

"Freddy!" someone shouted. They detoured and Freddy greeted someone who was, from what Karla could tell, a coworker of his. He chatted for a moment, then they continued on.

"I guess it's hard to avoid Leviathan employees wherever you go, huh?" Karla asked, settling back into her wooden chair.

"We do seem to be taking over."

"So how are the robots coming along? Do *they* have any new party tricks?"

"Pretty good, if I do say so myself," Freddy answered. "The form lab has made some breakthroughs with agility and terrain adaptation over the past few months. Hyydra can now scale basically any landscape!" Karla got the feeling that Freddy had recently made this report to investors. "And the autonomous control system my team is building will ensure she makes good navigation decisions as fast as possible."

Even after years of hearing these updates, Karla still had trouble believing that Leviathan Labs was in the business of building robots programmed for Mars exploration.

"Congrats, Fred," she said, with a smile that she knew did not quite reach her eyes.

Freddy took a sip of beer. "Look, I know you're skeptical. Hell, I am too. But my boss is committed to building the least volatile product out there. So we're basically leading the way on harm reduction robotics."

"That's a great sales pitch!" Karla said. "Maybe you should join the marketing department."

Freddy rolled his eyes. "Joke all you want, Kar. But I don't think you can deny—it's pretty dope." He took out his phone and started scrolling. "Here, let me show you." He handed the phone to Karla, and she reluctantly pressed play on a video he had pulled up. Hyydra, a four-legged robot with a long rectangular torso, was dancing to a pop song that Karla kept hearing on the radio but did not know the name of. Hyydra's spry gray legs bent and crisscrossed to the beat. About twelve seconds into the clip, at the song's bridge, she spun around.

"That is in fact pretty dope," Karla said. "But somehow it just adds to my sense of existential despair."

"Ah. I can see where this is going."

Karla sighed. "How can I even consider bringing a kid into this world? Where there are more and more climate disasters by the week? And robots settling Mars?"

Just then, a waiter appeared with their nachos. He dropped them off without saying a word, and Karla wondered how much he had heard.

"I just keep waiting for a sign," she continued, "or some sort of feeling of clarity that it's the right time. And Vivian and I have both been so busy, and there's so much shit that—"

"I don't think there will ever be a moment that will seem perfectly right for procreating," Freddy said, interrupting Karla's spiral. "Everything will always be a mess. Sea levels continue to rise, and racism and sexism and transphobia—"

"And economic inequality—"

"And ableism and—"

"And xenophobia—"

"And antisemitism—"

"And a terrible lack of access to fried pickles, which I just realized is a human right," Karla sighed, noticing that part of their order had yet to arrive.

Freddy smirked. "And none of these seem to be going away," he said, popping a nacho into his mouth. "Though hopefully we will eventually get our fried pickles."

"I see your point. I guess it still doesn't feel right *enough* for us." Karla carefully lifted a tortilla chip chock full of toppings. "For me."

"You never know. Feeling clear enough may just sneak up on you. That's what happened to Camille and me." Freddy took a large gulp of beer and paused. "That, and we decided we didn't want these other assholes who have made terrible, greedy decisions to dictate our choices."

Karla sighed again.

"It's complicated," he conceded. "But just remember Xo's advice."

"And what's that?" she asked, leaning back.

"Fight the power."

. . .

Karla congratulated herself on timing it perfectly. Just as she and Freddy were paying their bill, Vivian texted that her train would arrive soon. Karla drove to the station, and when she pulled up, her wife was sitting outside on a bench, seeming to glow in the rays of the streetlights.

Vivian caught sight of Karla and stood up, rolling her suitcase toward the car. Karla hopped out to hug her, enjoying the familiar smell of Vivian's shampoo that hit her.

"I missed you," she said.

"Me too," Vivian murmured into Karla's neck.

Karla pulled back and glanced at Vivian's bag, thinking about how their demanding and uncooperative work schedules, not to mention the years she was in graduate school, had often kept them from vacations, together or on their own. She wondered when they would next get to pack their matching suitcases—wedding gifts from Karla's favorite uncle—together. She grabbed the bag and shimmied it into the trunk.

"Off we go," Karla said, as they settled into the car. "So how was it? Any highlights, besides hanging out with Mimi?" She remembered the video clips and reports of karaoke that Vivian had sent the night before. "Oh, and of course drunk-spexting me!"

"What?! I did *not*…" Vivian shifted into a whisper, "sext you, Karla Dixon."

"No, no. Spext," Karla said, enunciating the *p*. "It's texting about sperm donor prospects."

Vivian cracked up. "Just call me Director of Donor Relations."

"Oh, that's good!" Karla said. "You should add that to your business card…next to Senior Rabbi."

"Noted," Vivian replied. "And yes, there was more. For example, in other news, you'll appreciate that Tekiyah is focusing more resources on work dealing with the impacts of climate change at the local level. This one rabbi from Florida talked about how her clergy group pushed their city council to develop a surprisingly strong resiliency plan. And now they're keeping up the pressure so it actually happens."

"Glad to hear it!" Karla enthused, careful to keep her eyes on the road. "If I had known rabbis could do all that, it might have taken a lower bar than marrying you to get me back into a synagogue."

Vivian giggled. "It turns out there's still lots to do to improve the one you do come to. Now that my contract is set, I think it's time to push for some other changes to make Beth Abraham more into the community I know we can be."

"Hmm. Sounds like you found a little inspiration on your travels." Karla put her free hand on Vivian's. "Well, I believe in you, and I'm sure you'll be very convincing…and I've already gotten what I want, now that you'll have more Friday nights off." Vivian flipped over her palm and squeezed Karla's fingers.

"And it seems good to start pushing for change now," Karla continued, "you know…." Her sentence trailed off as she peered ahead, looking for a parking spot. "Before a baby," she found herself adding finally. She furrowed her brow, wondering if she really meant what this suggested. Vivian, seeming to echo the question, cocked her head, though Karla couldn't tell if she was pleased or wary.

They found a parking spot near their house—which was no small victory ever since a huge building of condos had gone up a few streets over. Karla put the car into park and exhaled.

Perhaps there was more to discuss, but they were both exhausted. Karla leaned over and kissed her wife. They gathered their bags and made their way inside.

CHAPTER THREE

"**I**'M IMPRESSED THAT YOU had time to cook, given the season," Reverend Heather Wu said, placing a dollop of sour cream onto a bowl of butternut squash soup at Vivian and Karla's kitchen counter.

"Karla deserves the credit. She did all the prep," Vivian said. "Plus, I needed the break, and meals between the services provide just the opportunity."

"Ha! So hosting a Rosh Hashanah dinner with a priest is a break from ritual and community?"

"Totally. It's like an all-star break in the middle of the season." Vivian passed another bowl of soup to Heather, who was tasked with adding the fixings.

"I get that. I mean, not the sports reference, as usual, but the sentiment. Sometimes you just need a moment away from *your* community." They both continued their tasks, absorbing the errant sounds coming from the dining room where the others sat.

Vivian had been friends with Heather, who served an Episcopal church across town, ever since arriving in Providence. For years now, they had been confidantes who could regularly commiserate about the challenges of working with and tolerating older male superiors. And each offered the other cover when they brought their boards suggestions from "other clergy around town" for cross-faith collaboration.

"Viv…what's this?"

Vivian turned around and saw that the priest was neglecting her job. Instead, she was peeling a pink Post-it from the side of the refrigerator. If Vivian recalled correctly, it had been pretty well hidden among a jumble of magnets and outdated New Year's cards featuring friends' adorable children.

Vivian gulped as she set down another bowl on the counter. "Um. It's, uh…." She turned back to the giant pot, calculating that after scooping one last bowl, she could "accidentally" overturn it as a diversion. It would be wasteful, though, and messy. She tried to think of a believable lie instead, but quickly realized that her response had already taken too long to avoid suspicion.

"It's our list of potential sperm donors," Vivian mumbled in surrender.

Heather stared at Vivian. Then she roared with laughter, her gesticulating arm accidentally shoving the tub of sour cream like a hockey puck across the slick counter, dislodging a few of the glass bowls from their original spots.

So much for avoiding mess. Vivian wondered if anyone else heard the commotion and might start asking questions. In the other room, Karla was chatting with her friend Freddy, his partner, Camille, and their one-and-a-half-year-old, Xiomara, plus Heather's husband, Paul, and their five-year-old, Addie.

Heather continued to study the note sticking to her finger. "And this 'Paul' on the list. I'm guessing that's my husband, Paul?"

The running list of potential donors had been on the side of their refrigerator for a few months now. There was Karla's friend Matty from college. Kind, smart, very funny, San Francisco resident. Gay. Obviously. There was Vivian's cousin Rafi, checking most of the same boxes. Phil Schulman, who Vivian had added after the Tekiyah retreat. And….

"Um. Yes. That Paul," Vivian said. "It's just, well, we don't know too many amazing men. And if he was local, it could make the logistics so much easier. Plus, he has clearly already dealt with the existential questions that come up for men when you ask about procreation."

"Unlike Rafi, I suppose?" Heather said, pointing at the penciled strike through his name.

"Right," Vivian said, although Rafi wasn't completely scratched from the list: he just wasn't a top contender anymore since he had recently taken a job in Brussels.

"Have you actually asked anyone?"

"Not yet. We've started to write an email once or twice, but…." Vivian finally turned back to the stove and handed Heather the last steaming bowl. "Do you know, through this process I've learned that there isn't even one Etsy vendor that sells 'Will you be my sperm donor?' cards? Seems like a market just asking to be cornered. Though I did find a shirt sold by someone in California that says, 'I donated my sperm and all I got was this lousy t-shirt.'"

Heather bobbed her head. "Hmm...let's think." She had also returned to her task, sprinkling croutons over the dollops of sour cream. "How about 'roses are red, violets are blue'...no, no, that's not going to work." She continued garnishing the bowls. "Okay! I've got one! 'This egg is swiping right on your sperm.'" Heather pantomimed it, drawing a cheeky check mark in the air with her free hand.

"Ooh!" Vivian yelped. "Or, 'Seeking donations for 100 million...reproductive cells.' And then we could send a follow-up: 'Thank you for your meaningful contribution.'"

"Oh, that is good! Perhaps even tax deductible. Let's go with that," Heather said, dashing green onions onto each serving. "Now that that's settled, I'm not opposed to you asking Paul, if this is your strange and passive way of investigating that option."

"Thanks, though I'm not really clear on where we are in the process. We've gone back and forth for a while now." Vivian stretched her neck, trying to get a glimpse into the dining room, as she wondered what Karla might say. "But who knows, perhaps a curious card will soon grace your mailbox."

"I'll keep a lookout," Heather said. "Though I have to warn you, Addie is getting very sassy. So beware!"

"Oh, that definitely comes from you, though, not Paul."

"Right, okay. You can just go on believing that you will be able to fully control the behavior of your future children." Heather refastened the Post-it to its original spot, but it didn't stick. She rubbed it with more force and it stayed in place.

"I will do just that," Vivian said.

Heather rolled her eyes, balanced three bowls of soup on a tray, and turned toward the dining room. Vivian stared at the Post-it as she hoisted the second tray. In her mind, she drew a small star by Paul's name.

The kitchen contingent entered the dining room to the cheers of a hungry crowd already demolishing a second challah. Once everyone had been served, oohing and ahhing over Heather's decorative flourishes, they settled into their seats. Xiomara, sitting between Freddy and Camille, clapped her hands expectantly.

"Uh-oh. Ever since we let her taste some, Xo seems to think that anything served in a bowl is ice cream," Freddy said. "I hope she's not too vocal about her disappointment."

"She won't be," Paul said. "This is delicious, Karla! You've got to give me the recipe. I'm always looking for new ones."

"Will do, Paul," Karla said.

Vivian smiled in Heather's direction.

Addie picked up her own bowl and started slurping. "Addie seems to like it, too!" Heather said. "But honey, we use our *spoons* for soup." She slid the spoon her daughter wasn't using closer to her hand.

"But why, mommy?" she whined. "*Drinking* soup is more easy."

"Because that's the rule, honey."

"Says who?" Addie retorted.

"Says the manners police," Heather said, rolling her eyes.

"But you don't like the police," Addie shot back.

Vivian and others failed at holding in their laughter.

"She makes a strong point," Karla whispered loudly.

"It just seems like we're supposed to train her to have 'good manners' or something," Heather said. "But then—I mean, it is indeed *more easy* to drink soup." She threw up her hands. Paul took over unsuccessfully nudging the spoon toward their child. "When you guys have kids, you can make your own decisions about which social constructs to leave by the wayside," she said, looking straight at Vivian.

Karla turned toward Heather and then elegantly shot the briefest of glares Vivian's way, plainly asking with her eyes what Heather knew.

"So Viv! How's the, uh, the planning for Joseph's retirement going?" Heather asked, seemingly aware that a change of subject was in order.

Vivian swallowed. "There's still a lot to figure out. But at least after years and years of his waffling, change is afoot."

"Why has it been so drawn out?" Paul asked.

"I think Joseph's whole identity has been wrapped up in being a rabbi. Even though he's seemed tired of many parts of the job for years, I don't think he has a sense of who he is without the title."

"Does he have any hobbies?" Camille asked, trying to feed a resistant Xo a spoonful of soup. "That's what most people throw themselves into in retirement. Most of my writing classes are made up of recent retirees." When she wasn't writing her own queer sci-fi novels, Camille taught fiction classes at a few places around town.

"That's the problem with humans," Freddy tsk-tsked. "So flawed and irrational, even when the obvious answers are right in front of us."

"And this is why robots should be in charge, right?" Karla asked.

"You said it, not me," Freddy said, folding his arms and leaning back in his chair. "But seriously, if we had all the information in front of us, all of the relevant inputs as well as all the possible outcomes of our decisions, and were able to logically and mathematically weigh them out, don't you think we'd make better decisions?"

Vivian and Paul nodded their heads politely. "I think that's B.S.," Karla said. "There are lots of people who make the right calls when given the right information. The issue isn't that all humans are flawed, it's that the people making the most consequential decisions are often the most flawed of the bunch." She paused to sip her wine. "I'd much rather Margaret Heath or Winona MacLean make important decisions about the fate of our planet than robots."

"Okay, Kar, you've got a point. And yet, most people with decision-making power—especially global decision-making power—are not even in Heath or MacLean's league," Freddy countered. "So, let's reframe the question. Would you prefer a well-trained robot, programmed to have at least a modicum of moral discernment, calling the shots—or the vast majority of our political leaders, elected through an increasingly less democratic system? Not to mention the shortsighted billionaires hoarding unchecked wealth and influence outside of public view."

Paul sighed. "When you put it like that, the robots don't sound so bad."

"I'd still go with the humans," Heather said. "It just seems like there is a clear ethical line we cross if we cede our politics and power to machines. Even if they are trained to weigh out data better than us."

"Look," Freddy said. "I share y'alls ambivalence. But these

machines are coming—they're already here—and they are going
to be relied upon more and more, whether we like it or not. And
the ones my company is building will be a real improvement, if
not over elected political leaders, then at least over the alternative
first explorers on Mars."

"Mars?!" Heather yelped. Addie, startled, stopped slurping
for a minute, and the absence of that noise made Vivian realize
how unpleasantly loud it had been. She surreptitiously inched the
twice-abandoned spoon back toward the child.

"That's right," Freddy said. "Our prototype will be exploring
Mars in a few years. And again, the technology is inevitable, so
we may as well make it the best it can be." He tossed an extra
crouton into his mouth. "I'm telling you, Hyydra's been trained
to be way more careful than a colonialist human has ever been."

Camille spoke up. She was still optimistically holding a spoonful of soup up to Xiomara's sour face, even though the kid had
firmly closed her lips after her first taste ten minutes earlier. "And
that kind of change can only happen if there are good engineers,
who make good decisions, in on the ground floor." She looked
at Freddy lovingly.

"Sounds familiar," Karla whispered to Vivian. Vivian nodded,
knowing that she and others at the table could relate.

Xiomara suddenly sneezed, sending bright-orange droplets of
soup all over her highchair tray and the left side of Freddy's button-down. Freddy automatically wiped her nose with his napkin.

"What I still can't get over," Karla said, undistracted, "is the
amount of investment pouring into robotic Mars exploration when
we are living in a climate emergency, when this hurricane season
has already wreaked havoc on Florida and Texas. Again. When

fires are raging in California. Again. The leaders enabling these out-of-whack priorities are the decision-makers we need to oust! And while Providence is certainly ahead of the curve on preparation, we are so not ready to handle that kind of chaos." Karla scraped the sides of her bowl for the last bits of buttery squash. "Can you get your robots to solve *those* problems?"

"We've each got our part to do, baby," Vivian said, patting Karla's knee. "It's not all on Freddy."

"Well," Heather piped up. "My church just put solar panels on our roof, after talking about it for about a decade. So, we've pretty much done our part."

"Oh, great," Karla said. "Glad to hear our problems are solved."

"Jeez. If I'd known that was all it took to assuage your fears about investment in space exploration—and bringing kids into the world, perhaps?—I would have told you months ago," Heather said. "From now on, you'll be the first to know. In another 10 years and 10,000 vestry meetings, we might even go fully compostable or something."

Karla dropped her face into her hands. Vivian rubbed her wife's back. And Addie continued to drink her soup straight from the bowl, as no one bothered to correct her.

CHAPTER FOUR

THE DAYS OF AWE were Rabbi Joseph Glass's favorite time of year. Every Rosh Hashanah and Yom Kippur, and the days between them, jolted him back to his sense of purpose. While the weekly sermons might have felt stale on occasion—after all, he'd spent decades finding different ways to articulate the same insights (for example: maybe Abraham actually *failed* the test of the binding of Isaac; paying shul dues is akin to building the *mishkan*; it's good that kashrut is hard!)—he always saved his biggest, most earnest questions for this season.

This year, throughout his preparations, he hadn't been able to shake his excitement about moving to Israel after retirement—nor his guilt that, at this age, he was still living in the diaspora, when as a young man he always thought he was just a few years away from making the ultimate commitment. A particular vision of the future kept coming to him. Somewhere in Jerusalem, he would finish studying a page of Talmud and walk to a nearby café to get lunch…but without leaving the alef-bet behind in his office. The holy language of his texts and his people would finally accompany him everywhere.

Meanwhile, he had a little more time here, in Beth Abraham's sanctuary, sitting in the senior rabbi's chair while Vivian chanted the end of the Torah portion for Rosh Hashanah's second day. He scanned the packed room. Ever since the fire that raged through the building six years earlier, ever since the consequent rebuilding of the sanctuary, he had not felt fully at home here.

The seats were situated closer to the *bimah* than they had originally been, and the rabbis now sat with the *kahal* in order to minimize what the design committee called "experiential distance" between the clergy and the rest of the community. And all the chairs were movable now, though they were nearly always positioned, as they were that day, in a semicircle—so that members of the community could "be present together." (Before the rebuilding, had his congregants been present *separately*? Or absent together?) More windows welcomed an abundance of light into the space on sunny days, and the walls had been painted a color called *oatmeal*. Upon hearing that detail, Joseph had been quite distracted by the thought of a PR team promoting unattractive foods in the color lexicon. The company could just as easily have called this shade *gefilte fish*. Maybe that one had made the list for Israeli paint manufacturers.

And so, each time he entered the sanctuary nowadays, he

would think, *This is beautiful, but it must be some other rabbi's shul.*
At least the *aron* looked familiar; they had been able to salvage a
few pieces of the sanctuary's original wood paneling to make it.
And the Torahs inside of it, thank God, had been pulled from the
old ark before the smoke and flames got to it.

Joseph tuned back into the service just in time to hear the
melody that cued the dressing of the Torah. After the scroll was
tucked away on its stand in the corner, waiting to be returned to
the ark, Joseph approached the bimah. He looked out at the few
hundred faces in the crowd and began to address his congregants.

"For decades, a particular piece of art has hung in my living
room, always in the same place. Even when we moved, even when
my wife Miriam did a beautiful redecoration—the same spot.
Why? Because it points us in the direction of Jerusalem. East.
The direction we face each day when we pray. This piece of art,
this *mizrach*, is one of the first things I see each morning. And in
my heart, I can feel its magnetic pull. To the east. To Israel. To our
people, to the place where our millennia-old dream of a Jewish
homeland—a Jewish home—has come to fruition."

Joseph could feel the rhythm of the sermon starting to flow
through his body. Slowly getting going, then beginning to pick
up speed.

"You might wonder why, in what is arguably the very center of my life—the living room where friends and family relax
after dinner, where my grandchildren play, where Miriam and I
compete at Wheel of Fortune every night, except on Shabbos, of
course—why, in the very center of my home, is there a signpost
pointing elsewhere? What could be more important than the

family, the relationship between spouses, the study of holy books in a comfortable chair?

"On this Rosh Hashanah, I want to talk to you about home. Where is our home? Where do we set down our roots? Cultivate them so that they can grow?" Joseph looked up, briefly fixing his gaze on the Tree of Life wall installation that commemorated congregants who had died. After the fire, he had insisted that it be restored, not replaced. The golden tree looked almost new now, from where he stood. But up close, the traces of damage were visible.

"Beth Abraham has been my home for decades. And this community has been a kind of family, with generation after generation moving through it. And our congregation has even helped build real homes for other families, those who live in the Two Rivers complex just next door.

"And yet, I still pray—we still pray—facing east. Facing our *true* home." Surprising himself, Joseph felt his hand land over his heart. "Israel is on unstable ground these days, threatened from so many directions. And so are our people, here and across the world. How do we stay connected to her? How do we ensure that she is a safe haven for each of us in the face of rising antisemitism? And how do we do our part to ensure that even when she veers off course, this little miracle of a country that we love lives up to her potential?"

In his mind, the drumbeat of stories began to sound, stories from *this* country. The horrific attacks on synagogues in recent years. Desecrated cemeteries here. Swastikas graffitied in middle-school bathrooms over there. And everywhere, of course, the constant and unfair vilification of Israel. Whenever Joseph calmed down after one incident, another story would break, echoing the steady escalation his parents and grandparents used to describe when they talked about Germany before....

He inhaled deeply. "Sometimes I wonder: Have we neglected our Jewish homeland? Have we not taken the risks that we should to safeguard it, to guarantee that our sovereignty will not have been one more blip in history, but an eternal guarantor of safety for persecuted Jews everywhere? Yes, there are stormy waters rising all around us. And that certainly includes in Israel."

Joseph almost laughed, realizing he had accidentally sounded like Vivian. There were always plenty of storms and rising waters in her sermons, while curiously, she'd only addressed antisemitism four times in seven years. But who was counting? (He was.)

"Next week, we will recite Kol Nidre," he continued solemnly. "We will ask, again, that the vows we inevitably broke not taint God's judgment of us. I have been thinking about the vows that we have broken. That *I* have broken. For years, I vowed in my heart to make aliyah, to move to Israel. To really commit. And I will soon make good on that. As you know, this is my last year before retiring from this congregation, from the home of my last four decades. And so it is also the year I can finally make plans for my next home, plans to fulfill a vow I took long ago.

"I am old. I no longer sow seeds for trees that I will live to see grow. All I can do is find my place to eat the fruits others have sown, and to sow the fruits others will eat. And it is time, in the dusk of my life, to do that. *This* is my retirement, *this* is my investment, this is where my life, like the *mizrach* on my wall, has always pointed. It is time for me to finally love Israel with all my heart and soul and resources."

Joseph paused to look around him. He briefly caught the eyes of a few of his longtime members: Harry Mermelstein, Tamar Benayoun, Joel Fishman, Gert Fineman, Shlomo Seidel. While some of them had known this move was in the cards, he had not announced it publicly. He couldn't focus long enough to read their body language, but he sensed they were with him. Especially Shlomo, his vigorous nodding easy to decode.

"And I know that this is not the case for every Jew or every person in this congregation. But my plea to you is that you don't lose the connection. Israel is our home. Mine and yours. Sometimes people leave home only to come back many years later. I hope so much that this is your experience. That you hold on to that pull to the east, no matter how faint it might be. That you hold on to that pull to the east, even when things happen there that you disagree with, even when life here feels comfortable enough.

"You can plant seeds now, wait for the tree to grow, and eat of its fruits later. This is my charge to you." Joseph cupped both hands together and lifted them toward his congregants. "Plant seeds of hope for our homeland. Set aside some of your savings— figurative ones and real ones—to invest in this vision. And let us together, from wherever we sit, watch the trees of our commitment, of our hope, as they sprout."

He rocked back on his feet, folded his hands behind him, and finished up. "Now you have an opportunity to do just that. It's my pleasure to call up our eminently capable president, Tamar Benayoun, to make our Israel bonds appeal." Joseph walked back to his chair.

He cherished the annual appeal; he loved encouraging congregants to participate in the tradition of investing their money
by lending funds to the Israeli state. *A mitzvah of the modern day
that our ancestors could only dream of*, he would say. He thought back
to his very first Israel bond, which he received—along with a U.S.
bond, though it seemed of lesser significance—as a bar mitzvah
gift. Now that had been a good investment!

In years past, Beth Abraham had always made the appeal on the
first day of Rosh Hashanah. This year, Vivian and a few supporters
she'd whipped up had advocated to change it to the second. They
insisted that, because the first day of Rosh Hashanah was many
people's singular visit to shul all year, the appeal should not be the
"only thing" that they heard. (He supposed the other four hours of
prayers, sermons, hymns, and Torah reading didn't count.) Joseph
disagreed, but finally relented. He was constantly accommodating
Vivian's changes, but it never seemed like she appreciated or even
noticed his concessions. How could she not see?

And how could she not see that even if Israel was never going
to be perfect—for that, no doubt, was why she basically objected
to the country's name even being mentioned in shul—that no
country was, and yet, it was still *ours*? And wasn't that true here
too? In the U.S.? In Providence? He didn't see Vivian pausing her
own appeals to engage with the "wider community" whenever the
cracks in American democracy widened; in fact, the opposite was
true. The bonds were an investment, a ballot cast for a vision of
the *best version* of Israel.

At the lectern, Tamar was introducing herself and arranging
her papers. She began to repeat a familiar introduction, which,
to Joseph, always felt like part of the liturgy of the holiday. He

enjoyed hearing it, but he wished that she spoke with more gusto. More heart.

From his chair at the corner of the semicircle, he could see some people folding down tabs on the pledge cards that had been set out on each seat. But now that congregants were directed to place them in baskets at the end of the service, instead of handing them to ushers circulating around the sanctuary in real time, he couldn't estimate the number of respondents—another modification that he found distressing. He wondered what else would change at Beth Abraham when he was gone.

Leaning back in his seat, Joseph found himself feeling grateful that, in the new layout of the sanctuary, no one was looking straight at him. He closed his eyes and envisioned being in Israel, in a small crowded shul in Jerusalem, the next time Rosh Hashanah came around.

· · ·

After the last of the congregants had filed out, and the greeters had turned over the sanctuary for the next service, and the security officer hired to stand outside during the High Holidays had completed his shift, Vivian returned to the rows of chairs, straightening out a few prayerbooks left askew on the seats' thin cushions. She could not stop thinking about Joseph's sermon. She walked over to the greeters' table and shuffled through the Israel bonds pledge cards, curious to see what sort of investments her people had made this year. Some small amounts. A bunch of gifts of $500. Several in the thousands. Even two for $3,600.

Months ago, when the small tweaks to the appeal—moving

it to the second day, nixing the public collection—had made it through a board vote, Vivian felt like she had won something. But now, having just sat through it, she didn't feel so sure.

"Ready to lock up, Rabbi?" The voice belonged to Raymond Weeks, the Chief of Building Operations. He had been at Beth Abraham almost as long as Joseph. After the fire, he had managed the rebuilding process. Raymond had done his own advocacy within Beth Abraham to ensure that the rebuild complied not only with the city's requirements for environmentally sustainable development, but its stated "recommendations," too.

"Yes," Vivian said. "Thanks for pulling me back to reality, Raymond."

"What's holding you up?"

"Oh, Raymond, you know me, always fussing about one thing or another."

He chuckled. "That I do, Rabbi. But I figured now that your Cincinnati Bengals finally won the Super Bowl, maybe you'd be less troubled," he said, continuing his and Vivian's ritual of teasing each other about their conflicting team loyalties.

The edges of Vivian's mouth curled upward. "It turns out the joy and contentment that brought could only last for so long."

"Ah yes. I learned that lesson after the fifth time the Patriots won."

"Rub it in, why don't you?"

He smiled. "So," he said. "What's eating at you this New Year?"

Vivian explained sheepishly that she was sifting through the Israel bonds commitments, which she figured Raymond knew something about after all these years. "I just keep wondering what this community is most invested in," she said. "You know, *where*…." Raymond cocked his head quizzically. "Like, do they—do we—even look outside the window and consider the needs right in front of us, in our own…." She trailed off.

"I see," Raymond said quietly. Then he leaned to one side. "Well, at least you can look right through *that* window"—he pointed—"when you need a reminder that this congregation has done some good for this city."

Vivian turned around and fixed her eyes on Two Rivers, the mixed-income housing project that she and others had helped make a reality, the one Joseph had referred to in his sermon. Through the window she could see a stretch of the playground, including a handful of small children playing together on the elaborate jungle gym and an older woman who was reliably reading a romance novel on her usual bench. Vivian's hand migrated to her heart.

"That's true, Raymond. Thanks."

"I'm going to get my coat and then we are leaving this building. That is a commandment!"

Vivian smiled as she gazed out. "Okay, Raymond. As you know, I'm a sucker for commandments. Most of them, anyway." She heard him walk away.

Through the window, something beyond Two Rivers caught her eye. She sighed. It was a *COMING SOON!* banner flapping over the construction site for a luxury condo project. While the new buildings would contain a few affordable units here and there, that could only do so much to stem the tide.

And then there were the actual rising waters. Under Karla's influence, Vivian's sermon the day before had been about climate change, about the collective vows they needed to make to fight against the prioritization of profit over people. About how individual choices were not the primary problem. The choices that resulted in rising sea levels, and in the displacement of so many people, and in the once-in-a-thousand-year storms now coming every few years—these were bigger than any one person, and so the problems could only be faced as a community. As a city. As a state. As a country. As a world. We needed to say *hineini*, here I am—*hineinu*, here *we* are.

There were certainly times when Vivian wanted to escape, though unlike Joseph, her dreams were usually of Canada or of a magical place untouched by climate change. But—she remembered vividly—there *had* been a time when she dreamed of life in Israel. When she was young, she could feel the love pulsing through her, especially when she was there: speaking Hebrew with her cousins, walking on the same holy dirt her ancestors had tread. There was a time when she believed Israel was in fact a home, a refuge, of some sort, for her, for her people.

That tether had been severed years ago, since callous politicians with a totally different vision of Israel—and Judaism—had maneuvered into power and stayed there, chipping away at the hope of any tenable democratic future for Israelis *and* Palestinians. And since she visited in her twenties and a cousin with whom she had been particularly close sat across from her at a café, army-issued gun hung across his chest, and chatted casually about the enemy Arabs. Now, when people spoke of Israel as home, and of Israelis as family, all Vivian could feel were pangs of disconnection, as though the whole country were an estranged relative.

Home. Her thoughts returned to Joseph's sermon. For Vivian, the answer was clear. She was already home. And she desperately wanted to help her community recognize that Providence—where they actually lived—was as deserving of their investment as Israel. *More* deserving, in fact, since Israel was…well, it was…okay, she still didn't have the words for what Israel was to her. But whatever it was, it was not going to get in the way of her being an active citizen *here*, and doing what she could to bring her congregants along with her.

"This way to the inspirational viewing of Two Rivers," Raymond shouted, leaning through the door of the sanctuary, interrupting Vivian's cascade of thoughts. "Let's go." She followed him through the atrium. He held the front door open, keys jingling in his hand, as Vivian made her way out of Beth Abraham.

CHAPTER FIVE

"I T LOOKS LIKE we might be in for a few later storms this season," Winona MacLean said to the group. Karla kept her eyes fixed on her monitor as she clicked through the slide-show they were presenting. She had surprised herself by feeling guilty about working on the second day of Rosh Hashanah, but she was hopeful that traces of the holiness of the holiday would seep into the planning inside City Hall.

In a small room, her team was meeting with representatives from the Executive Office of Budget Management, led by Secretary Clarissa Fox. Having failed to get the room's projector to work, the little group was huddled behind and to either side of Karla, poring over the colorful slides she had compiled. "According to the National Weather Service, there are some strange patterns starting to form as a result of the warmest October we will likely ever have on record," MacLean said. She stood up abruptly and gripped the back of her chair. "We've got to remain vigilant and be prepared to get resources to every neighborhood if a storm is on its way."

"We'll set aside funds to support evacuation and have the mobile rapid-response units ready to distribute what's needed to those who stay if and when the time comes," Secretary Fox said, simultaneously jotting down notes. Karla snuck a look at her. A former city councilor, Fox was a rising star in the Heath administration, and it still took a fair amount of restraint for Karla not to fangirl her every time they were in the same room. Everyone understood that the position the mayor had appointed her to was basically chief financial officer of the entire city. In her time as city councilor, she had pushed for the shifting of budget priorities; now she was implementing and overseeing those very changes—and as the first Black woman to hold her role. Karla was among those who firmly believed—and hoped—that Heath was grooming Fox to replace her as mayor in the next election cycle.

"And I've confirmed that we've got stores of food and supplies and a few hundred extra generators that the wind farm should be able to power for a few days," Karla said.

"Good to hear," MacLean said. "Clarissa, what do we have after the mobile units, for recovery?"

Fox gave her deputy, Amir Noori, the signal to pass around their own packet of colorful graphs and statistics. "If we aggregate the state and federal grants and the new city line items," Fox said, "then we should be able to prepare for, respond to, and recover from storms, potential flooding, and power outages with a program of proportionate and equitable resources. This year and for the next decade or so at least."

The room was quiet. *A decade*, Karla thought. It was so much and so little time all at once. Amir, who Karla often found to be more cheerful than others she encountered in his line of work, chimed in. "Wow! Isn't it something to see what you get when you redistribute twenty percent of the police budget?!"

"It is *something*," MacLean said, immune to Amir's good cheer. "But I worry that down the line, there is only so much that a fixed pool of public funds can do. The challenges are monumental, and they won't be any smaller ten years from now." She sipped her ever-present travel mug, which sparkled in the glare of the fluorescent light. It smelled to Karla like a Bengal Spice meeting, or perhaps Vermont Maple Ginger. "If we could only get a fraction of the venture-capital dollars going into the damn tech companies I drive past every day."

"At least they now pay their fair share in property taxes," Fox said. "The mayor has certainly made sure of that. Though I wouldn't say no to donated computers. Mine and Amir's are competing to die first."

Karla thought about Freddy and the video he had shown her of Hyydra's rocking dance moves. She tried to imagine Hyydra zipping around their warehouse, interpreting spreadsheets and loading supplies onto pallets destined for distribution sites, pausing to breakdance every few minutes.

"I suppose we should plan for what's in front of us," MacLean said. "Let's touch base with the utility companies to make sure the grid is as resilient as it can be. And review the deployment plan for the mobile units. If there are any gaps, now is the time to identify them."

"Roger that," Karla said, willing the robots out of her mind. "I'll also get in touch with the food pantries and confirm our distribution strategy." She typed out a few notes while others did the same. "You know," she mused aloud. "Today is the second day of Rosh Hashanah, the Jewish New Year, and one of the prayers we say is about how humans have the power to 'reverse bad decrees.' When I first heard it, I couldn't understand how people might believe that. But now I'm getting it. It's like we ourselves have the power—through responsible government interventions, for example!—to shift things as a result of our actions." Karla paused and then gulped. "Or at least make sure they aren't as bad," she added quietly.

Everyone stared at her while she slowly regained her senses. *Oh my God. Did I just give a spontaneous sermon? Am I turning into Vivian?*

"That's really nice, Karla," Amir said finally, nodding heartily, as if to make up for everyone else's silence. "Oh, and happy New Year."

"Yes. What Amir said. And on that note," MacLean said. "Karla and Amir, make sure we are tracking and sharing the data. It's easy to let that fall by the wayside, but if we are going to make the case for more resources down the line, and cultivate public support, we need good data."

Karla pounded the keys of her laptop especially loudly, wondering if her face was still as red as the apple she had dipped in honey the previous day. As her mortification subsided, her thoughts returned to the prayer. And to Clarissa Fox, Winona MacLean and Margaret Heath. These women showed her what public service could be at its best, what holding and implementing strong visions could look like. If there were "bad decrees"—and there certainly were—maybe they could be reversed by this legion of government superheroes. Maybe.

CHAPTER SIX

A COOL BREEZE BRUSHED Vivian's face and sent ripples through the shallow creek. She scanned the park. About forty-two congregants, she estimated, were gathered for Beth Abraham's annual communal *tashlich*.

She took a deep breath of autumn air before addressing them. "From what we know," she began, "the ritual of tashlich came into practice around the thirteenth century. People connected it to the verse in Micah: *You will cast all their sins into the depths of the sea*. But the rabbis of that time initially rejected it. They were afraid that people would believe it was this simple ritual, rather than the practice of actively seeking forgiveness, that had the power to change their lives, to reverse their bad decrees.

"Yet, despite that rabbinic opposition, tashlich only grew in popularity. And now it is broadly practiced throughout the Jewish world. Why is that?"

Vivian paused, noticing the other people who roamed the park, probably wondering what her group was up to. She was always gratified by seeing her congregation collect outside the four walls of Beth Abraham. Wherever it happened—in a nearby church for an interfaith event, at the local food bank before Passover, while dancing in the streets on Simchat Torah—she was reminded that they existed as a body, as a community out in the wide world, to be seen by others, to try to bring light wherever they went. They all shone in this municipal park, the colors of their holiday clothes glowing in the afternoon sun.

"I believe it's because we crave an action," she continued, "some marker to initiate our commitment to change.

"Today as we symbolically rid ourselves of our misdeeds by casting something into the water, I wanted to remind us that tashlich is a custom, a *minhag*. Like most of what we practice today, it is *not* a requirement that was commanded in perpetuity.

"And so, though people have often cast breadcrumbs into flowing water, we are going to make a modification. We know now that breadcrumbs can impair this beautiful ecosystem, potentially causing harm to geese, ducks, fish, and whoever else might ingest them. So instead, we will collect and then cast out objects that are already part of this natural habitat—stones, twigs, pinecones, or whatever else you might find. We don't want to injure any of God's creatures while we make meaning in this custom of cleansing ourselves."

Vivian looked around at her congregants and caught the eye

of Tamar Benayoun. Vivian had developed a deep warmth toward her, witnessing as she became more vocal and confident in her leadership over years of service on various shul committees. It was Tamar who had recruited the right team to overhaul the Hebrew school curriculum that had languished in the same three-ring binders for thirty years. And it was Tamar who consistently made clear, during contract negotiations, that she would do whatever she could to keep Vivian at Beth Abraham.

Vivian's mind wandered back to Tamar's Israel bonds appeal that morning, and the way it had unsettled her. Had it unsettled Tamar too? Had she felt that she could opt in or out of the task, or had she thought that the custom was simply too well established: *that's just what we do, it's the president's job, ever since anyone can remember*? Maybe all the way back to the thirteenth century?

Mimi's voice whispered to her. *You have power here. Now is the time to push for what you need.*

And for what the community needs, Vivian replied silently.

"Sometimes our traditions need to change," she found herself improvising. "Sometimes they no longer fit into our lives as they did for preceding generations. Or we learn something that compels us to try something different.

"Today we do that with tashlich. But we can also strive to do this every day, training our muscles as a community, as individuals, to create rituals and meaning anew. Just as our ancestors did." Vivian stepped under the canopy of a large birch and leaned down, running her hand lightly over the ground, to gather its loose twigs and golden leaves. "Now, let's get to it!"

Her congregants followed suit, scattering to hunt whatever they could find.

Finally, the group fanned out along the creek bed, each person finding their own spot. Holding siddurim open to the tashlich prayers, they either mumbled the text to themselves or meditated on the words of their hearts. Every so often, Vivian chanted one of the verses aloud and the community joined in.

"*Min ha-metzar karati Yah; anani ba-merchav Yah.* From the narrow place, I called to God, who answered me with the breadth of Divine relief....

"*Ve-ya'alu kol nitzutzeh ha-kedushah asher nitpazru.* May all the sparks of holiness that have been scattered rise up before You...."

Vivian loved that line. As though the pebbles of wrongdoing could be transformed into sparks of holiness if we summoned our power.

After the final verse, Vivian and her congregants tossed their individual collections into the glistening creek. A few ducks took notice, swimming toward them. Whenever they detected a new offering, they changed course sharply, repeatedly disrupting the reflection of the oak trees growing over the water. Then they swam off as quickly as they had come; maybe they too remembered the breadcrumbs, and were disappointed. But things change, Vivian thought. Sometimes even for the better.

She sucked in the cool air. *One more ritual complete!*, she congratulated herself.

While the holiday season required months of work to pull off, now that Vivian was accustomed to the routine, she had developed an appreciation for this time and how it brought the congregation together. A past president, Harry Mermelstein, had once told her that the High Holidays were akin to the annual strategy retreats he had at his company. While she and Harry did not see eye to eye on many points during his tenure, and though she initially scoffed at that comparison, his interpretation had stuck with her.

"Hey, Rabbi," said a voice behind her. "I wonder what *you* could possibly have to repent for." Vivian turned to see Gordy Silver, who had moved to town with his family and joined the congregation a few years earlier. He held some kind of high-power position at Leviathan Labs.

"We've each got our shortcomings, Gordy."

"Sure, but you must have enough points on the other side of the scale to cancel those out."

"You never know." Vivian raised an eyebrow, trying to play along. She immediately wished she could take back her comment and replace it with something more earnest. Perhaps she had missed a teachable moment. Oh well. As the Rambam said, true repentance is making a different choice next time you're faced with the same situation. Gordy slipped back into the crowd of chatting congregants, and Vivian picked up another pebble. She made a mental note to toss it into the water when the schmoozing was done—less a confession of sin and more a reminder for the future.

Gordy Silver embodied one of the reasons that Vivian had questioned staying at Beth Abraham. He was a nice guy, full of ideas, and a triumph for the shul as a younger person—one with money and a willingness to be involved. He even led Shabbat prayers sometimes. He even seemed to respect Vivian. Sometimes. To a handful of board members, and to Joseph, Gordy represented the future of the community. They had lobbied hard for him to join the board, but he had apologetically declined, citing a busy work schedule.

And yet, he managed to make things happen at Beth Abraham

from the sidelines. Like when he proposed an "innovative program for Israeli Independence Day" to showcase advancements in tech coming out of Israel. And so, on an evening the previous spring, Vivian had looked on as congregants gathered to eat falafel and watch a documentary about the country's contributions to facial recognition technology, which, it was shown, had massively benefitted the global tech sector more broadly. There was no mention of the fact that technologies like this were responsible for reinforcing the militarized surveillance of millions of Palestinians under the guise of innovation. Or the fact that falafel clearly originated in other parts of the Middle East.

Woops. Defiance was swiftly overtaking Vivian, her moment of humility clearly past. Well…not everything could be forgiven so easily.

Vivian shook her head to clear it and shifted her attention. A few clusters of people were still symbolically ridding themselves of their transgressions, but most of the group had moved on to schmoozing. She reminded herself that she enjoyed doing what was hers to do in this moment.

Vivian spotted Flora Moore chatting with Vera Cohen under a sprawling birch tree. Flora and her husband, Ben, were in their thirties, though unlike some of their peers in the congregation, they were not in tech. For a few years now, Flora and Vivian had learned together regularly. Flora wanted to understand the theological and textual underpinnings of Shabbat, so Vivian compiled traditional Jewish texts on the topic along with more contemporary takes on the need for regular, societally sanctioned rest… from Marge Piercy poems to labor laws.

"Shana tova!" Vivian said, stepping into their circle of conversation.

She loved these in-between moments. The blank spaces for connection after committee meetings ended, over kiddush after a Shabbat morning service, with volunteers during an event setup. It was at kiddush a few years back that she had planted the seed with Tamar that someday she would make a fantastic president of Beth Abraham's board. Kiddush was also where Vivian had proposed the idea that she and Flora learn together.

"Shana tova," Vera said, grinning. Ever since Vivian arrived at Beth Abraham, Vera had been one of her biggest allies. When Gordy's Israeli Independence Day program was being planned, Vera had decided she would not attend, in protest, and she had even emailed the board a thoughtful critique. In it, she suggested a different documentary for the community to watch, one about a mixed Jewish and Palestinian soccer league that came together to resist extremist violence in their community. But nothing had come of it. *Maybe in the future*, they had replied.

"I'm loving this new take on tashlich," Flora said, a few twigs peeking out of her clenched fist. "And I'm glad to hear that my procrastination and judginess won't hurt the ducks anymore."

The group caught up about how the holiday was going for each of them. Flora detailed the scrumptious menu of a meal she had hosted for friends. Vera shared tales from her grandkids' visit and bemoaned the fact that every nook and cranny of their house was now mysteriously sticky with honey.

"I want to ask you both about something," Vivian said. "I was, um…I was thinking about the Israel bonds pitch—"

"Whatever other tweaks you're proposing," Vera interrupted, "I'm assuming I'm in, Rabbi."

Thank God for Vera. "The appeal raises so much money," Vivian continued, feeling bolder. "And it's an opportunity to put a stake in the ground about who we are and what we care about." She gripped the little rock in her hand more tightly. "Now might be the time for a big change, bigger than just moving it from the first to second day. I'm thinking that we could use our collective resources to invest in, um, local efforts."

"Yessss!" Flora said, clasping her hands together excitedly. Vivian was happy to see her immediate enthusiasm, though not surprised. The two of them had discussed their grief, both about the Israeli occupation and Jewish institutions' tendency to condone it, often enough.

"I could research organizations that might be options for a future appeal," Flora said.

"Please do!" Vivian said, pumping her clasped hands as if she was shaking a *lulav*.

"I'm obviously on board," Vera said, folding her arms. "But how do we get the *actual* board not to shut this down right away? We did just spend a good amount of capital getting the tweaks to the pitch approved. And that was already quite radical for the old timers."

"Well, then it's a good thing I just joined the board!" Flora said.

Vivian grinned. A few months earlier, as they were learning together at their regular spot, Flora had mentioned to Vivian that her leadership term in the Black Teachers Collective, a subgroup of the Providence Teacher's Union, was ending. She wondered aloud what she would do with the extra time, and on a whim, Vivian had pitched joining Beth Abraham's board. She had thought for a while that Flora could be a great addition, but wasn't sure if being the only Black member would be a deterrent. It was clearly the time to discuss it. "You could help usher in a new era at Beth Abraham, now that Joseph is retiring," she urged her. "Just like the rabbis did thousands of years ago." Flora had laughed when Vivian pulled out that line, an oft-used refrain. Flora shared that she was fascinated by boards, and governance structures in general, and decided that she was up for it—as long as they could check in about any needs for support that might arise. Vivian had switched out their coffees for spiked hot ciders to celebrate.

The group of three chatted and strategized a bit longer before saying their goodbyes. There was more to discuss, but they knew they would be seeing a lot of each other over the course of the holiday season.

Out of the corner of her eye, Vivian glimpsed Joseph still sitting on the bench by the river where he had spent most of tashlich. He looked tired and alone. Recently, he had been doing the same during most kiddushes and the schmoozing periods at the ends of meetings, disappearing into his office for one reason or another.

Vivian felt a sadness for Joseph. But mostly, she was angry—a feeling that came up more and more often now, even as this dance of sharing leadership with him neared its end. While he moped around, she had to do a disproportionate amount of the work they should have shared. She had hoped that Joseph would be repenting for *that*, but she presumed that their relationship dynamic was not one of the things on his mind.

Vivian picked up one more pebble. When most of her congregants had dispersed, she walked back to the edge of the creek and released the objects that remained squeezed in her fist.

CHAPTER SEVEN

F REDDY'S COLLEAGUE Jacqueline Saito bent over to inspect
a three-foot-tall, four-legged machine. "The demonstration
will commence," she said—first to the machine, then to the small
crowd huddled together on Buck Creek Peak, an hour outside
of Providence. The air was crisp, the sun was just setting, and
the leaves on the surrounding birch trees glimmered in its glow.

Buck Creek contained smooth and rough terrain, plenty of
elevation, and creeks and crevices everywhere. It was not recommended for children under twelve to traverse the particular trail
on which the team of engineers found themselves...but the park's
guidelines said nothing about advanced robotic technology. The

Devil's Snare was a perfect place for Leviathan Labs to test the cutting-edge navigation skills of their crown jewel, Hyydra.

It was all systems go.

For years, Freddy and his team had fed into Hyydra's system millions of instructions, pictures, and videos that detailed scenarios and conditions in which she might someday find herself when on Mars. And now, there was no weather pattern or sound or topography to which Hyydra could not respond. Nor any obstacle she could not overcome.

Freddy had never seen her tested in conditions anything like this. This was the first time she was putting her physical skills— along with the artificial intelligence Freddy and his team built into her—to use in the wider world. There was a dissonance between her thin metal rods, rubber-tubed hydraulic joints, and bright orange torso, and the green vegetation and brown earth of the mountain. But Freddy knew he would grow used to it. They all would. This was their new world: evolving robotics, humanoids, and the earth's elements, all coexisting.

Freddy glanced over at his boss, Sal Maraj, whose uniform of suit pants, a polo, a puffy green vest, and white sneakers were oddly harmonious with their surroundings. Sal was the company's founder and CEO, and along with Gordy Silver and other members of the executive team, he was here to observe their prize prototype in action. Freddy wiped clammy palms on his pants, trying to quantify his excitement-to-nervousness ratio, and wondering what it was for his colleagues. And his boss.

The vision of Hyydra had been Sal's PhD thesis as a graduate student at MIT, and then he had set out to make it a reality. *A new generation of space explorers*, he had said. Investors ate it up and the funding poured in. Leviathan Labs had opened its doors with $100 million of dedicated investment.

There were lots of problems in the tech sector, and certainly many questions surrounding robotic space-exploration technology, but Freddy wanted to stick around and make sure these companies considered all of the angles. And Sal prioritized creating machines that would be as morally capable as robotically possible—*well beyond the capacities of humans*, he always said. Freddy was comforted by Sal's leadership. And his mentorship, too. From day one, Sal had taken Freddy under his wing, meeting with him monthly about his own goals and progress.

It also didn't hurt that this job—and the whole industry—paid engineers well. The side hustles put him through college. They made it possible to pay for the components of his gender transition. And now, with a sizeable salary and an impressive title—*associate director of machine learning and moral advancement*—he could help out his mom with her mortgage and his little sister with her college fund.

"Hyydra here is the future of space travel. She is an explorer, a diplomat, a master navigator," said Jacqueline, who was director of robotics, working closely with Freddy and the other programmers. She turned toward him.

"Now we set her loose," he said, taking the cue, "and see how she responds to a variety of external elements. The changing terrain. The dimming light. The cliffs. The streams. Her control system has been built and solidified through tens of thousands of hours of learning, closely studying the possible scenarios in which she could find herself. Hyydra is indeed a master navigator."

Jacqueline jumped in. "The park's brochure says that the Devil's Snare loop takes about two hours to complete. We believe that Hyydra can do it in under half an hour, with waning light."

"Let's see her in action!" It came out louder than Freddy intended.

A human-controlled drone hovered above Hyydra, ready to follow her. The group looked on transfixed, though Freddy noticed a few who had closed their eyes. He wondered if they were saying whatever constituted a prayer for them. That was certainly what he was doing.

"Ready, Hyydra?" Jacqueline said. The four-legged robot turned back toward Jacqueline and galloped in place, indicating that she was indeed ready. "Set. Go!"

Hyydra sprinted around the first ledge of the peak. She disappeared from sight within seconds. In unison, the observers shifted their attention to their iPads, which were streaming video taken by the drone following her. They watched as Hyydra ran up a narrow path composed of rocks of varying sizes. Some were firmly wedged into each other; others were loose. Hyydra stumbled initially, but quickly got a feel for which ones were solid.

"I can't believe this is happening," Freddy whispered to Jacqueline. She smiled, her eyes staying on her screen.

Hyydra's speed, along with a handful of other stats calculated by her control system, ran across the top of the iPad display. She was moving at 12.07 miles an hour. The team watched as she rounded the mountain dexterously and soon came upon a creek. With no hesitation, she plunged into the water and made her way through, not even bothering to jump from rock to rock.

On the other side, she continued to run while the forest grew dimmer around her. Freddy felt as though Hyydra was chasing the sun. And winning!

She now found herself at a section of the trail where two pointy rocks jutted out from either side, forcing hikers to choose between crawling under or climbing on top of them. Hyydra was not slowing down as she approached this obstacle. She leaped through the air, clearing the rocks with a full foot to spare.

The team let out a collective gasp. Freddy thought back to incorporating the study of Olympic long jumpers and pole vaulters into her algorithm. His team spent weeks on it, and now Hyydra looked as if she herself could be a gold medalist.

Right as she landed, the most important test began, giving Hyydra no time to rest—just as they had intended. An older, larger robot model had been situated around a sharp corner. It stood on two legs and would tower over Hyydra once they came into contact. As Hyydra rounded the corner, a member of Jacqueline's team remotely activated the other robot and charged her with it. Hyydra acted fast. She extended two legs in front of her, tripping the second robot before it could reach her. She did so at just such an angle that the spot where its torso and legs were attached hit a rock on the side of the path, dislodging one of the legs and incapacitating it.

They were testing how intense physical demands on Hyydra, like the soaring jump she had just executed, would impact her decision-making when encountering a threat. For months, Freddy and his team had been training her on applying just the right amount of force in any given situation. *Stop the threat; don't destroy it.* That was the goal. Freddy could almost hear Hyydra saying this mantra to herself throughout the sequence. And she had succeeded; she made the right decision. Without skipping a beat, she continued down the trail.

The gathered group finally looked up from their iPads and at each other. Freddy could feel the sense of victory pulsing through all of them, almost pulsing through the mountain. They were doing something great. *He* was doing something great.

Freddy's focus settled on Sal, who flashed a big grin and two robust thumbs-up in his direction.

As usual, Sal's clarity and support made him feel even more confident. They were a balm when he doubted himself, too. A few years earlier, at a time when Freddy woke up most mornings wondering if he had made the right choice to work at Leviathan, he had found himself sharing a few of his questions aloud with Sal one day. Sal had confided that whenever he was overcome by his own qualms, he would take hold of a compass, ever-present in his pocket, that was a gift from his grandfather, who had served as an Indian naval officer. *But Hyydra's compass is built into her*, Sal had said. *We are going to be able to trust her to make the right choice. Always.* Sal had trusted Hyydra, completely. And Freddy had trusted Sal.

Sal's actual voice filtered into Freddy's thoughts. "Her decisiveness is masterful!" he was saying to the group, though he looked in Freddy's direction. "Good work, everyone!"

Hyydra continued on, moving quickly through the dark. *Night vision activated* displayed on the iPad screen. She continued to meet every impediment with the same certainty she had shown at the protruding rocks. Freddy was finally relaxed enough to notice his colleague's running commentary.

"Would you look at that incredible balance control!"

"That's the way, girl!"

"Those independent finger movements—I could cry."

Hyydra was a star!

As she swiftly approached the end of the trail, the team cheered her on like they were fans at a marathon finish line. She arrived back at the beginning and abruptly halted. No heaving, no collapsing. Hyydra just stood still, like it had never happened at all.

"Twenty-seven minutes and forty-six seconds!" Jacqueline shouted.

They were stunned. The cheering stopped. And then there was just silence, the crickets growing audible in the vacuum of human noise. Freddy held out his hand, rotating it, marveling at his own power. Seeing Hyydra in action made him feel as though he knew something about the future that few others did.

Sal was first to break the silence. "Wonderful! Just excellent. Freddy, Jacqueline, everyone—Hyydra and her incredible autonomous control system are a revelation. She—*we*—are going to change the world. No. The universe!"

Gordy Silver, the vice president of marketing and partnerships, chimed in. "That was amazing. Just phenomenal." Freddy braced himself. He could pretty much count on Gordy's observations about anything differing substantially from his own. "It looks like we are ready for the public simulation!" Gordy continued. Well, that made sense. As the contact for Leviathan's collaborators, which included investors, Gordy worried about everything public-facing that Freddy, thankfully, didn't have to think about. And he might have been Leviathan's biggest cheerleader. Gordy liked to say that while there were other robotics companies developing exploratory robots, Leviathan had a leg up. *Four of them, in fact!* he liked to joke…again and again.

"That's right!" Jacqueline said, examining Hyydra's limbs, looking for any signs of wear.

"The PR team from SpaceRace has given us their invite lists, and we've got press enquiring from the right outlets," Gordy continued. "And after that—we set her loose in the world, and beyond! We're so close, I can taste it."

Freddy's feeling of accomplishment was turning to unease. He and Gordy often operated at different speeds.

"Hyydra is certainly acing every test we throw at her," Freddy spoke up. "But we'd like more time after the simulation to keep training her. There is still more to work out."

"Sure, but we can make any necessary tweaks as we go," Gordy said. He was responding to Freddy but facing Sal. "You see, the simulation is a clear deadline." The excitement had drained out of Gordy's voice and he sounded serious. "It's important on the investment side that we hold to that."

Neither Gordy nor Sal had ever told Freddy, Jacqueline, and their respective teams that there were such clear time constraints.

"We've always said, 'It will take the time it takes' to do such important and groundbreaking work. Right?" Freddy asked. It was hard to see in the dark, but he could just make out Gordy nodding slowly, not saying a word. Sal was standing closer to him, and Freddy could see his hand go to his pocket. He wondered if Sal was reaching for his grandfather's compass.

"Of course, of course," Sal said. "But enough logistics. Let's celebrate!" He pulled his hand from his pocket. The winged cork-screw he held glinted in the light of an iPad. Someone handed Sal what looked like a champagne bottle, and he wedged the fulcrum into its cork and opened it, liquid spilling over the top.

The evening wind was picking up, and Freddy noticed suddenly how cold he was.

Sal raised the bottle. "To Hyydra!" he said. The group, their faces obscure in the dark, echoed his toast.

CHAPTER EIGHT

THE BELL OF Witches' Brew Café dinged as Flora walked in, papers and fresh tests spilling out of her messenger bag. Vivian waved at her from their usual table toward the back.

For a few years now, the two of them had met here monthly to study texts together. Flora had chosen the Witches' Brew because it was just two blocks from the high school where she taught, but after they started meeting, she had discovered that it was also a hangout for witchy healers across Providence. Flora had seen enough fliers on the community bulletin advertising tincture-making 101 workshops and full-moon herb gathers to drive away any feelings of bashfulness about the piles of leather-bound, gold-lettered books filled with Hebrew and Aramaic that Vivian often brought.

"Ooh, it's good to be here," Flora said, sitting down in a creaky wooden chair. "Today was exhausting, but learning always gives me energy."

Vivian grinned. "That has always seemed like one of your superpowers, Flora."

"I bet lots of people feel that way," Flora said, settling her bag on the floor and then stuffing back in the papers that fell out.

"Some people, definitely," Vivian said, "but I have a suspicion it's a smaller number than you might think. I'm not even sure *I* feel that way. Though learning with you is certainly very energizing"— Vivian stood up—"especially paired with my afternoon coffee."

They walked over to the register and ordered. Once they had their drinks, served in mugs imprinted with a witch stirring a pot of coffee, they settled back into their seats.

"So, how's it been balancing the holidays with the beginning of the school year?" Vivian asked.

"It's always a challenge. But it's been enough years now that my department head asked me in advance about the dates, so she could avoid scheduling important meetings that would conflict."

"That seems like progress!" Vivian said.

"It is. Though she still thinks Simchat Torah is totally made up, since no other Jews she knows celebrate it."

"She's not wrong. I mean, they *are* all made up."

Flora laughed. This is what she loved about studying Jewish text, and specifically what she loved about studying texts with Vivian: Deconstructing tradition from its origins, not for the sake of disproving it, but in order to bolster their understanding of how it exists today.

Ever since she had first encountered Judaism, alongside her then-boyfriend, now-husband, Ben, Flora was drawn to the explicit acknowledgement that Jewish communities, Jewish rituals, Jewish beliefs, were always subject to change. Nothing was fixed, and the communities and lives that grew from them were dynamic and committed, rooted in the world around them. Or at least had the potential to be.

This orientation was poles apart from how her devoutly humanist parents had disdainfully characterized religion to Flora growing up. They had even rejected her countless appeals for a Christmas tree. When she begged for *any* kind of annual family tradition around the time everyone else had one, her parents finally agreed. On December 25th that year, they handed her a thick package enclosed in a neutral silver wrapping paper. Ten-year-old Flora lit up.

But then she opened it. Inside was *Mutual Aid* by Peter Kropotkin. And she was subsequently informed that the Moore family tradition each December 25th would be reading aloud from it.

"Right, just don't go telling my department head that," Flora concluded. "My strategy of bringing her challah before each holiday is working well. She seems to have given up on trying to understand why I do things other Jews don't. Or at least she graciously accepts my bribes."

"Ooh! Speaking of," Vivian said, "I've seen your challah pics on Instagram. Your braid-swirl method for the round ones is ingenious!"

"Thank you for noticing." Flora preened and took a sip from her mug. "Okay, we should probably get to it, right? I bet you've still got holiday prep to do."

"Right, right. Where were we?" Vivian took out a large tractate of Talmud and flipped through the pages.

"*Eruv!*" Flora said. "And I've been thinking about it *a lot*. I'm still confused about whether it's a real physical boundary or just a metaphor with a symbolically physical element."

"So, my read is that it's kind of both," Vivian said. "Initially, the markers were plates of food that you'd put where you'd want to go on Shabbat. They connected two private residences in order to create one public space. And that enabled you to travel there. And then the focus shifted to establishing broader public borders so that people could move more freely and carry within their communities."

"The food plates I get," Flora said. "It's like…it's like bringing your potluck offering to the host before Shabbat. But if the thing itself is just made out of fishing twine or whatever, how do people even know if they are still within the defined boundary, which is impossible to see? And what if something happens to it?"

Vivian clasped both hands around her coffee. "There are usually maps available so people can see what is and isn't inside the eruv," she said. "And it's also customary for groups of people to go out and check the eruv each week to make sure it hasn't fallen."

"And if it has?"

"My dad used to volunteer to help check the eruv in Cincinnati every few weeks. There was this one time, after a big storm, that a portion of the twine disconnected and the eruv was down. It was a *big* deal. A lot of people couldn't go to shul that week."

"Well?" Flora twirled her hand, demanding the rest of the story. "What happened?"

"Someone had to fix it the next week—a contractor who was familiar with the ins and outs, and did the upkeep for a few of the *eruvim* in the area."

Flora tilted her head to one side, pondering. "Hmm. I can't tell how I feel about this," she said. "Like, I appreciate the commitment to this hack so people can override the prohibition of carrying on Shabbat, but it sounds like a whole lot of work, physically and mentally."

"Financially, too," Vivian said. "Those are some of the reasons why a lot of communities don't abide by it."

"Right," Flora said, her words coming slowly, "but there still seems to be something salvageable and…beautiful…about it. About what it enables to take form within the boundaries."

"You know, you could go see the Providence eruv for yourself." Vivian pulled out her phone and began typing. "I'm going to send you a link to the map." A few seconds later, Flora's phone buzzed with a text. She clicked the link and found herself on a website dedicated to Providence's eruv.

"Wow! Who knew?" Flora said. Holding the phone close to her face, she studied the tiny map. There it was, that magical demarcated boundary the Talmud was describing. "This is rad!" Flora scrolled through the rest of the website. "And there's a signup page for new volunteers! Should I do it?" She raised an eyebrow.

Vivian plopped down her mug. "Oh my goodness. I waited six years to ask you to join Beth Abraham's board, and you might have been ready twenty minutes in?"

"Maybe!" Flora scrolled back up to the map. "I—oh, crap!"

"What's wrong?"

"It looks like I live right outside of the eruv," Flora wailed. "By like two blocks!"

"Ah! It turns out that there are hacks for that," Vivian said.

Flora gave a small smile. "Of course there are."

"First off, an eruv can be extended," Vivian said. "But also, if you look right at the section we are up to, you'll find another one."

She rotated the large book on the table and pushed it toward Flora. With a finger marking her place in the open tome, Flora read aloud. "Nechemiah, son of Rav Hanilai, was once so engrossed in his learning that he did not notice he was going out beyond the Shabbat limit. Rav Hisda said to Rav Nachman: 'Your student Nechemiah is in distress. What can we do for him?' Rav Nachman said to him: 'Establish a human partition for him so that he may reenter.'"

Flora stopped and reread the story to herself.

"So—they basically use a literal line of people to extend the eruv and allow Nechemiah to come back in," Flora said. She shook her head from side to side. "I love that. The eruv is not set in stone."

"Right. I think this is quite stunning," Vivian said. "Though if you read further, you'll see that not all the rabbis accepted Rav Nachman's position."

"Sure, but that's always the case. And I love imagining that this happened. That when people were—are—beyond the limit, there are ways to use our people power to bring them back in."

"Are you thinking about something else you'd apply this to?"

Flora bowed her head, willing the connections to form. "I mean, I *am* imagining having some friends create a human partition for me every time I walk to shul on Shabbat. But I'm also thinking about my students. What it looks like to help them find a way forward, to create space for a little movement where it wasn't before, or where we thought it couldn't be."

She thought of how often her classes shrunk and grew because kids' families constantly had to move. And how many kids couldn't study because they needed to work after school. "These institutions—education, housing, healthcare—are failing them because they were set up to serve only some people, people within a boundary. So fighting for better access to those systems, for expanding who is served, feels like an extension of the eruv. And it takes real, individual people to do that. People power. A 'human partition.'"

Flora took a sip of coffee, then she chuckled. "Well, it took me less than two minutes to connect this text to systemic injustice. What does it bring up for you?"

"For me, it offers a frame for thinking about the lines we draw around our community and how we shift them," Vivian said. "You know, like in what situations does the phrase 'the Beth Abraham community' include Two Rivers…or other neighbors who don't come to shul? And how do we determine 'the issues' that matter to us—and who's even included in the 'us?' I can sometimes see the boundaries growing and shifting in my mind."

Vivian abruptly clapped her hands. "Speaking of which! Before I forget, any leads on a potential recipient for funds in future shul appeals?"

"Actually, yes!" Flora leaned over to and riffled through the papers in her bag, but couldn't find what she was looking for. She looked up and swatted a hand at the air. "Whatever, I can email you more about it, but here is the gist: There's this amazing organization that raises investment money to grow Black-and Brown-owned businesses in Providence. It seems perfect. It's called Rainbow Capital."

"That does sound perfect," Vivian said.

"I was teaching a unit on macroeconomics, and one of my favorite students—even though I don't have favorite students—they wrote a paper on it." Flora cupped her face with her palm. "Viv, you'd totally melt over this queer kid. They came into class today with this fresh new undercut and their curls pinned to the side. It was…." She cleared her throat. "But back to the point. Didi mentioned in their report that a key part of Rainbow Capital's strategy is recruiting new investors from local faith communities."

"Bingo!" Vivian said, banging on the table.

"Bingo is right. Do you think the board would approve it?"

"I honestly don't know. But I do know that now is the moment to try for things like that."

"Hmmm." Flora attempted her witchiest smile, waggling both eyebrows. "Our very own eruv extension!"

CHAPTER NINE

As the right-hand man of Sal Maraj, Gordy Silver did it all. Marketing. Investor relations. Staff management. There was lots of important work to do and money to be made, and for Gordy, life in the tech world was a constant hustle.

None of the initial timelines that Gordy and Sal had sold to Leviathan Labs' investors were being met. They were making good progress, sure, but not enough, not at the pace that Gordy had been begging Sal to get to for months now. "The new financial analysis isn't looking good," Gordy had told him as soon as he'd seen it. He had explained it clearly to Sal: The seed money was gone, the incoming investments didn't match the budget, and they were going to need cash. Quick!

But Sal had just nodded, looking far less stressed than Gordy felt. "Good thing I've got you to go find it!"

That was all he would get from Sal, who often seemed powered by the sheer assumption that everything would work itself out. This challenge was Gordy's to manage, like so many at the company. And Gordy would manage the hell out of it. He pored over his records of stakeholders—there were lots of people who wanted in on what Leviathan had to sell—but it often took months to cultivate investors, and it was clear to Gordy that he did not have months. He racked his brain for who to call. One of the handful of investors who had gotten in on the ground floor? Or *should* he expedite a pitch to one of the new targets he had been researching?

And then he remembered. Avner Ben Ami. The CEO of the Tel Aviv-based company KiTov Robotics.

Gordy had stayed in touch with Avner after they met at a conference in New York. KiTov was building autonomous robotic soldiers for the Israeli army. Avner's vision, primarily funded by the Israel Defense Forces, was for these new soldiers to adopt responsibility for the more—in his words—*delicate* work, which humans often bungled. Especially these days, when tensions in the region were only growing. The moral differentiation technology in Leviathan's autonomous control system had impressed Avner, and since then, he had called Gordy up several times to ask for guidance as KiTov worked to develop its own ACS.

In their most recent conversation, Avner had mentioned an upcoming trip to the Boston area for a summit of U.S. and Israeli companies working on new military technologies. When Gordy called, the timing was perfect. He would be thrilled to take a meeting with Gordy and Sal in Providence.

. . .

Reclining in a buttery leather chair and surrounded by the mahogany-paneled walls of Radclyffe's Lounge, Gordy sipped his Scotch.

"I'm glad you got in touch, Gordy," Avner said. "I think we could do such big things together."

"Our industry can be so cutthroat," Gordy said, "but we at Leviathan see ourselves as collaborators, as peace-makers, as we build the most effective products to benefit the whole world."

"And beyond," Sal added.

Gordy knew that Sal had been hesitant, at first, about the idea of collaborating on a project funded by a foreign military. On Mars, Leviathan Labs and Hyydra would be *starting from scratch*, Sal would say. He often acted like exploring an uninhabited planet was immune from the complex moral quandaries of other robotic projects, though Gordy questioned if they were that different.

But Gordy had had a hunch that the possibility of breaking into a whole new market would appeal to Sal's ambition. The possibility of accessing a lot of money fast, when they really needed it, could seal the deal. And he had known the right angle to take. If Leviathan's moral differentiation technology was used to mediate complex military operations, he told Sal, it could well end up being the most meaningful work they did. And voilà! Here they were.

"From what I've heard and read, Hyydra will be an incredible explorer. And I think her ACS could be a great fit for our military technology…which is also about peace-making and collaboration, and of course for the good of the whole world," Avner said. He took a slug of his whiskey. "We call him ISAC. Israel Safety and Autonomy Corps."

"Can you explain what ISAC is being trained to do in more detail, Avner?" Gordy asked, stroking his glass. Gordy reveled in the moments when he knew more than Sal.

"Of course," Avner said, picking up his fork and knife to cut the prime rib on his plate. "You know how the Israeli army oversees security checkpoints for Palestinians in the West Bank?" Sal nodded. "You see—" Avner paused. He put down his utensils. "The IDF has found it…em…more and more difficult for soldiers to…em…manage these operations. They want to enlist a fleet of ISACs to do this work in the future. The IDF has been at the forefront of utilizing robotics, but is only now catching onto the possibility of using them to handle human interactions, and in doing so to…em…minimize collateral damage.

"ISAC's form factor is incredible, and building him is proceeding right on schedule." Avner's hand hovered over his knife. "But we've been experiencing…em…glitches with the ACS we have built internally, and at this point, we are looking for other options."

"I have to be honest with you, Avner," Sal said, gazing out the window at the dramatic view of the Seekonk meeting the Providence River. "I never envisioned using our innovations for military operations."

Gordy had just put a bite of his steak in his mouth, but he needed to cut off Sal's line of thinking. "The IDF is one of the most moral armies in the world, always trying to minimize civilian casualties and defending the only democracy in the Middle East," he said, steak heroically shoved into one cheek. "If there was ever a way for our work to be in service of a military that shares Leviathan's values, it's this one."

He allowed himself a moment to swallow, then continued.

"And the beauty of this plan is that it does not require very much work on our end, Sal. KiTov would purchase access to our ACS using money from their contract with the IDF. They would run their own training program for ISAC in order to fit their context, with minimal initial training by our team." Gordy sat back in his chair. "Think about the advantages here, Sal. We'd get to see what this technology can do in other scenarios. The research possibilities are endless. Everyone wins!"

"It's a good idea," Sal said, his fingers clasping together. "Though I wonder how we sell this—you know, get out ahead of the story. Since Israel is often, um, battered in the press."

"I've already thought of that," Gordy said. "Of course we can pitch stories to favorable outlets, but we also have an exciting opportunity to cultivate public support. Listen to this, Sal. Synagogues across the country encourage their congregants to buy Israel bonds. It's a financial strategy, sure, but it also promotes goodwill among American Jewish communities and investment in Israel's security, which can help counter the disproportionate amount of negative attention.

"The pitches, though—and I just sat through one at my own synagogue—have gotten stale in recent years. We could package a brand-new pitch for synagogues that highlights the IDF's innovative security technologies as investment opportunities. People could even travel to Israel and see ISAC in action at the KiTov lab!

"The U.S. Jewish community becomes our ambassador, see?" he continued. "And the taglines write themselves. 'IDF robots are the new trees.'"

Avner laughed, and Gordy kept going, feeling his momentum building. "Or how about this: 'Not your bubby's Israel bond!'"

Avner guffawed even louder. "Oh Gordy, that is very good," he said, collecting himself.

Sal tittered and his shoulders loosened. Gordy crossed his arms and leaned back in his plush leather chair. Everything was sliding into place. His heart was still pounding, but he tasted victory.

Gordy's mind wandered to his younger brother, Simon. When the Silver boys were growing up, Simon had proved his excellence on the baseball field while Gordy became a master debater. His parents used to sit in the front row at every debate tournament, bringing Simon along to watch. But as their lives progressed, Gordy felt his parents' pride slowly detach from him and amass on his brother, like a flock of birds quietly relocating from one tree to another, one by one. And Gordy knew why. Ever since Simon moved to Israel, changed his name, and became a lifer in the IDF, it was all *Major Shimon, who made aliyah to serve the Jewish nation.* Now the mantle above his parents' fireplace even had one more picture of Simon's family than of Gordy's. If anyone was counting.

"It never ceases to amaze me how many of our personal—I mean, our global problems can be solved through advanced robotic technology," Gordy said.

"Indeed!" said Avner, polishing off the last of his steak.

"Avner, can we move quickly enough to announce the partnership at our simulation and press conference coming up in a few weeks?" Gordy asked.

"I don't see why not."

"Good," Sal said. "That timeline works well for us."

"Phenomenal," Gordy agreed. He pulled out his phone and texted Jacqueline and Freddy to set up a meeting for that afternoon. "I'll also call a few rabbis to take their temperature on the bonds pitch. Thank God the High Holidays are over."

"And who says relations between Israel and the U.S. are strained?" Avner joked.

"Not here they aren't," Gordy said, lifting his glass.

Gordy took an extravagant gulp of his smoky Scotch. He had won Sal and Avner over, and Leviathan Labs would soon be financially stable. Take that, Major Shimon!

. . .

Without much warning, Freddy and Jacqueline had been summoned to a meeting in Sal's top-floor office, which was replete with a panoramic view of the river, framed degrees and awards, an ergonomic chair that looked like a spaceship, and a suspiciously sparse desk made of black glass.

"We have some exciting news to share!" Gordy began, while Freddy and Jacqueline were still taking their seats at the conference table, also black glass. The oversized smirk on Gordy's face was already making Freddy nervous. "Sal and I have been in talks with Avner Ben Ami, CEO of the illustrious KiTov Robotics," he continued. "They're based in Tel Aviv. They are wildly impressed with the progress we've made on our ACS, and they've decided to buy the rights to it."

Freddy swallowed hard. He thought he could hear that sound of unease echoing off the office walls.

"KiTov would tailor it to the needs and uses of the Israel Defense Forces," Gordy went on. "And they already have an incredible military robot that will work perfectly with what you've—we've—built." Gordy clasped his hands together. "We plan to announce this exciting partnership at the press conference."

Freddy tried to repeat each sentence in his head to make sure he was hearing Gordy right.

"The plan is to give KiTov access to the ACS immediately so they get to work on it right away," Sal added, leaning forward. Freddy noted that he spoke with far less gusto than Gordy.

"If we move fast enough, they can even perform their own simulation for our stakeholders," Gordy added. "It's very exciting!"

Jacqueline looked at Freddy. He shook his head, wordlessly asking Jacqueline to speak, as he was having trouble finding words. Though they worked in different departments, the two of them had grown close over the years. They spent most lunches together, and, over takeout containers or Tupperwares from home, they had confessed more doubts about the value of their work to each other than they had to their own spouses.

"Wow," Jacqueline said. "That's really, um…something."

"Yes, it is! Glad we're on the same page," Gordy said. "We move quickly around here. There is so much important work to do!"

Freddy continued to try to communicate with Jacqueline with his eyes, but it proved difficult to develop a collective response in real time without words.

"What happened to KiTov's original control system?" Freddy finally asked. He tapped on the table, the glass producing a louder sound than he had intended. It didn't make sense that they would only be getting to this part of the project now.

"Their in-house system didn't work out," Gordy said. "Your usual trial and error. And they saw our product as the best one out there to replace it with. A real testament to your work!"

"Umm," Freddy said. He needed a few more words. "I think we should learn more about that. And maybe run more tests to see where this integration may lead, we wouldn't want to—"

"I don't think you understand, Freddy," Gordy said, leaning forward in his squeaky leather chair. "This is a done deal. It's happening. And it's a win for all of us. This is exactly the right path of expansion for the company. Our technology has been in the works for several years now and Hyydra has passed the thousands upon thousands of tests that we've given her. ISAC will be able to do the same."

"Who is ISAC?" Jacqueline asked.

"Israel Safety and Autonomy Corps," Gordy said. "That's the name of KiTov's robotic soldier."

Freddy's stomach dropped. There was something about that name. He swiveled toward one of the windows. This was not the work that he signed up for.

Sure, he trusted well-made algorithms to make better decisions than most humans, but it took good humans to make good algorithms, and he sure as hell didn't trust militaries. His own family's experience in Honduras made sure of that. How could Sal and Gordy make such monumental decisions so fast? Weren't there people they answered to, people they had to run these things by? A board? Investors? And why was Gordy doing all the talking?

He spun back toward Gordy. "I think we should spend more time figuring this out, hearing from…KiTov"—Freddy wasn't sure if he was pronouncing that correctly—"about their plans. We need to make sure they know the ins and outs of the technology, and the importance of a diverse machine learning regimen. We need to make sure that our companies' independent goals are—"

"The beauty of this partnership is that we don't have to do any of that. They can!" Gordy said.

"But how can we trust them?" Freddy blurted out.

"With all due respect, Freddy, *we* make the decisions here," Gordy said. "Your job is to build control systems so that our amazing machines can function autonomously. And you have done that! Leave the rest to us."

"We have the best product," Sal spoke up. "And much of that is thanks to your work, Freddy. There's nothing to worry about."

Freddy kept his eyes on Sal—his boss, his mentor—willing him to give more of an explanation, more reassurance, more of *something*. But Sal had gone silent again. He stared past Freddy, seemingly past the whole conversation, hands in his pockets. Was that all he had for them?! Freddy exchanged a look with Jacqueline again. The energy between the two executives seemed packed with worry, refuting Sal's claim.

"Alright then. I guess we have work to do," Jacqueline said, not bothering to conceal her lack of enthusiasm. Freddy was grateful to her for finding the words that at least allowed them to get out of there, since he had none.

CHAPTER TEN

Vivian sat across from Joseph, thumbing through her tractate of Talmud, searching for the right page. Beth Abraham's two rabbis were holding their weekly meeting in a corner of the community sukkah, where a dry spot had been spared by the previous night's rain. Fake fruit and paper chains flapped up and down as the autumn winds howled around them.

When she had found their page, Vivian read aloud in Aramaic and then translated into English. "Leaving the sukkah is permitted from the point that it is raining. Raining so hard that...hmm... that the 'congealed dish' will spoil."

Years ago, upon Vivian's suggestion, the two rabbis had incorporated regular text study into their weekly meetings, which offered them an alternative language with which to address issues that had gotten stuck in the space between them. Vivian knew that Joseph's love language, too, was Torah. She knew that it could often soften him—and her—into more conversation, into a sincere grappling, perhaps even away from the usual tensions.

"The Sages told a parable," she continued. "To what is this matter comparable? It is comparable to a servant who comes to pour wine for his master, and the master pours a jug of water in the servant's face to show him that his presence is not desired."

"Hmm." Joseph leaned back in his plastic chair. "So, God doesn't want us to stay in the sukkah, even when we've created this structure for Him to dwell in."

Vivian looked up from the text toward Joseph. "What do you make of this?" she asked.

Joseph stroked his beard. "It makes me think of my retirement."

"What about it?"

"About how hard it is to tell when something has spoiled, when it's run its course. About how hard it is to leave."

Vivian studied Joseph. His tired eyes, his uneven collar, the wrinkles on his hand as he pointed toward the text. "Interesting," she said. "So what do you think the dish is then?"

He looked up, away from the text, away from Vivian. "I'm picturing a feast of dishes," he said. "Chicken, tzimmes, the broccoli Miriam makes me eat." He cupped his chin. "Maybe they're different relationships I've had with congregants over the years. The ones I've learned with, the ones whose funerals I've done. The ones who have been here for decades."

Vivian closed her eyes and pictured Joseph sitting in the sukkah with different generations of Beth Abraham members, some who she knew, some whose stories she had heard, and some she could only imagine.

"Why are you smiling?" Joseph asked.

"Oh. I didn't realize I was," Vivian said. "I guess it's because I haven't heard you talk about this part of retirement. You know, the things you'll miss. The people you'll miss."

"What do you think has kept me here so long?" he said, his tone a little sharper. "Even as the rain was clearly falling on me and the food." Vivian wondered if he meant, *Even as I haven't been able to give everything I should.*

Vivian took a deep breath, consciously creating a space in her heart for the warmth she was feeling toward Joseph. "That makes a lot of sense," she said.

"What do *you* think the dish is?" he asked.

Vivian looked toward the *s'chach* that made up the sukkah's roof, noticing a gap between a few of the bamboo poles. "I'm not quite sure," she said, almost in a whisper. "But whatever it is, I'm not sure it's spoiled just yet."

Joseph looked like he was trying to make sense of what she had said. If Vivian were being honest, so was she.

"You know, Vivian," he said, turning toward his colleague, "I want you to know that it's you who has inspired me to act on my instincts more. I've seen you do that time and time again and it's led to a lot of changes in our community…good changes, of course.

"And I've gotten a lot clearer on my own convictions recently. That's why Miriam and I are taking this trip to Israel after the holidays—to start planning for our move. Just like the scouts in the Torah!" He gazed away again, dreamily. "I think our commitments change over time, and I wonder if that will happen for you too."

The warmth Vivian was feeling was starting to turn into some-thing else. Maybe even congealing. After seven years of working together as colleagues, Joseph still did this—still talked about any opinion of Vivian's that differed from his own as if it was merely a function of her youth.

Her mind wandered to an email thread she had read on Teki-yah's listserv. A rabbi from the network had led her congregation through a process to adopt an alternative Prayer for Israel, dif-ferent from the one printed in their Conservative prayerbook. The new prayer, written in the voices of Palestinian and Jewish mothers who had lost children to violence, asked for peace for all the people of the land and declared the dignity and human-ity of every inhabitant of Israel/Palestine. Vivian had started an email to the rabbi, wanting to congratulate her as others on the thread had done, but for some reason it had gotten stuck as an unsent draft.

And stuck was what she was with Joseph. They would not move each other, so she would just let his words wash over her.

"Just yesterday," he continued, "when I was buying a new suitcase for our trip and I told the salesclerk where I was going, he said, 'Israel, huh?' And then he told me the sale tag was expired and charged me extra. He said, 'You can afford it.'" Joseph pointed to his kippah. "I'm not sure if these things happen to you, but they happen to me, to a lot of people. And that is never going to stop."

Before Vivian could respond, Raymond passed through the sukkah. She was grateful for the interruption. He stopped near the two rabbis and looked up at the s'chach roof. "You want me or Alton to fix that?" he asked, pointing to a section that had been jostled and shifted by the wind, leaving a few gaps.

"Thanks, Raymond, but we aren't supposed to fix it," Joseph said. "Whatever happens to the sukkah, we have to live with."

Vivian tried to square this additional directive into the metaphor about rain, but she was losing her grip on it.

"Ah, right," Raymond said, still looking up and examining the bamboo mats. "You tell me that every year. I guess I have trouble accepting it." He scratched his chin. "But you know, I like that rule. We can't always fix everything. Sometimes we got to live with the damage." He chuckled. "Though Mac might disagree with me. He never gives up on a fight."

"How is Mac doing?" Vivian asked, gladly accepting the conversational detour. "He's been gone, what, a year now?"

Raymond's son had moved to the farm of a cousin of theirs in Georgia, where a public reparations program scaffolded agricultural property ownership for descendants of enslaved people. "He's doing good," Raymond said. "Working hard. He's eaten more vegetables in the last year than I think he had in his whole life before that. Got real into canning, too. Sheila's so proud. She's down there now, visiting."

"Happy to hear it, Raymond!" Joseph said. "Sometimes you have to leave to find your true home."

Raymond nodded, and went back inside the building. Joseph grinned in Vivian's direction. Vivian felt skeptical of how the original text was getting absorbed into Joseph's understanding of his own decisions, and how they related to Mac's. But wasn't that always the case? We see what we need to see. We see what we want to see.

And Vivian's vision, too, was getting clearer. Her sukkah, her city, her people, getting rained on steadily. But if the waiter threw water on one face, maybe the ones who'd stayed drier could help wipe the water away, wait it out together and regroup. Like the time she and her family hung around at a Cincinnati Reds game despite a two-hour rain delay. And then the Reds won on a walk-off double!

"Ah! I almost forgot," Joseph said, interrupting Vivian's consideration of whether it was worth testing the limits of Joseph's baseball savvy in order to add this to the conversation. "I got an interesting call from Gordy Silver this morning. His company is starting up a partnership with an Israeli robotics company to improve the IDF's security systems. He's working on a new pitch for Israel bonds that would highlight that work. It sounds very innovative. Maybe even a way of bridging this generational divide!"

Vivian gulped.

"He had this great line," Joseph continued, beaming. "'Robots are the new trees.' It's a good investment opportunity and it can help those so far away to stay connected. Something to perhaps keep in mind for next year's appeal."

Vivian did not know what to say. The tenderness she had been feeling toward Joseph was now fully congealed, and her calm had turned to urgency. But Joseph would be gone by next Rosh Hashanah, and she would do what she could to ensure that this was not, in fact, Beth Abraham's High Holiday appeal. Joseph could have his memories—not a say in future shul decisions.

Her mind shifted to Freddy. Was he working on this project of Leviathan's? He hadn't mentioned it at dinner a few weeks earlier. How could he think it would be a good idea to mix robots and militaries? Oh, God.

Vivian looked back toward Joseph, who was still smiling. "On some days," he said, "I think that the sukkahs we've built might not be so bad." Vivian certainly wanted that to be true, but she hoped it was *her* vision, however blurry it was, that would come to pass. Not his.

CHAPTER ELEVEN

"THANK YOU, MIAMI!" said the cheerful face peering through a box on Karla's computer screen. "It's inspiring to hear about so much public money getting invested in marsh creation." The moderator of the call sounded like he was about to move on, but then he added in a fake radio-announcer voice, "Sea levels aren't the only things rising down there, folks!"

Every other month, Karla found herself on a video call with hundreds of municipal climate-resiliency professionals from around the country. They were gathered by the Intergovernmental Climate Adaptation Network: ICAN. It seemed obvious that *WE*CAN would suit the organization much better, but apparently everyone had more important work to do than rebrand a little-known group of government bureaucrats.

Karla looked forward to these calls. Knowing that so many people were out there building strategies, thinking creatively in order to bypass political gridlock, working in some of the most vulnerable areas, rooted her more deeply in her own tasks.

The calls also made her, and surely everyone else, uneasy. It was hard enough to face the challenges within Providence. Looking closely at the countless ways that sea-level rise, and escalating temperatures, and draught, and so many other disastrous consequences of climate change were impacting areas across the entire country could sometimes be too much. Which is why, it seemed, ICAN's director, Lino, joked around whenever he could. Sometimes that led to group chants of *Yes, ICAN!* Other times, he attempted to make light of the apocalyptic challenges that they all faced both in their current realities and in the projections.

But facing the doom with this group gave Karla strength.

Today the call had started with a presentation by a team in Miami. After years of fighting with the state of Florida, they had secured funding to grow their coastline through marsh expansion and creation, borrowing strategies from a project that had been active in Louisiana for over a decade. And while the wildfires, hurricanes, and heat waves kept coming, so did the ingenuity in many places. Karla and her colleagues had been asked to present more than once on the topic of future planning. Providence was certainly ahead of the game, as these calls made even clearer to her. Knowing that filled Karla with simultaneous pride and dread.

The theme of the rest of today's presentations was "private

economic investment in public resiliency programs." Lino got very excited, bouncing up and down in his Zoom box as he introduced a northern Californian whose city government had collaborated successfully with several social-networking companies. The companies had each committed a significant cut of their philanthropic budgets—thirty percent—to local and statewide wildfire prevention and cleanup efforts. That was a huge win. "And we'll take all the wins we can get," the presenter concluded.

Someone who essentially held Karla's position in a small coastal city in South Carolina was next to present a victory. A local manufacturer that was moving out of its waterfront operation had committed to sell the campus to the city at a heavily reduced price. The city would build it into a natural buffer against storms. From all over the country, others chimed in, making the case that it was indeed possible to get corporations to invest in protecting and defending their host towns.

This was not an area where Providence was leading the way. In fact, they were definitely behind. They got *crumbs* from the local powerhouse businesses. Leviathan Labs restored a small public park near their headquarters. Wow. A medical records company offered discounts to the city's safety net hospitals. Double wow. NVTN Technologies gave old iPads to middle schools, and that did, admittedly, enable more equitable remote learning during school closures—for the few kids who got them. Start the parade. But none of their offers even hinted at acknowledging the ways these companies shifted the makeup of the city—increasing housing prices, expanding development in areas vulnerable to flooding, putting more of a drain on the public resources that would become more and more scarce.

But thanks to ICAN, Karla and her team had a bit of inspiration. A roadmap.

"Thank you, everyone, for being here," Lino said, concluding the call. "And one last time…if you could all come off mute…"

"Yes, ICAN!"

There was a note of beleaguerment in Karla's chant as she joined in with all the others in their separate virtual boxes. After signing off the call, she exhaled and whispered her version—"Yes, *I can*. Yes, *we can*"—and that time, it came out with a little more oomph.

CHAPTER TWELVE

V IVIAN EYED THE paper chains, which weren't looking so hot after the rain shower a few nights prior. Colorless and misshapen, they looked like a string of shriveled potatoes creeping around the sukkah. The folding table in front of her held leftover desserts from earlier holiday celebrations, recycled as fuel for this month's board meeting.

"Tonight we'll review key pieces related to the rabbinic transition. But first," Tamar Benayoun said, clasping her hands together, "we'll start in our traditional way. A go-around! Let's each share a highlight from the High Holidays."

Vivian smiled. Tamar went first, sharing how glad she was that a few of the prayer leaders had incorporated Sephardic tunes into the davening. Vera Cohen's highlight was decorating her own sukkah with her grandchildren, plastering signs of protest from various demonstrations on the walls. Shlomo Seidel's was his wife's extra-special multilayered gefilte fish, which she had been making for Rosh Hashanah for decades. It took him a while to explain. Flora shared the joy of building a sukkah for the first time. When her turn came around, Vivian mentioned how happy she was to see so many new faces at the different services over the past few weeks.

"Now that wasn't too painful, was it?" Tamar said, after a few more people had shared. Vivian's shoulders loosened. Having Tamar at the helm made her feel like the community was in good hands.

She moved on to business. "So. We are very glad that Rabbi Vivian has chosen to stay and become our senior rabbi! The next part of the process is figuring out what we want in the new associate rabbi, and what their portfolio would be, so we can put together a job description." Tamar passed a pile of papers around the table. "Here is our starting point. It's the job description we used when we hired Rabbi Vivian. We'll begin by discussing any edits we want to make to it."

Once each board member had gotten a copy, they each looked down, and a rare moment of silence overtook the sukkah.

Barry Katz was first to speak up. "It says here that this rabbi would be committed to engaging young adults," he said. "That's so important. But I wonder if we might lose sight of the needs of the older congregants. If, you know, both rabbis are on the, um, younger side."

"Okay, thank you, Barry," Tamar said, jotting down notes. "Maybe we could make that more explicit in the description."

"And here it says that the associate rabbi would manage the social justice work." Joel Fishman pointed to his sheet. "But since Rabbi Vivian said she will keep that area within her responsibilities, we'd obviously need the new rabbi to fill in the gaps that Rabbi Glass's departure will leave open, instead. So perhaps we should scratch it from the new rabbi's list of duties?" Several heads bobbed slowly in what looked like agreement.

"Some responsibilities, like prayer leading and adult education, inevitably fall on both rabbis' plates," Vera said. "Perhaps justice work should be one of those things."

"I don't know," Shlomo said. "I think we need to make sure that we get someone who has similar skills and, um, interests and, um…you know, a similar *disposition* to Rabbi Glass."

Does he mean that we need a man? Vivian wondered. For Pete's sake. How was Shlomo Seidel, who must surely be 120 years old by now, even still on the board?!

"That is one way to look at it, Shlomo," she said, butting in earlier than she usually would at a board meeting, where she technically was not a voting member. But she felt the need to remind the board that she was, in fact, *in the room* as this conversation about her continued. "And another way to look at it is that there is so much important social justice work to do." Vivian paused. "*And* adult education *and* prayer facilitation *and* pastoral care for congregants *of every age*," she added, looking at Barry. "Both rabbis being partners in all that work would only make our community stronger and more—" *More coherent*, she thought. There was that word again. But she stopped herself, for some reason, from saying it out loud.

"But," Shlomo interjected, wagging his finger, "if you are too alike, then how will we know who to go to for what? How will this work?" A few more nods followed.

"I don't think it would be that hard," Flora responded. "The new rabbi and Rabbi Vivian would figure out which projects and areas of work make sense for each of them based on their strengths and interests." She clasped her hands on the table and leaned in toward Shlomo. "Think about it like a good partnership—a good marriage." Shlomo stared blankly. "You probably have your domains, and your wife has hers," Flora said. Shlomo kept staring blankly. "Like she makes the gefilte fish, but you probably, um, cook other things. Right?"

"We do the normal roles for men and women," Shlomo said, scowling. Vivian noticed Flora crumpling a corner of the job description sheet. Glancing down at her own copy, she realized she must have been doing the same.

"No," Vera chimed in, "what you and Phyllis each do is based on the roles you have *chosen*, Shlomo. For instance, I do the food shopping and Charlie most often does the laundry and takes out the trash."

"Please don't tell Phyllis that," Shlomo said, arms folded. "She's always told me maybe I could learn to do the laundry, but I've stuck it out this long."

Vivian had a sudden burst of inspiration. "Maybe think about it like a good basketball team," she said. "Like how lots of players these days play multiple positions so that they can switch things up on the court depending on the opposing team. To get the best match-up, right?"

"My memory of the Celtics is that each player stuck to their role," Shlomo said. "Danny Ainge would never play center, and

Larry Bird would certainly never play the point. That would be...."
Shlomo chortled. "That would just be laughable!"

Vivian sighed, realizing it might be best to let this metaphor go.

"Now is a moment to put our stake in the ground," Vera said,
looking at Vivian intently. "Whether the basketball people do it
or not. To say that this is who we are. We are a synagogue committed to justice, at all levels."

"But we already *are*. We do the annual food drive and we support Two Rivers somehow, don't we?" someone said. "Are there
more things to do?"

Flora rolled her eyes. "So many things."

"Like what?" someone asked.

Vivian looked at Flora, then Vera, then Flora again, wishing
she could will a strategy into existence that they had not in fact
put into words yet. Vera took the cue. "Well...for instance." She
took a deep breath. "The Israel bonds pitch on Rosh Hashanah.
That is something that started decades ago, and I wonder, is that
still a commitment that makes sense these days? Or might there be
an option that allows us to engage in a more local justice effort?"

The room went completely silent.

Oops, Vivian thought.

"But that's our tradition," Joel said.

"What would we do instead?" Barry asked.

Vivian, Vera and Flora looked at each other again, their eyes
darting back and forth. It was too soon. They didn't have a plan.
They had not yet worked through the kinks of what they might
say, how they might soften their language to make it possible for
some members to hear. But here they were.

Vivian was about to jump in when Flora beat her to it. "One

idea is raising money for a deserving organization in our city," she said. "For example, there's this amazing one called Rainbow Capital." Her voice was a little shaky at first, but Flora soon found her footing and described what Rainbow did. When she had finished, Vivian looked around the sukkah. It felt like a wax museum. Everyone was perfectly still. She could hear the wind blowing through the cracks in the s'chach.

"But supporting Israel matters just as much," Joel finally said. "No. It matters more! Who else is going to do it? And besides, selling bonds is something we've done forever."

No, not forever, Vivian thought. *Not since the thirteenth century. Just, like, the eighties.* But she was determined to avoid going down that rabbit hole. Instead, she said, "The world has changed. Providence, the U.S, Israel, everywhere." She suddenly remembered robotic Mars exploration. *The whole universe.* "There is so much work to do *here*, and we have the opportunity—some would say the obligation—to partake of it." She wasn't sure this was the right argument for the Shlomos and the Joels of the board, but apparently she had fully entered improvisational mode.

"It's an intriguing idea," Tamar said. "Very, umm, innovative." Gah! Tamar sometimes took the role of referee when Vivian wished she would get out there in the game, a player on the field. On Vivian's team, of course.

"Maybe *too* innovative?" Barry Katz asked. A half dozen board members started nodding so vigorously that it hurt Vivian's neck just to watch.

Shlomo chimed in. "The point of shul is that we know what to expect, we do things the way they've always been done."

"I don't think that's true," Flora said. "I certainly don't know

THE RABBI WHO PRAYED FOR THE CITY   99

how things have always been done, but I do know that I wouldn't feel comfortable in a community that never changed."

A chorus of *mhm*s filled the space. Sensing a little momentum, Vivian spoke up. "I think this is a moment, as Vera said before, when we as a community have an opportunity to really commit to who we want to be. We can figure out the details of what that looks like over time. But one first step is finding an associate rabbi who ascribes to that vision, who understands that Torah and prayer are needed as we face the challenges of our moment, who believes in the importance of allyship with other faith communities so we can face our respective challenges, who—"

"What does Joseph think?" Shlomo asked. "I think we should get his input here."

Joseph wasn't there. He hadn't come to a board meeting in months, abandoning that responsibility to Vivian. And—*wait*. Why was Joseph's input needed to hire *her* associate rabbi?!

Vivian had learned a useful trick from Heather for whenever she needed to scream at the top of her lungs in a situation in which it would be inadvisable to do so. And so, she imagined a separate miniature version of herself screaming as loud as she could. She had gotten so good at this that she could conjure up her own incensed analogue even with her eyes wide open.

"Right, yes," Joel said. "It seems to me like we need more information before moving forward on the job description. And any other changes."

"I move that we table this discussion," Barry said.

"I second," someone else said swiftly.

Tamar responded automatically, in a monotone. "All in favor of tabling this discussion and returning next month." Eight hands went up. "All opposed?" Four went up. "Abstentions." One. "The motion carries," Tamar said.

Vivian glanced at Vera again, then Flora, who looked surprised. In her mind, analogue Vivian was cursing Robert's Rules of Order at the top of her lungs.

"It looks like we'll reconvene about this next month," Tamar said, a note of exasperation breaking through. "Let's take five, then we'll move onto plans for the spring fundraiser."

During the short break, the board members stood up, mingling or heading inside for a few minutes. Vivian felt defeated. She forced herself to think of her beloved Bengals. For her entire life, they had ended almost every football season in shambles, but then they had finally done it. A Super Bowl win. *My win is coming*, she told herself.

"That wasn't great," Flora said to Vivian and Vera, the three of them coalescing in a corner of the sukkah.

"I'm sorry," Vivian sighed. "I think I set us up for that. We were so not ready for this conversation. And Flora, I promise—board meetings aren't always like this."

Vera tilted her head and pursed her lips.

"Okay, maybe they often are," Vivian conceded. "But they can get better?" She had meant that to come out as a statement.

"They can and they will," Vera said. "We'll regroup and be more prepared for the next one." She put a hand on Vivian's shoulder. "Revolutions take time," she said.

"No," Flora said, folding her arms and shaking her head. "Shlomo Seidel takes time."

Vivian's Super Bowl hadn't come yet, but her team had the kind of players who could get there. Someday.

CHAPTER THIRTEEN

G ORDY SIPPED HIS fourth coffee of the day.

"We were up all night looking into the hacked engineer's account," announced Jack Phillips, Leviathan's head of security. He flattened his tie against his chest. "As far as we could find, Horizon didn't reach anything else. We've contained the threat and let the authorities know, but we need to ramp up security for the event."

A small team was sitting at the glass table in Sal's office, preparing for the press conference and simulation that would show the world—and beyond!—the heights of what technological innovation could do. There was only one day to go.

As a result of recent developments, the company's financial troubles had been resolved, mostly, and Leviathan now had an opportunity to make a big splash by unveiling the new partnership with KiTov Robotics. But there were a few last-minute hiccups to address. Horizon Systems, a Chinese robotics company, claimed to be making a product similar to Hyydra, and they were now racing for a patent. Gordy knew the situation had already been worrying Sal for weeks, and yesterday's hack had unsettled them all.

"Jack, we can't take any chances," Sal said, his hands folded together in front of his face. "We know there is a possibility of more tampering."

Jack proceeded to lay out his plan to ramp up cybersecurity. He reassured Sal that he was bringing in an additional expert to keep a close eye on Leviathan's digital systems and detect any infiltration. And physical security for the following day's event would be even tighter than planned.

"There's one more thing," he said. "Some group or other—they seem to be very angry about Mars exploration—is planning a protest across the street during the event. Given the variety of security concerns, I propose that we move the press conference into the inner courtyard, rather than blocking off the street out front."

Gordy folded his arms. "But think of the visual," he said. "No one can see the logo on the building from the courtyard."

"Sometimes you've got to be cautious," Jack replied, "and I would recommend caution right now."

Gordy and Jack both looked at Sal, who was gazing beyond both of his colleagues and frowning, silent. Gordy tapped his foot on the floor, waiting. "While I often resist caution," Sal finally said, "we're going to follow Jack's advice here." Gordy huffed, but he knew that if Sal's mind was set, he would not change it.

He scrolled through his emails restlessly. Jacqueline and Freddy were still asking for more time. Hiccups and more hiccups. Gordy kept scrolling, hoping for good news to hold on to, tuning out the rest of the conversation between Sal and Jack.

Then an email caught his attention. It was the head of finance, letting him know that the first installment of funds had come in from KiTov. It was a hefty amount; the company would be set for many months. Gordy could feel the tension in his shoulders relaxing.

Some things were moving in the right direction. In fact, any minute now, Avner Ben Ami and the ISAC prototype would arrive. And within a day, the whole world would know about the game-changing contributions that Leviathan Labs was poised to make. And the money, of course. Even if they couldn't have photo ops with the company logo, it would be an amazing day for Leviathan. An amazing day for Gordy Silver.

At some point, in between emails, daydreams, and the drone of Jack's security plan in the background, Gordy's phone rang. He picked it up without excusing himself from Sal's office. It was Avner.

"They're here!" Gordy said.

. . .

Two floors below ground, in the most secure room in all of Leviathan Labs' headquarters, Freddy came face to face with a six-foot behemoth of steel, rubber and aluminum. As he sized up ISAC, Freddy could feel ISAC doing the same to him. And Freddy knew who would win that fight.

"Amazing, isn't he?" Gordy said.

"How many hydraulic joints has he got?" Jacqueline asked Avner, sounding more excited than Freddy would have liked.

"Twenty-four!" Avner said. "Along with whole-body mobility, and the most advanced depth sensors to detect surroundings and calculate the appropriate motion."

"ISAC is certainly a marvel!" Gordy said. "I can't wait to see his state-of-the-art agility merge with our control system."

Our control system?! Freddy thought. *What have you done to build this, Gordy? Nothing.*

"We've written and filed most of the contracts and the paperwork already," Gordy said. "So, Freddy, now we just have to give KiTov access to a copycat ACS and they can start tailoring it to ISAC."

Another bald man had arrived with Avner—and looked unsettlingly like him—but had not been introduced. Now he passed something to Avner. "Here is the information to access ISAC," Avner said, extending it toward Freddy. The USB flash drive's shape was a miniature version of the prototype standing next to them.

Freddy started to reach for it, but everything in his body tightened. His own control system was telling him that this was one hasty and irresponsible human-made choice. He looked across the room at Sal. The compass of Leviathan. The reason Freddy accepted the job in the first place. He was stoic, inscrutable, as he always seemed to be these days. Hands ever in his pockets. For an instant, Freddy got the sense that maybe the same conflict was raging in Sal's gut too, and he was doing all he could to hide it.

But Sal just lifted his chin toward his protégé, cosigning Gordy and Avner's directions.

Freddy finally allowed his hand to make contact with the flash drive. He held it far away from his body. "What went wrong with the first ACS built to sync with ISAC?" he asked suddenly.

"Em…." Avner said, tapping his foot. "It was just…what's the word…there were…em…glitches." The guy's English seemed to have deserted him for a moment, Freddy noticed.

"I'd be interested to know more about those—"

Gordy cut in. "Freddy, we don't have time for this," he said, stepping closer and sort of smiling, clearly trying to exude a collegiality he didn't feel. "We have built the best product out there, and KiTov needs it to do important work in the world."

Freddy stared at Gordy, deciding whether to keep fighting this losing battle. He twisted toward Sal, pleading one more time with his eyes for his boss to intervene. All he got was another nod.

Surrendering, Freddy walked over to the table where he had set down his laptop and plugged in the flash drive. He opened up the file from Avner and commenced the uploading process, handing over years of work to a company whose mission he was clear he did not share.

Freddy looked back toward ISAC, toward wherever his eyes might be if he were human. But he was no less opaque than Sal.

CHAPTER FOURTEEN

THE ART ON THE WALLS of Ocean State Fertility and Obstetrics was not very interesting. Pleasant but generic photos of seas, sunrises and flowers were everywhere Vivian looked. She wondered if the images were intentional—perhaps metaphors for conception and birth? Or, maybe, reminders that the ocean was dying, the sun was getting too hot, and flowers may soon be an endangered species?

A nurse named Gray Nicholson reviewed Vivian and Karla's paperwork and then looked up from the desk. Nicholson wore a red-and-black checkered shirt and a fleece vest adorned with a clinic logo and a *they/them* pronoun pin.

"So, have you decided on a timeline?" they asked.

Vivian and Karla sighed in unison. "We keep putting it off," Vivian said, reaching her hand over to the next chair to hold Karla's. "We'll reach different markers of time, like with work, or family, or politics, and then just make new ones." Nicholson jotted down notes.

"But we are here," Karla added, "and that seems as much a sign as anything that we are ready."

Vivian leaned forward. "*Almost* ready," she clarified. She grasped in her mind for the image of their future family unit that she was starting to access more readily, but sitting in this office, with the steps forward getting more and more real, oddly made it blurrier. "Or, like, *almost* almost ready."

Nicholson smiled faintly. "Do you have a preference for a donor you know versus one through the sperm bank?"

"We like the idea of a known donor," Karla said. "Someone who might be around every now and then to get to know our kid in case they have questions. We've started making a list of possibilities. We've gotten that far."

"And?" Nicholson waited for a response. Silence. "Have you made any asks?"

"Um, sort of?" Vivian said, thinking back to when Heather found the potential donor Post-it note.

"Yeah," Nicholson said, elongating the word as if it were two syllables, "I'm going to classify that as a no." They jotted down more notes on their clipboard. "That will clearly be key. Okay, next question. Have you decided which one of you would be the gestational parent?"

Vivian and Karla looked at each other. They started to speak at the same time, and Vivian ceded the floor to her wife with relief. Karla said, "We've, um, talked about me going first, so…."

"So Karla would be the one pursuing pregnancy, then?" Nicholson pointed their pen at her.

"Um, yeah, mhm. We think," Karla said, as Vivian nodded slowly in a semblance of clarity.

"She even downloaded one of those ovulation-tracking apps," Vivian added.

"Oh, so you've already started tracking?"

"No, we just have the app for when it's time."

Nicholson put their pen down. "You know, a lot of people come here in a similar place, still working through some of the biggest questions. More so now than in the past, given how, um"—Nicholson tapped their desk—"uncertain the future can feel."

Vivian took a deep breath. Imagining their anxiety and uncertainty as a collective experience was somewhat comforting.

"That said, you folks are a bit all over the place," Nicholson continued, their voice growing more serious. They leaned back into their leather chair. "I wonder if you may be finding it hard to look past the obstacles. I'm going to give you a little homework. Make a list of the pros—the reasons why, despite the cons, you are still here trying to get to yes."

Nicholson gave them a few pamphlets and pointers about the fertility-tracking process, and recommended vitamins for Karla… or whoever might get pregnant. And Vivian and Karla sheepishly said their goodbyes.

They walked out of the clinic and into the half-empty parking lot. Listening to the sounds of cars whizzing by on the main road,

Vivian noticed a couple walking into the clinic. One partner's belly looked like it was about to explode, and the other rested their hand on the pregnant one's back, holding them up.

"I mean, I do see it, for us," Vivian said. "I know I want kids."

"Yeah, same. You know that."

"But...."

"Yeah," Karla said, as they arrived at their car and stood in front of it. "But there are always *buts*."

"How about we each think of a pro right now?" Vivian suggested. "I'll say one and then you'll say one." She thought for a moment. "I think...." The words came slowly. "I think I just have a primal desire for us to be a bigger family." She nodded, feeling satisfied with herself. "Sometimes," she blurted out.

"That's a good one," Karla said. "Here's mine: more people to love while we wait for the end of the world."

Vivian laughed. "Seems like a con disguised as a pro to me, baby."

"Okay, let me try again. More people to love while we *fight against* the end of the world."

"That's a little better," Vivian said, catching Karla's chin with a finger and leaning in to kiss her. "This is good! We now have the beginnings of a solid pros list."

"We should put these on another Post-it!" Karla said. "To celebrate, want to stop by Freddy's robot reveal with me? It's near here, and when I told him we were heading to this part of town he said he'd put our names on the list. I think it could be valuable for my office to get a better grip on the kinds of things Leviathan is doing with all that investment money."

Vivian had the day off, the first since the condensed schedule of Jewish holidays had ended. She had just taken out a new sci-fi book from the library that she was excited to read. But perhaps this could scratch the same itch.

"Okay," she said. "And *I* heard from Joseph that Leviathan has a new project with the Israeli army." She shook her head. "Apparently they are going to be looking for support from Jewish communities, so it could be good reconnaissance for me too."

Vivian sighed, finally opening the car door. "But I have a funny feeling this won't add too many pros to our list."

CHAPTER FIFTEEN

THE FERTILITY CLINIC was less than a mile from Leviathan Labs' headquarters. Vivian drove herself and Karla through Providence's ever-changing landscape, heading toward a neighborhood near the water that was ripe with luxury condo development—despite, as Karla was quick to point out, projections that the area would flood more regularly in the coming years.

As Vivian parked, she could already see a crowd outside of Leviathan. Something about the day's activities—meeting with Gray Nicholson, being introduced to Freddy's robot prototype—felt almost sequential to her, like a themed day: *The Future.*

She and Karla walked toward the action. As they made their way into the crowd, a repeated clicking sound caught Vivian's attention, and she swiveled her head to locate it. *There*. She spotted the red point of a laser. Then another one. And another. There was very visible security everywhere, and apparently plenty of invisible surveillance as well.

The company's main building, made up mostly of panoramic windows, had a silver sheen to it and a huge logo across its front, the word *Leviathan* inside a simple stencil of a large fish. Next to it was a construction site where large posters plastered the chain link fence, making it very clear what was in progress: more tech campuses.

A commotion across the street attracted Vivian's attention, and when she turned, she found herself facing a group of protesters. She caught a few of their signs. "HELL NO! COLONIALISM 3.0." Another read, "INVEST IN PROVIDENCE, NOT MARS." Then there was "CLEAN UP THIS MESS FIRST." That last demand, Vivian thought, sounded especially reasonable.

Karla tugged on Vivian's shirt, and they fell into the line to enter. From here, Vivian could see two canopy tents tucked into a courtyard between Leviathan's main building and another one, the tents' silver awnings also printed with the fish logo. At the front of the line, Karla pulled up a QR code on her cell phone and slid it under a machine, which beeped. The plexiglass turnstile opened for them. Once inside the courtyard, they found themselves in an immaculately kept garden, which they passed through in the direction of the tents. Soothing electronic music played in the background. Flowers outlined their path, each bunch a different shade of red. Vivian appreciated the homage to the Red Sox, who had made it to the playoffs once again. Then it hit her. Of course. *Mars*. The red planet.

At the canopies, Vivian surveyed the crowd. Lots of men. Not too old. Lots of suits. Frequently paired with white sneakers. As she pondered what certainly could not just be a sartorial coincidence, a man approached the podium in a well-fitted suit. And white sneakers.

"Good morning!" he said. "I am Sal Maraj, CEO of Leviathan Labs, and we are here today to celebrate the future!" The crowd broke out in loud applause. "Some would have you think we are headed for a time of doom, of scarcity. But those people are just not creative enough. They are not dreamers like you, and you," he said, pointing out into the audience. On the second "you," Vivian was sure Sal was pointing and looking right at her.

"And me," Sal continued, angling his finger toward his own chest.

"We are standing on the precipice between who we are and who we might be as a species, between what is possible now, and what could be within our reach if we stretch our dreams and work together to ensure their fruition.

"Today, we at Leviathan Labs will be introducing you to Hyydra, our prized prototype, controlled by our innovative moral differentiation technology. Hyydra is a robotic marvel who will help build the future. She can dig, she can build, navigate any terrain, identify any danger. And she possesses the most advanced machine-learning intelligence model in robotics right now.

"I want to welcome a few special guests here with us today. Firstly, Colin Creed, the CEO of SpaceRace, who has been working tirelessly for almost two decades to build a spacecraft that will soon be traveling to Mars on a weekly basis. And SpaceRace, as you saw in the news just a few months ago, has now landed their fourth rover on the red planet!"

A tall man with perfectly coiffed brown hair, whose age Vivian could not determine, turned his head back toward the crowd and waved. "We cannot wait for Hyydra to climb aboard and work with us to shape the future!" Creed said. His voice was amplified as if he had a microphone, but Vivian couldn't see one.

Sal smiled. "And I'd also like to introduce a special new partner from KiTov Robotics," he said, "all the way from Tel Aviv: Avner Ben Ami." A shorter, brawny-looking bald man standing very straight turned and waved from a spot next to Creed. He didn't make any comments, and Sal continued. "While the world knows of our efforts to get Hyydra to Mars, we have an announcement to make today about another exciting frontier. Leviathan Labs has entered into a groundbreaking partnership with KiTov and the Israeli military in order to create a robotic soldier more evolved than you can possibly imagine."

Vivian couldn't be sure, but it sounded as though the thrill in his voice was waning. Sal's volume was building, but his enthusiasm didn't seem to be. But she was probably just projecting. Right?

"KiTov has built ISAC," Sal said. "Israeli Safety and Autonomy Corps, an incredible humanoid machine that will dazzle you all. ISAC will be endowed with the same autonomous control system that we have built for Hyydra, adapted to his own context."

Vivian noticed that though Avner Ben Ami's expression did not change, he somehow stood even straighter, maybe even gaining a few inches of height.

The audience clapped wildly. Vivian's stomach dropped. The partnership that Joseph had mentioned seemed pretty far along.

This must have happened quite fast. Everyone around Vivian seemed far more excited than she did about this news. Or than Freddy did, for that matter. She spotted him toward the front, fidgeting and looking glum within what Vivian assumed was a group of beaming colleagues.

"There is no time to waste when trying to build a better world," Sal said, his initial pep returning, "or a better galaxy. Someday—sooner than you might think—our creations will be on the ground floor exploring and building on the surface of Mars, making peace in the Middle East even. The future is now. And Hyydra—and ISAC—will lead the way."

Vivian scanned the crowd. Everyone stood still, seemingly captivated by the visions of Sal Maraj. She worked to grasp the appeal. *Why trust flawed humans to solve our problems? Why not leave it to these magical beings?*

It almost sounded messianic. As a child, Vivian had gone through a stage of being obsessed with the idea of the Messiah. Her Orthodox cousins often talked about what they would do when *mashiach* came, when everyone would be safe and everything would be exactly as it should be. After a Passover spent with them in Israel, Vivian started wondering the same thing. Would there be no more school? Could she have dessert after every meal? She would ask her parents all sorts of questions, and they would roll their eyes, waiting for her to come back to earth.

Later on, in rabbinical school, she became very interested in the ancient rabbis' thoughts on the matter. In her search through the sources, she found that some rabbis in the Talmud expounded upon the idea of a messianic savior, but she was never convinced that any of them wholeheartedly believed in one. She concluded that the idea held spiritual and emotional value in challenging times, when it was difficult to identify a way out. Kind of like robots going to Mars. And, certainly, solving the Israel Defense Force's problems.

"We look forward to taking many of you on a more in-depth tour today, where you will experience a simulation that will blow your minds." Sal lifted what looked like a silver water bottle. "To the future!" he toasted.

"To the future!" the crowd chanted enthusiastically, with many pantomiming their own toasts.

Karla whispered into Vivian's ear. "This is…I mean…"

Vivian shook her head. "I know, baby," she whispered back. "I know."

"Rabbi!"

Vivian turned around to find Gordy Silver standing right behind her. "Oh! Hi, Gordy."

"What a surprise!" Gordy said. "What are you doing here?"

Vivian shared that Karla and Freddy were old friends, hoping that constituted enough of an explanation to satiate his curiosity.

"Well I'm glad you're here! What do you think of our ground-breaking collaboration with KiTov?" Gordy asked, arms spread outward, taking up as much room as was possible in the crowd. There was that word again. *Groundbreaking.* "Exciting, right?"

"Mhm. It's really, uh," Vivian said, willing words to come out. "Really something! It sounds so new. And there are so many people here!" Vivian noticed that she was just stating facts, but if she could do it with a smile on her face, perhaps Gordy would not detect her real feelings. "And there is so much happening on this huge campus. And these flowers are just so…so red." Karla squeezed Vivian's arm. She got control of herself and stopped talking.

"Right?!" Gordy said. "Hey, why don't you both come to the simulation for VIPs?" He was looking at something over Vivian's head as he spoke. "I'd love your feedback. I have this dream that synagogues might want to invest in ISAC. We could highlight this work through Israel bonds appeals and spread the good will throughout the Jewish community." Gordy's eyes found Vivian's again. "Joseph sounded very excited about it when I told him. I've already thought of a marketing plan: 'Not your bubby's Israel bonds!'" He sashayed one arm through the air as if visualizing the tagline on a poster. "Genius, right?"

Vivian bobbed her head without saying anything. Possible answers to his questions were proving more difficult to find. Luckily, someone appeared and pulled Gordy away before Vivian could answer.

As he made his way back toward the podium, Karla seemed to be following him with her gaze. "Now, I wonder if *he* would make a good sperm donor. Successful, handsome-ish, you know—once you get past the robot obsession."

Vivian glared at her. They both burst out laughing.

. . .

Half of Vivian wanted to leave Leviathan Labs as fast as she could, but the other half of her couldn't help but be intrigued. So when a young man, presumably sent by Gordy, brought over two VIP passes with their names scribbled on them, she allowed herself to get swept up in the flow of people moving into the building.

Once they had gotten inside, she realized they had ended up situated between press and what looked like a group of investors. It was pretty easy to tell the difference between the two groups: the sneakers.

A crowd of about sixty people stood in the spacious lobby. The sun was shining through a wall made up mostly of windows, a few of which were open. In the light, the Hyydra prototypes were glowing. They looked like headless robotic dogs.

"Those are terrifying," Vivian whispered.

"I don't know," Karla countered. "They seem kind of cute to me."

At the front of the room, an engineer named Jacqueline Saito introduced herself and addressed the crowd. "Hyydra is a physical marvel—quick, strong, decisive and, of course, graceful. Her body can withstand any conditions she is faced with. Blistering heat. A physical attack. You name it!

"And we've been working with NASA to break down thousands of different scenarios into narratives, each moment of which has millions of images or videos associated with it, training Hyydra to decipher the most rational action for any situation: resource exploration, combat, infrastructure construction, diplomacy, and on and on. Her corporeal flexibility and unparalleled moral decision-making capabilities allow her to adapt to anything thrown her way.

"Now let's see her in action, shall we?" Jacqueline paused. "Please welcome the star of our show: Hyydra!"

Two Hyydra models approached her from the side of the room. The crowd clapped, and an echo boomed off of the glass walls. "She can do it all! Our legion of Hyydras will be able to construct full hospitals and schools, to establish complex underground water systems at ten times the speed of humans and in any conditions.

"And now, watch in real time as they construct a building. Perhaps it's a school for the first generation of human children who will grow up on Mars." Vivian, whose imaginary future children were already at the top of her mind, now pictured them in a school on Mars, in tiny space suits learning their multiplication tables.

The two robots swiftly made their way toward a set of building materials piled up behind Jacqueline. Extending thick rods from their torsos with what looked like claws at their ends, they hauled and re-piled the materials in the center of the room. Once that was completed, they began constructing the building, right inside Leviathan Laboratories' atrium.

A large digital clock timed the process. A few attendees wandered off toward tables of snacks and drinks, but most observed with rapt attention as the robots swiftly built a sound structure of multiple stories with no hesitation. In order to build the second level, one Hyydra climbed atop the other, both growing a few feet by extending their limbs. At some point, a small bird, presumably having flown into the atrium through an open window, began circling the structure in progress. Vivian's attention moved between it and the Hyydras, a contrast she found unsettling.

Karla leaned toward her. "Can you imagine if they used all of this investment and innovation to repair the schools that already exist? You know—for 'human children' on planet Earth?"

"Maybe someday they will?" Vivian wanted to comfort her wife, but she herself didn't believe it. Instead, she pictured everyone who could bolting for Mars—or Israel—while the vast majority of people, not having those options, would somehow have to survive whatever came their way. Without the benefit of Leviathan's technological innovation.

When they were done installing glass panes that made up the walls, the two Hyydras carried a table and chairs into the transparent structure and sat down for effect. The clock read seventeen minutes and thirty-two seconds. A bell dinged. And the crowd erupted in applause.

Sal Maraj came forward again, clapping as he walked. "Now, *that* was something! Goes to show you, we have been putting your investment dollars to good use." Vivian noticed many of the people around her looking quite pleased with themselves.

Gordy stepped up and took over as Sal dropped back into the crowd. "Later we will demonstrate Hyydra's unmatched discernment capability," he began, grinning as he spoke. "But before we do, in honor of our budding partnership with KiTov Robotics and the Israeli army, we have planned an additional demonstration to show how quickly our evolved technology can adapt to new contexts and challenges."

Vivian spotted the Israeli CEO that Sal had pointed out during the press conference. His face remained unmoving; Sal's did too. But Gordy Silver was certainly excited enough for all of them.

"Please draw your attention to the other side of the room," he announced.

The crowd turned in unison. And in the far corner of the room, Vivian spotted a humongous machine. It looked like a professional basketball player in a sleek aluminum space suit. She instinctively grabbed Karla's forearm. She didn't remember seeing it when they came in, but now it seemed way too big to have missed. So that was ISAC. A chill overtook her. She wasn't sure if a breeze was flowing through the room or if it was purely her own fear.

Avner stepped into the center and took over. "Now, this machine right here, ISAC, is the future of military technology. He can surmount any physical obstacle."

ISAC stood next to a monkey bar structure that had also just mysteriously appeared. With no warning, ISAC jumped up and traversed the monkey bars with ease, skipping two bars each time. Once he had switched directions and returned to where he started, he flipped on top of the structure and carefully but quickly made his way across. He dismounted like an Olympic gymnast with a tumble, landing on his feet.

Everyone's mouths were agape. "ISAC's hydraulic control system and full-body mobility make him the most advanced humanoid robot we could dream up. But partnering with Leviathan, continuing to build upon their exceptional work, will ensure that his autonomous control system is just as advanced. We are in the beginning stages of this partnership, but it's clear that there is no ceiling on what ISAC will be able to do to ensure safety for—"

A sudden, horrible screech reverberated through the room. Avner stopped talking. Vivian grabbed Karla's forearm.

"Ow!" Karla whispered.

"Sorry." Vivian loosened her grip, but only slightly. She didn't understand what had happened. Her attention had been focused on Avner, but now she, along with the rest of the crowd, turned it to ISAC. One of his arms was raised in the air, his agile fingers clenched into a fist. The room grew silent.

ISAC lowered his arm from its raised position and extended it in front of his torso. He opened his fingers, and out of his hand dropped what looked to Vivian like a crumpled-up piece of trash. Vivian and Karla looked at each other, puzzled. It was hard to see from afar. Vivian focused on the nondescript object, and then she made out its shape. And its feathers.

ISAC had crushed the bird that Vivian lost track of. It had happened so fast, it was almost undetectable but for the sound. And it did not seem planned.

"You...um...you see?" Avner said. "ISAC's agility knows no bounds. And as I was saying, there is no ceiling on what ISAC will be able to do to ensure safety for my homeland. And beyond!"

The room erupted with applause once again. Vivian scanned the crowd. All of them seemed to be buying everything that Sal, Gordy, and Avner were selling. But when she caught sight of her friend across the room, Freddy's furrowed brows, crossed arms, and raised shoulders conveyed a different message.

"Isn't this just amazing?" Gordy said. Vivian jumped, not realizing he had somehow traversed the room and was standing right behind her. "And to think that this technological marvel will contribute to a stronger, safer Jewish state!"

He raised his bottle of mineral water close to her face. "To the future, aye?"

"Mhm. The future," Vivian repeated, instinctively bringing a hand to her stomach. She was suddenly very, very aware of her ovaries.

CHAPTER SIXTEEN

T HE DINING ROOM TABLE was festooned with boxes of take-out as Vivian and Karla unwound from their outing. Vivian scooped pad Thai onto her plate.

"What a day," she said. "I wonder how Freddy's doing."

"I texted him after we left," Karla said. "He seemed so uncomfortable once the Israeli robot stole the show and, you know, crushed that bird to death. But I haven't heard back."

Vivian paused mid-bite. "From how he's described the robots in the past, with their advanced moral-reasoning skills and everything, it just seems like mission drift to me."

"Not if your mission is making money."

"Fair point." Vivian sighed. "I'm worried about Gordy Silver pushing Beth Abraham to support this, since to him, and to Joseph, it's clearly mission-aligned." She tilted her head and a piece of art, their wedding present from Mimi, caught her eye. It was a papercut of the skyline of all of Jerusalem's holy sites, with a verse embossed around them: *None of us are free until all of us are free.*

"Even though Leviathan Labs has suddenly invested in robotic soldiers," Karla said, "I'd bet that the Beth Abraham bureaucracy can't move that fast, so I think you may have time before confronting that problem."

"That is strangely reassuring."

"God, what a bleak future we have ahead of us." Karla shook her head.

"Speaking of which," Vivian said, "you know, something about seeing those robots today made me like 100% percent sure, or maybe like 95% percent sure, that I'm ready for us to have a baby. Actually, maybe like 89% percent."

Karla laughed through a mouthful of food, and Vivian continued. "I was thinking about what you said earlier. About having more people to fight alongside in this brave new world. There is so much to fight. And I want to invest in humans who can chart a better path."

"Something tells me having a kid will introduce an additional set of fights. And probably on a more regular basis," Karla replied. "But maybe that will be a good distraction from the doom and gloom of climate predictions and robots settling Mars."

Vivian raised an eyebrow, wordlessly asking Karla if she believed her own argument.

"The thing that is hard for me to get over," Karla continued, "is this myth that our kids' lives are supposed to be better than ours. It seems so impossible that that could ever be true in the world we live in."

"In some ways, yeah. But baby, you work in an impactful government office that does incredible work, adapting to the times. And you sit in rooms with so many amazing, powerful women who are making better decisions than their predecessors. And think about Raymond's son, Mac—that farm they got in Georgia through the land-redistribution reparations project. And Beth Abraham is growing in positive ways. Maybe. I'm between ninety and forty percent sure. And—"

"And Leviathan Labs is building a legion of robots to settle Mars and maintain the occupation," Karla interrupted.

"Well. You can't win them all." Vivian swallowed a bite and took a sip of white wine. "Things have always been unsteady, and that's certainly evident right now. But so is the resistance. And we can try to bring a child up in the vibrancy of all of it. Even as the rain comes pouring through the sukkah."

"I'll just bypass that last part, assuming it's a part of a sermon you've written in your head that makes sense to you."

Vivian kissed her and then leaned back. It was a pleasure being so well known. She watched as Karla fumbled through her phone and then held it up so Vivian could see the screen. It was the app she had downloaded several months earlier, but not yet used. "I was pretty excited about starting to keep track of my ovulation cycle when I downloaded this." Karla stared at it. "Maybe we could start using it? Like, for real?"

"That would be a manageable step," Vivian said, taking the phone from her and scrolling through the app's features.

Karla leaned back in her chair and rubbed her chin. "Hmm," she said. "It seems like we may have done our homework."

"It does seem that way!" Vivian downed some wine triumphantly.

"So maybe we're ready to move on to the possible donors?"

"Maybe we are."

"How do we feel about Paul?"

Without skipping a beat, Vivian ran through the specs. "I mean, I like the idea of him living nearby, and he's had Addie—who's a great kid by the way—so he's already dealt with the existential questions of procreation. And Heather is fine with it, so that's another big hurdle we won't have." Vivian rested a forefinger on her cheek while she thought. "And he's like nice and feminist and doesn't ever seem to talk too much."

Karla chuckled. "I don't think those are genetic traits."

"It's got to count for something," Vivian insisted, scooping rice onto her plate.

"I do wonder if he's a bit too close to us," Karla said, as she stood up and walked to the kitchen. She returned quickly with their Post-it note. "Hmm," she said, examining the list. "We *could* go with someone we are more peripherally connected to, like your friend Phil."

"That's a good point...though he's kind of far away. If Paul said yes, we could try the DIY route at home." Vivian paused. "What if we put out a few asks at a time?"

Karla squinted.

"What?" Vivian asked. "Do you think that's bad etiquette?"

"I don't know. I don't think a clear etiquette has been developed around this kind of ask just yet." Karla put her hand on Vivian's arm. "So maybe we get to do whatever we want."

"Right, that makes sense," Vivian said. "I just sometimes find rules helpful." Karla squeezed her.

"So should we invite Paul over?" Vivian asked. "And email Phil? Should we email both of them? Should we *spext* them?"

Karla shook her head. "That is so not the proper use of spext. *Spexting* is just between us."

"So, right now, we're spexting?"

"Definitely not."

Vivian rolled her eyes. "I'm just trying to help you make it a thing."

Karla laughed. Getting up again, she went into the living room to retrieve her computer and brought it back to the table. She rubbed her face, opened a new email window and started to type while Vivian looked on.

Random favor, she wrote in the subject line.

"Hmm," Vivian said. "Maybe we should make it sound more enticing?" Shimmying her chair closer to Karla's, she pulled the laptop toward her. She deleted Karla's subject line and wrote instead, *Exciting invitation*. Karla nodded. Vivian moved her cursor into the body of the email and kept going. *We were wondering if you might be open to exploring being our sperm donor.*

"No, no, no, baby. That is *not* an exciting invitation." Karla shifted the computer back toward her. "How about..."

Vivian watched her type. *Get in on the ground floor...of our future.* She spit out her wine. "Oh my God!" she coughed. "That would be the perfect pitch for Gordy Silver. But maybe not Paul."

"Fine, fine," Karla said, deleting it and starting over. *We'll get right to it. We're on the prowl for a sperm donor.*

"I like it!" Vivian said. "It sounds fun, like a great opportunity he wouldn't want to miss out on. Certainly an exciting invitation."

They spent another twenty minutes crafting the email. Then they personalized one for Paul and reviewed it several times.

"So, are we really going to do this?" Karla asked.

"I think we are."

Karla curled her finger and held it above the mouse while the onscreen arrow hovered over the *Send* button. "Three...two...one!" Vivian counted down. Karla still hadn't moved. "Come on. You can do it," Vivian said, and Karla finally clicked. The email disappeared. *Done!* They tailored a second one to Phil, Vivian's friend from rabbinical school, and hit send on that one with more ease.

As she reread the sent emails, something caught Vivian's attention. Something bad. "Crap!" she shouted to Karla, who was carrying leftovers to the kitchen. "The email to Phil says 'Take care, Paul' at the end. Do we have to send a follow-up? What's he going to think?"

"It's going to be fine," Karla said, reappearing and resting her hand on Vivian's knee. "He probably won't even notice." She closed the computer and kissed Vivian, then picked up a pen and circled Paul's and Phil's names on the Post-it.

"So...I guess we might have a kid someday," she said.

"That's right," Vivian replied. "A real, breathing, *human* kid!"

CHAPTER SEVENTEEN

FREDDY DREAMED OF ISAC that night. A whole legion of ISACs, in fact. That was not so out of the ordinary for him. Ever since he was a kid, visions of powerful humanoid robots would come to him in his sleep. But this time, they were coming *for* him, and for his family. And they were not like the prototype sitting in the basement of Leviathan Labs. They were bigger, more aggressive, and certainly not morally discerning. An army of them had surrounded his house and were knocking on the doors and the windows as Camille and Xo glared at him, asking what the hell they should do. But he could not move.

He woke up sweating.

"Robots again, Fred?" asked Camille, lying beside him.

As they got up and prepared for the day, Freddy remained quiet. He fed Xo breakfast in a kitchen cluttered with dishes and food containers from the day before.

"This is the closest I've come to working on an autonomous control system that will actually be used out in the world," he finally said aloud. "And I'm worried." He was watching their daughter eat while Camille, behind them at the counter, put a few handfuls of blueberries into a Ziploc for her lunch.

"I confess," Camille said, "according to social media, I think some of my friends from grad school went to the protest."

"I don't blame them." Freddy shook his head. "I might have been on that side of things too if I didn't build the damn thing."

"You're doing the best you can…and making things less bad."

"That will be my legacy, huh?" Freddy said. "'Making things less bad.'"

"You joke, honey, but that's important work to do. Plus, you've got lots of other things to be remembered for. You're an amazing parent. A caring son and brother. And don't forget about your band."

"Ha," he blurted out half-heartedly. After college, he and a few friends had formed a metal band in New York called Noise Machine. The one promotional poster they had made still hung on Freddy and Camille's living room wall. It featured Freddy on electric guitar, his goatee only just coming in, wearing a sleeveless shirt with a glitter lightning bolt and black leather pants.

One of Noise Machine's old songs popped into Freddy's head. *Who you gonna be at the end? Who you gonna be at the end? Na na na. Who you gonna be at the end of the world?*

While he drove Xo to daycare, he sang the words aloud. She

started to mimic him, putting together sounds that did not quite form words. Her head bangs were pretty on point though, Freddy thought.

From daycare he drove to work, with the song, and the images from his dream, still running through his head.

He could already hear it before walking in the door: a very loud alarm spilling out onto the street. When he got inside, security officers were everywhere...*human* security officers. The hallway to Freddy's lab was blocked by yellow caution tape.

Someone shouted through a loudspeaker: "No one leave! Everyone to the atrium immediately." Freddy wondered if this was another simulation, but that didn't seem right. Too many humans, not enough machines. He moved toward a clump of colleagues gathering in the same spot where yesterday's event had taken place.

"ISAC's gone," he overheard an engineer from another department saying. Jacqueline appeared, walking with Sal, the two deep in conversation. Freddy gulped. Sal continued up a few steps of the atrium's wide staircase, then turned to address them.

"The ISAC prototype has gone missing," he said. "We are looking into security footage from last night, but are having difficulty recovering the recording. It seems as though our security systems were tampered with." The crowd let out a collective gasp. "If anyone has any relevant information, come talk to me or Gordy immediately."

Freddy got more of the story from Jacqueline as they waited aimlessly in the very bright space. The huge atrium was usually empty save for one welcome desk, several plush neon-green chairs, and a humungous sculpture of one of the first known robotic machines. But today it was full of people again. Freddy used one hand to block the sun from his eyes so he could see Jacqueline's face as she spoke. In horror, she recounted walking into their maximum-security lab, where ISAC had been spending the night until he could be returned to Israel. After an initial jolt of fear, she figured that ISAC's absence must have been intentional. Perhaps a different team was working on him, and they forgot to notify her amid yesterday's excitement?

But on her way to check that theory, it became clear that the true scenario was much worse. Gordy was running every which way, presumably figuring out damage control, and officers were pouring in. It certainly would not be a good look, Jaqueline noted—Leviathan Labs losing the prize project of the Israeli military.

"They said they are 'exploring all of the possible angles,'" she went on. "Sal said they would look into anyone who might have been at the press conference who wanted to cause us harm."

Freddy was nodding more expressively than usual.

"Do you have any idea what could have happened?" she asked him.

His whole body tightened. Glancing to his side, he saw Sal, who was talking to someone from the security team but looking straight at Freddy. At first his look felt like an accusation. But then, for a moment, it felt like Sal was trying to divulge something *to* him.

Jacqueline snapped her fingers to get Freddy's attention. "Any ideas, Freddy?" she prompted him again. He shook his head, and she sighed.

"Same here. Oh, and they'll probably ask you—do you know who was last to lock up the lab last night?"

Freddy stared at her. "Yeah," he said, his voice cracking, and his hands beginning to tremble. "It was me."

CHAPTER EIGHTEEN

K ARLA SAT AT her desk eating her go-to lunch purchase, a Caprese sandwich, and doing a little research during her lunch break. As soon as she had typed *How long does it take...* into the Google search box, a drop-down offering of questions appeared. *How long does it take to boil eggs? How long does it take to get a tax refund? How long does it take to get to Mars?*

She snorted at the third question, and peered outside of her cubicle to see if anyone had noticed. When no one appeared suspicious, she returned to the task at hand and typed in the rest of her question: *...to get pregnant through insemination?*

Now that she and Vivian had decided they were ready, and since Paul had quickly written back saying he and Heather would consider their "exciting invitation," all Karla could think about was pregnancy. Her internet searches were dead giveaways: what prenatal vitamins were recommended before conception, which STI tests a potential donor should take, how cervical fluid viscosity can indicate the best times for insemination.

As she was watching an animated YouTube simulation of the sperm's great life journey through the fallopian tubes in search of the egg, Winona MacLean announced herself (and her sparkly travel mug) with a cough at the opening of Karla's cubicle.

"Oh! Hi Nona," Karla said, swiftly closing the seven tabs she had just generated in the last two minutes.

Nona sat down in the chair next to Karla's desk. "We were just notified by the National Weather Service about a potential Category 3 hurricane starting to form. It could hit in a week or so. It's a strange and slow pattern, one of those later October storms we were warned about. Caused by warming temperatures." The rhythm of her words sped up. "But it looks like it's coming for Rhode Island, with a tail of heavy rains and winds that could hit most of New England. We don't know the exact trajectory; it's too early to tell. And it might *just* miss us, like Julieta did. But this one's bigger. We've got to be prepared."

Karla thought back to Hurricane Julieta a few years earlier. Their office had prepped, setting up shelters and everything, and then the storm had sharply curled off the coast of Long Island and out to sea before reaching them.

"What's this one called?" Karla asked.

"Vincenzo," MacLean said, sipping her tea.

"Vincenzo," Karla repeated. "Sticking with the trend of men's names, I see."

The last few years had seen many significant developments at the National Weather Service, as its public funding increased. In addition to getting sharper storm-prediction technology that offered projections further in advance, the NWS had also decided on naming the more dangerous hurricanes after men, to compensate for a sexist track record.

"Men do tend to make the biggest messes," MacLean said. *Yup*, Karla thought.

"The NWS has made changes to their website," she continued, leaning over so she could reach Karla's keyboard and beginning to type. "So here's how you can now find the most up-to-date storm tracking. I need you to check on—" She paused.

"Cervical fluid viscosity?"

For a moment, Nona just sat there looking at the tab that Karla apparently had not managed to close in time, while Karla bit her lip. Hard. Then Nona's shoulders seemed to loosen and she turned away from the screen to face her.

Karla felt her cheeks flushing. Nona let out a small, almost imperceptible smile. Then she turned back to the screen and continued to explain the updates to the NWS's tracking system.

What was that smile?! Karla wondered, unable to take in her boss's continued instructions. *And is it finally a clue to Nona?*

"—so let's get the team together ASAP," MacLean was saying. "And make sure we get a good showing from comms. We've got a lot to do. Fast."

"On it!"

Nona stood and started to leave the cubicle, then abruptly turned back around. "It's a real trip in this line of work. Being a parent, that is. But sometimes it's…." She didn't finish her sentence.

She shook her head, turned back around, and quickly walked on down the hall.

Karla was still blushing, and now her mind was racing too. *It's what, Nona?* But there wasn't time to connect those dots right now. Right now, she had to notify the relevant government offices about the coming storm and wrangle them together for a meeting. A whole lot of meetings.

. . .

The phone rang just as Vivian, snuggled on the couch, was texting back and forth with Flora.

"Hey baby," Karla said. "I'm almost home. Sorry I'm late. I'll explain when I get there."

"Okay, see you soon."

They hung up and Vivian navigated back to her text messages. There was a new one from Flora. *Did some more research on Rainbow Capital today at their office so we can hone our pitch. And guess what?!?*

What? Vivian wrote.

The intersection where the office is sounded familiar. So I checked back to an open tab in my phone and I was right! Rainbow Capital is in the eruv!!!!! Vivian wondered if anyone had ever, in the history of texting, used that many exclamation points when discussing an eruv.

And so close to the edge that I spotted it!! This one included a selfie of Flora, a huge grin on her face, pointing to a tangle of electrical wires above her—and right atop them, a very thin and taut line of fishing twine. If you knew to look for it.

That's amazing! Vivian replied. *You hereby get 1,000 eruv points for spotting that.*

Right? I bet we can totally work this into the pitch to the board! Also, an old lady asked me why I was so excited about the utility wires, and I tried to explain the concept of eruv to her and it did NOT go well. LOL. I need a better elevator pitch.

Vivian giggled. As she was typing a response, the front door opened and Karla walked through, looking more awake than she normally did at the end of a workday. She threw her suit jacket onto the couch and turned toward Vivian. "We have some prep to do," Karla said, her voice sounding serious. "A storm is coming."

CHAPTER NINETEEN

G ORDY, SAL, AND Jack Phillips sat in the boardroom, at the end of a large glass table surrounded by windows. Gavin Gladstone, a private detective specializing in cybersecurity, appeared on a very large screen in front of them. Gladstone's brown hair was slicked back and he was wearing a white button-down shirt with a slim black tie. Also onscreen were Avner Ben Ami and a few members of his team, calling in from Tel Aviv. Avner had returned to Israel as soon as the disaster broke to deal with the fallout from the IDF.

"One group of interest is the protestors," Gladstone said. "We are looking into every one of them. So far, they're mostly college and grad students involved in a group called Planet Earth

Investments. However, none of the footage shows any of them breaching security or getting any closer than a few dozen feet from the building."

"Could they have hacked into our systems?" Gordy asked, tapping the table.

"That seems almost impossible without access to the building or the robots themselves. And then there's the fact that the alarm system was disarmed. Anyone who could manage to do all of that and escape with ISAC undetected would need incredibly high-level hacking skills, which, at this point, we don't believe any of them have. They are largely students of literature and philosophy and...sexuality studies," he said, shaking his head. "So I'm not putting my money on any of them."

Avner rolled his eyes. "There is no way they could have breached security. This had to have been done by professionals."

"Yes. Mr. Ben Ami, we agree," Gladstone said. "But we need to rule out the other suspects in order to find the culprit." Avner waved his hand at the screen dismissively.

"The most likely scenario is that it was someone with access, someone at HQ that day," Gladstone continued, "since no one even knew about Leviathan's partnership with KiTov aside from members of your own teams."

Gordy looked toward Sal, who was staring off toward one of the windows overlooking the Seekonk River. *Earth to Sal,* Gordy screamed internally. Someone in their orbit, someone they probably trusted, did this! *What are we going to do?!* But Sal was quiet, as he seemed to be so often lately.

Gordy closed his eyes, trying to avert Avner's large virtual gaze for a moment. Everything felt so fragile. There had been so many frantic calls from Avner about the trouble they all might be in, the potential lawsuits that could come if the ISAC model was not found. Leviathan Labs had moved so fast to bring in the prototype for the press conference that they did not have all the paperwork in place to waive liability. Gordy's thoughts drifted to his brother. If he was being completely honest, he was frustrated that his dream of a success to rival Simon's was in jeopardy. He could just imagine if Major Shimon got wind of this epic failure.

"There were hundreds of people here that day," Jack Phillips said, jolting Gordy's attention back to the boardroom.

"What about Horizon?" Gordy asked. "They've been on our radar already. Was there anyone at the event we can link to them?"

"That brings us to our next lead," Gladstone said. "We have identified a potential suspect from the crowd of invitees. What do you know about Calvin Chen?"

Gordy swiveled in his chair. "He's been a very hands-off investor of ours," he said. "He just gave us a million bucks without much fuss or solicitation and left it at that."

"Turns out that he gave twenty million to Horizon and is on their advisory committee," Gladstone said. "Seems pretty hands *on* over there. He's got a PhD in engineering, to boot."

"Do we have anything on him?" Gordy asked.

"My team has been studying tape of him from the event. He was fidgety that day. Nervous."

"*Fidgety?*" Gordy scoffed, leaning back in his chair.

"Don't discount body language, Mr. Silver. Sometimes, it tells us more than words can."

Jack Phillips positioned his elbows on the table and clasped his fingers together. "We also had a security badge reported missing yesterday by a lower-level engineer," he said. "And according to footage, that staff member was in Mr. Chen's vicinity at certain points of the event. Obviously, we will also be verifying his story."

"We're digging deeper into Chen," Gladstone said, taking over from Jack. "And his whereabouts. We know he had a flight scheduled that same night heading to Beijing, and I've got someone checking if he was in fact on the flight. But you obviously don't have to be in the building, or in the country for that matter, to wreak havoc if you've got advanced programming capabilities." Gladstone paused to write something down. "We're digging through the ACS instructions, and also trying to access his computer and phone."

"And if it's not Chen? What then?" Sal asked, finally contributing to the conversation. Or at least registering awareness that it was happening.

"We study the list of everyone who had access to the building and to the general Leviathan Laboratories operating system—that day, and the week leading up to it," Gladstone said. "And we zoom in on those who had contact with the robots *and* possess strong coding skills."

Just then, Gordy's phone and several others beeped within a few seconds of each other. Probably an Amber Alert, or notification of a rush-hour lane closure on I-95. Everyone ignored it.

And then the texts started coming in. Gordy finally looked down as Gladstone was urging everyone to be patient during the investigation. *What are we going to do?*, his wife had written. *Should we go to my parents' place?*

Jostled out of his focus, Gordy scrolled to the alert on his phone. Apparently, a hurricane was on its way. The notification urged Gordy, and the rest of Providence's residents, to make plans.

"We'll deal with that later," Gordy murmured to himself. It couldn't be that bad, and this was not the time to get distracted. Right now, a key partnership with KiTov Robotics, many millions of dollars of research and investment, and the future of Israeli military security—not to mention Mars exploration—were on the line. A glance at Sal, whose closed body language accurately reflected his level of engagement, made it all the more clear that Gordy needed to stay focused.

I'll be home soon, honey. Still at HQ. Don't worry. We'll figure it out, he wrote back.

When the meeting finally ended, Gordy revisited the storm alert. What bad timing this was. It would surely disrupt the investigation. Rereading it, he noticed the storm's name. *Vincenzo*. He said it aloud a few times, trying to pronounce it.

CHAPTER TWENTY

"CAN YOU REMIND me why they build this?" Alton asked. He stood inside of a bare sukkah structure made up of metal poles, rolling up the mats of bamboo *s'chach* and placing them back in their storage bags.

"The holiday's a chance for Jewish people to experience the vulnerability of the elements," Raymond said, zipping up one of the bags. "And somehow, hanging out in the sukkah is supposed to strengthen faith in God. That's what I've heard the rabbis say, anyway."

Alton, Raymond's colleague, lifted a pile of crumpled construction paper off the ground. "And these little art projects help with that?"

"You got to get the kids involved, I guess," Raymond said. "They always seem to like it."

"Shoot!" Alton laughed. "Ray, you're basically a rabbi yourself. You know that?"

"I've picked up a few things here and there. Lots of the traditions don't make much sense to me, but I like this one." He carried a bag of bamboo to the entrance to the building, then turned back toward Alton. "Mac's been telling me about relying on the land and rain and all that ever since he got to the farm. So to have a holiday that can get people in that mindset...that seems like a good thing."

"Hmm." Alton considered Raymond's teaching. "With this storm coming and all, seems like they are on to something."

"What are you going to do?" Raymond asked, stretching out his back, getting in his physical therapy exercises.

"I don't know," Alton said. He paused for a moment from disconnecting the poles of the metal frame. "My mom and brother are in Boston. I might go stay with them. What about you?"

"Sheila's already down in Georgia visiting Mac," Raymond said. "I could go down there, but I don't know. It's a hassle and I've got to prep the synagogue and our house." He thought about the garden that he and Sheila had kept alive and flourishing for so many years. The herbs, the zucchinis, the tomatoes, the rainbow chard. And the potatoes and garlic that were still growing underground.

"We got some quick decisions to make, aye, boss?" Alton said.

"I bet the city will open up the convention center again," Raymond said, remembering a storm a few years earlier that had been predicted to hit Providence but ended up bypassing the city.

"And maybe the smaller community buildings and libraries and such. So those may be options, but waiting this out with hundreds of strangers sounds like hell to me." He paused and looked down at the growing pile of sukkah materials that, disassembled, were flat and one-dimensional. "I think the safest place we've got is this building right here."

"Huh? This hut?" Alton asked, raising his eyebrows.

"No, man. Beth Abraham," Raymond said, scanning the building. "After the fire, this place was rebuilt to handle anything. A lot of newer construction in the city has been, because of the new regulations. But I assume we'll just board it up and call it a day."

"Sounds like it would be the best option," Alton said. "Maybe we should wait out the storm here." He started to loosen another pole from its metal joint. "My neighborhood sure isn't ready for this."

"Hmm. Not a bad idea, Alton," Raymond said, folding up the canvas walls of the temporary structure.

CHAPTER TWENTY-ONE

F REDDY WAS DOING his part to calm Xiomara down. Funny faces. Songs. Bad jokes. It was well past her bedtime when Camille walked in.

"What are we going to do, babe?" she asked. It took Freddy a moment to realize that she wasn't talking about Xo's wakefulness.

"We could stick it out here," he answered.

"Sounds like there will be a lot of resources in town."

"Makes sense to me. And we can always get a second opinion from Karla if we need it." Freddy patted Xo's back, to no avail, as he paced around the room. "Ugh! Come on, Xo!"

"You seem fidgety-er than usual. What's wrong, Fred? You know, besides for everything."

He kept pacing. "It just feels like the threats are coming from every side. The detectives on the case were looking into the protestors, but no one got anywhere close to the building and they've gone through the list. So that seems highly unlikely—"

"And like a pretty ridiculous angle," Camille interrupted.

"The whispers around the lab are that they are now focusing on a competitor company, but it's only a matter of time before they start investigating me. I mean, no one's said anything just yet. Out loud, at least. But I can just *feel* Gordy's suspicion of me every time I'm around him, given that I was kind of resistant to the KiTov partnership to begin with."

"Uck-OO!" Xo started to cry. "Uck-OO. Uck-OOOOO."

"Great," Freddy said. "And now my baby is saying 'Fuck you.' She's coming for me too!"

"Come on, Fred. You know she just wants Cuckoo."

It was true. Xo loved her stuffed rooster, which had come pre-named by the manufacturer, and always seemed magically calmed by it. Though Freddy was now questioning the toy company's naming choice.

Camille put out her arms, and Freddy passed Xo to her. He sat down on a very low bench that had XIOMARA written on it in removable blocks. His head fell into his hands.

"What if you got someone else to vouch for you?" Camille asked.

"Hmm." He tilted his head, thinking of Sal. Of what they shared. Or of what Freddy *thought* they had shared. But ever since ISAC went missing, Sal basically did too, like he was in a different universe. He had even canceled the monthly meeting the two of them had been scheduled to have that day, which Freddy had been looking forward to as a much-needed chance to check in about everything that was happening. And then Freddy remembered something. He lifted his head.

"You know, Gordy goes to Vivian's synagogue. Maybe she could talk to him for me."

"I bet she would," Camille said, rocking Xo, who continued to whimper. "Why don't you call her?"

Freddy stood up and went into the living room, retrieving his phone and Cuckoo from their respective places. Back in Xo's room, he handed her the stuffed animal. She reached for it enthusiastically and stopped whimpering immediately. With his daughter settled, Freddy pulled up Vivian's contact in his phone and pressed the green call icon.

She picked up after the second ring. "Hey Freddy. How you doing?"

"Not great." By now the story of the missing ISAC prototype had gotten around Providence, so he imagined Vivian was caught up—either from the news or from Karla. "Everyone at work is on edge. The security team is looking into a few different angles, but nothing is clear yet. It's only a matter of time before they start questioning the staff."

"I'm sorry, Freddy. That sounds so stressful."

"ISAC is worth tens of millions of dollars, and he is one of the most advanced robots ever built for military use." He was speaking quickly. "So Leviathan and KiTov—not to mention the Israeli military—they won't stop until the mystery is solved."

"Or until someone goes down for it," Camille added from beside him, inclining her head toward the phone's mouthpiece and rubbing Freddy's arm with her free hand.

"Uck-OO," Xo said again, in a lower voice, sounding far less aggrieved than before.

"Yeah, and why not the Latinx trans guy?" Freddy continued. "Anyway, I'm calling because Gordy Silver goes to your synagogue, right?"

"He does," Vivian said.

"I can tell that he already suspects me," Freddy said. "I was kind of outspoken about not being on board with the ISAC project, and now it turns out I was the last to lock up before the security cameras went haywire, and…. I'm wondering if you could talk to him. He's so focused on the world of the lab that I think having someone who he knows and respects from outside of it vouch for me could make a difference."

"I don't know if Gordy respects me," Vivian said, "but I can do whatever you need."

"Well, you're white. So that's something."

"Point taken."

"Thanks, Vivian."

"You got it," she said. Freddy took a deep breath, in and out. "So what are you guys planning to do for the storm?" Vivian asked.

Freddy began pacing again, trying to recall the plan he and Camille had been discussing. "Oh right. We're probably going to stick it out here. Guessing you will be too, given Karla's job? I hope she at least gets overtime pay."

"Yes, seems like we'll be here. Let's stay in touch. I imagine we're *all* going to need each other."

Freddy hung up and looked over at Xo. She was asleep on Camille's shoulder, clutching her beloved Cuckoo. So that was one challenge, however small, that they had solved.

CHAPTER TWENTY-TWO

T HE OCTOBER SUN shone through the stained glass of Beth
Abraham's sanctuary, encasing the congregation in autumn
light. Vivian noted that the synagogue was fuller than was usual
on the Shabbat after the holidays, when even the regulars tended
to take a week off.

It was clear from the developing projections that Vincenzo
was going to be a big storm. Whispers filled the room in between
prayers, everyone sharing their plans and asking about others'.

Joseph was scheduled to give the sermon. The weekly parsha
was, appropriately, Noah, though he had told Vivian that he had
not had time to edit his sermon to account for the recent news
since he and Miriam had so much preparation to do for their trip

to Israel. *To scout out the land*, he was saying, to anyone who would listen. They were still planning to go. When he'd stopped her on her way out of work the day before to ask if that was okay, Vivian had reluctantly given him her blessing. But it had not struck Vivian as a sincere question. While Joseph continued to pursue his dream future, she and the board of directors would make any necessary plans for the hurricane coming the next week.

After the portion about Noah and his family surviving the flood had been chanted and the Torah scroll tucked temporarily onto its stand, Joseph rose from his seat and moved slowly toward the bimah.

He began by talking about Noah's loneliness, about the trials and tribulations of being, as the text said, the only righteous person in his generation. And how hard it is to take risks and face challenges from that place.

Vivian wondered where he was going with this. Maybe an exposition on the importance of community in facing challenges? Maybe he was about to explore the pitfalls of being separate and apart from the collective? Those, at least, were the angles she might have investigated.

"These days," Joseph continued, "I've been thinking a lot about leaving. I've been wondering how difficult it must have been for Noah to leave everything he knew in the face of crisis. We each encounter moments like this in our lives. In a way, that is where Miriam and I are right now. All the preparations that we are making for our trip—and for our eventual move—to Israel, have made me ask myself: What was Noah's inner life like before he boarded the ark? What was his relationship with God like? Did he trust God?"

Joseph coughed. "And I trust God. Even as things seem bleak. I do. I trust God."

He looked up from his notes. "And with this storm that is coming, I…I trust God too." Vivian guessed he was now off-script. "I trust that God will not destroy our world. God made that very promise to us in this week's parsha. When God made the rainbow appear in the aftermath of the storm and the flood, He promised never to destroy the world again. As we stand on the threshold of uncertainty, that promise gives me comfort." Joseph bowed his head. "Shabbat shalom."

Vivian looked around. The post-sermon silence felt discordant. No one was moving. Perhaps she was projecting? But no, the usual nods that accompanied the ritual end of a sermon were nowhere to be found. Tamar, sitting at one end of the half-circle seating arrangement, looked like she was trying hard to find the diamonds of wisdom to hold on to, her brow furrowed and head lifted toward the ceiling.

Vivian was stunned. Parshat Noah appears right before a threatening storm is set to hit their city, and *that's* the sermon her people would be left with?

Joseph returned to his seat in the center of the first row, head down, not making eye contact with any of the congregants around him. Vivian approached the bimah to continue the service, knowing that she could at least offer additional—or alternative—commentary through the tunes she chose. She closed her eyes and dug her feet into the floor, trying to summon what was needed of her in this dissonant and frightening moment.

Vivian did her best to wrest back control of the feeling in the room, slowing down the pace with minor melodies. As she led the first few prayers, Vivian could sense the community settling into the rhythm with her. When she had finished her silent Amidah, she turned around to examine her congregants, checking if enough of them had concluded their own prayers for her to continue with the service. She looked toward Vera and Charlie Cohen, then at Flora and Ben, wondering what was going through their minds on this strange day. Often she could tell; often it felt like many of them were having a shared experience. But not today. Then she noticed Gordy, and remembered that she still had another task to complete.

While leading the congregation through the Prayer for Israel—tuning out the words as she often did—she noted with annoyance how Joseph seemed to snap to attention for it and then immediately return to his daydreams. *If a massive hurricane was headed for Jerusalem*, she thought irritably, *you can bet he'd have edited his sermon.*

At the end of the service, Tamar thanked everyone who had volunteered—the Torah readers, the greeters, the ushers—and listed aloud the programs coming up over the next month at Beth Abraham, pending changes due to the storm, of course.

As Vivian listened, she knew that something else needed to be said. Something that could weave the community—each person's fears and hopes and prayers—back together. When the announcements were finished, Vivian arose from the first row and stepped once again toward the bimah.

"I know it's a scary time," she began. "During our service, I, too, was focusing on God's promise not to destroy the world. I closed my eyes when we read about the rainbow that symbolized just that. I thought of these storms that have been causing so much damage and will continue to, like Vincenzo. Yes, God promised not to destroy the world, but humans never did. And it is the actions of humans that have brought about such widescale destruction.

"And yet." She exhaled. "I trust that God is with us in the planning, giving us the wisdom and the strength to do what we can for each other, to make sure that the world is never fully destroyed again, ensuring that our ability to care for one another and rebuild—and do so justly—will endure." Vivian took another big breath, this time inviting her congregants to do so with her. "The board will be meeting this week. As the predictions develop, we'll be in touch with you about how we can support each another. And if anyone needs help preparing for the storm or finding a place to stay, please reach out to me or to the office. Shabbat shalom."

. . .

As people milled about schmoozing, several congregants thanked Vivian for her impromptu sermon, or at least her impromptu commentary on Joseph's sermon. They had questions that she was certainly not yet able to answer, given how little anyone knew about Vincenzo's trajectory. But she reassured them that she would be in touch when there was enough guidance on how to support community members. As she was repeating this to Gert Fineman, one of the shul's oldest members, she spotted Gordy talking to Shlomo Seidel in a corner. Gordy looked like he was trying to extricate himself from the conversation, pulling on his jacket as he talked. It seemed like a good opening.

She hugged Gert and promised to call within the next few days. Then she magically speed-walked toward Gordy without looking like she was rushing, a skill she had mastered in her time as a rabbi.

"Shabbat shalom, Gordy," she said. "How are you doing? It sounds like a hectic time, even without the storm."

"You could say that," he replied. "We have a few possible leads, but…. You know, I don't want to talk about this at shul."

"Yeah, I've heard a bit from Freddy," Vivian said, suppressing the pastoral training that would have required her to honor Gordy's clearly stated wish not to talk about this. She folded her hands in and out of each other, a habit she had picked up from Joseph. "I don't know if you remember, but he is a good friend of mine through my wife. He seems distraught over the missing, um, robot. I know he has put so much work into—"

"Look, let's not talk about this here," Gordy interrupted, zipping up his light jacket. "Shul is a place to steer clear of the hard stuff." Vivian wanted to roll her eyes, especially given the recent in-shul fundraising for military projects that Gordy had pitched to Joseph. She left that gesture to the analogue Vivian in her mind.

"Of course. I understand," she said…and then barreled forward. "But just one more thing. He seems to really care about getting to the bottom of this."

"Yes, yes, we all do," Gordy said, already making his way toward the exit. "Shabbat shalom, Rabbi." He reached the sanctuary door and disappeared behind it.

CHAPTER TWENTY-THREE

TAKEOUT CONTAINERS were splayed all over the meeting room table. The whiteboards were entirely scribbled over. Post-it notes were scattered across the wall, and a massive map of Providence was littered with green, red, blue, and yellow pushpins indicating four types of support infrastructure.

Karla focused her eyes on one particular Post-it near the top of the map. *Category 4*, it read. The news had come just hours earlier from the National Weather Service: Vincenzo had been upgraded.

"The convention center is prepped for shelter," Winona MacLean said to a small group huddled around her. "So are the smaller shelter sites—rec centers and libraries—which are marked with blue pushpins." She pointed to the map. "We can open up the atrium of City Hall, too, but we'll still need more. It's time to add houses of worship. Let's call the clergy. Hopefully this is when our relationship-building over the years bears fruit. Karla, you know a bunch of clergy, right?" Karla chuckled. "So you take point on outreach."

"Roger that. I'll start right away," Karla said, trying to spot congregations on the map. "And for those that say yes, I'll liaise between them and the rapid-response teams."

"Good. Moving on," MacLean said. She shifted her attention to Amir Noori from the budget office. "Amir, how are we doing?"

"We're in good shape with funds," he answered. "And we've locked up the grant from FEMA for preparedness projects, which allows us to save other monies for repairs after the storm."

"Excellent," MacLean said. "So what we need now are supplies, supplies, supplies." She ticked off items on her fingers as she spoke. "Food. Water. Medicine. Generators. Blankets."

Karla marveled at her boss's clarity and composure. MacLean turned back to look at the map. "I spoke with Mayor Heath about the potential for an evacuation order," she said. "It will be strongly recommended, and the city will provide free busses heading to safe destinations over the next few days. Everyone who stays will be given the option to go to a neighborhood shelter. And the comms office is working on translating the guidance and resources into a variety of languages.

"And for those that choose not to or can't leave their own homes—and we know there will be many—we make sure to publicize the mobile rapid-response units as much as possible."

She pulled a thick pile of paper flyers out of her leather folio and passed them around to the group. "Here are the routes. Thank the Lord we put this together several months ago with the transportation department. Karla, make sure to share the relevant ones with the shelter sites. The folks running them might have tips about houses that need visits." Karla nodded.

"Alright. Everybody's got their marching orders. Let's get to it!"

Karla knew that was as much of a motivational speech as she would get from her boss. But somehow, it worked. She was ready to go.

CHAPTER TWENTY-FOUR

G ORDY SILVER WAS AT his desk, the blue light of his computer glowing in the dark. The office lights had gone off automatically while he sat, perfectly still, and reviewed the security footage over and over, looking for clues. He could tell from Leviathan's digital timecard system who was last in the building on the night that ISAC disappeared. Six people had been there in the final hour: Freddy Fuentes, Jacqueline Saito, three janitorial staff, and himself.

The cameras from the basement lab showed that one of the janitors entered at 7:52 p.m. to sweep and left quickly. At 8:27 p.m., Freddy and Jacqueline entered. They plugged away for a few minutes, inspecting the two Hyydras that stood next to ISAC.

Jacqueline left at 8:45 p.m., and a few minutes later, Freddy did too. The hallway cameras picked up both of them heading back to their offices down the hall. By 9:18 p.m., everyone was out of the building. The lights in the lab automatically turned off at 10:00 p.m. And all the recordings and motion sensors cut off abruptly at 11:34 p.m.

Gordy thought back to his strange interaction with Rabbi Vivian. Why was she defending Freddy? What did she know? For what felt like the tenth time, he reviewed the lab tape from after the lights went out. A profusion of blinking computers and the bright red Exit signs provided a faint illumination, but any movement would be difficult to decipher. He thought he saw Hyydra or ISAC reposition themselves a few times, but was not so sure when he rewound and watched it again. How could a robotics lab that focused on security and innovation fail so spectacularly at surveilling itself?

None of Gladstone's so-called leads had *led* them anywhere just yet. It was a monumental mistake that was already proving costly for the company. Avner had called earlier to yell at Gordy once again, saying that the Israeli government was suing all of them. And unless ISAC turned up fast, KiTov would demand back the money that they had already paid, which would plunge Leviathan Labs into financial disaster.

Over the years that he had spent incubating Sal's ideas and building his prototypes, Gordy had given so much of himself to make Leviathan Labs into a leader in innovation and technological diplomacy. And now the company's reputation was on the line. *His* reputation was on the line. But to Gordy's chagrin, Sal was just leaving everything to the security team, who simply didn't understand enough about all of the complex pieces involved. So he needed to clean up this mess himself.

While he was reviewing, for the twelfth time, the grainy footage in the dark robotics lab from just before the security cameras cut out and the alarms deactivated, Gordy's phone rang. It was Gladstone.

"Yup," Gordy answered.

"I've got a few updates."

"I'm listening."

"The Horizon angle's a dead end," Gladstone began. "Calvin Chen boarded a plane an hour before the footage went dark, when the robots were still in place. The missing badge was located at the employee's house, so neither Chen nor any other unauthorized personnel ever used it, unless they also broke into his home and convinced the puppy to use it as a chew toy. And, most importantly, our cyber expert could not detect Chen's digital footprint anywhere in your system."

Gordy sighed.

"We also conducted a digital simulation of a break-in," Gladstone continued. "The culprit would have needed to make it through four different badge-only access points in the building just to get to the security system and disarm it, before even accessing ISAC. The system has no record of anyone doing that. So it seems like we can rule out a traditional theft."

"Did you call just to tell me we've only got dead ends?"

"Nope. I've also got good news." Gladstone's voice seemed to get higher. "We've made a significant break in the case."

"For God's sake," Gordy said, his eyes still fixed on the screen. "Go on."

"One of my guys just found a suspicious directive in the ACS which would override ISAC's behavior."

"What does that mean?"

"It means that there was additional logic written into the ACS that would stop ISAC from acting in alignment with his training. Whoever was responsible added it very late in the game, according to the timestamp we recovered—which, incidentally, they had tried to erase."

"And?"

"As far as I understand," Gladstone said, "if certain words were included in the orders given to or actions determined by ISAC, he would shut himself down."

"What were the words?"

"*Kill* plus *enemy* equals *shutdown*."

The phone line was silent for a moment.

Gladstone continued. "Basically, if ISAC entered a scenario where his training would lead to *killing something or someone that it had classified as an enemy*, that would do it. And that addition may have been incompatible with KiTov's training model. The integration could have provoked all sorts of unpredictable behavior."

"So someone," Gordy said, standing up and pacing around the dark room, which made the overhead lights click on abruptly, "but not Calvin Chen, set ISAC up to defy orders?"

"Correct. And we know that *someone* had to be on your team," Gladstone said, "since the buried subroutine was part of the original ACS shared with KiTov."

"I'll get you the names of everyone on the machine learning team," Gordy said. But as he spoke, he already knew. *Freddy*.

CHAPTER TWENTY-FIVE

IN GRAY SWEATPANTS, eating a piece of chocolate cake, Vivian searched for news updates. She could see the notifications online, but she needed to hear the predictions about the storm for herself. Finally, she found Channel Ten news streaming, but the anchors were just recapping the most recent Red Sox game. "Who cares?!" she yelled to no one...though if it were her beloved Cincinnati Reds in the playoffs, she would certainly still care.

Karla walked through the door just as Vivian started Googling again.

"I now understand why people still keep TVs around," Vivian said by way of greeting.

Karla sat down next to her and gave her a kiss. "Have you heard that the storm is now a Category 4?"

"Yeah," Vivian said, angling her body toward her wife. "How does that change things?"

"Heath is going to strongly recommend that those who can, evacuate, but we are also planning for a lot of people to shelter in place." Karla rubbed her forehead.

"We've been preparing for this," she continued. "We have a good number of shelter locations ready to go, to spread people out. But we could use a few more." She paused, biting into the cake she had spotted on the coffee table. "So…what are the chances we could add Beth Abraham to the list? I know we talked about this as a hypothetical a few years ago, but the need is real this time. And in case you're motivated by keeping up with the Episcopalians, I just talked to Heather and she is going to do her best to open up St. Paul's." Karla dug back into the cake.

"Hmm," Vivian said, leaning forward from the cushions she'd been nestled into. "Of course I wish the answer would be yes… but I just don't know." She stood up and paced around the room, then stopped in her tracks.

"What are you smirking about?"

"Joseph just left for Israel, so that's one obstacle we won't have to deal with. Or at least not immediately. And we already have an emergency board meeting scheduled for tomorrow to talk about the storm, so I could raise it then." Vivian scrunched her nose and rested two fingers on her chin. "So…this is really happening, huh? We're going to stick out this storm here?"

"Yup," Karla said, taking her hand. "But the buildings are in much better condition these days to handle what's coming. We have great leadership and a good plan. The city is ready."

"Well," Vivian said, squeezing Karla's hand back, "if there's a chance that Beth Abraham could be a shelter for folks in the city, I'm not missing that. You know that's kind of like my dream."

Karla laughed. "Baby, you have some weird dreams."

CHAPTER TWENTY-SIX

CROUCHING DOWN, FREDDY peered into Hyydra's torso. While eyes might be the window into a human soul, Hyydra's midsection was where her consciousness was located. Or at least her central computer.

"Okay, Hyydra," he said. "Let's see what you've got." Freddy looked back at Jacqueline.

Both of their departments had been running test after test to ensure that Hyydra's control system had not been tampered with when ISAC went missing. They had already run a variety of trials to assess her physical aptitude, and Hyydra had passed all of those as if she was her former self. But they were not out of the woods yet, and it would take a lot more before they could be certain.

Today they were testing her ability to categorize dangerous objects she encountered by running an advanced identification search, which would also direct her in how to handle the item. Jacqueline carefully assembled a pile of objects that clanked onto a low-standing table in front of them: a coffee pot, phone chargers, hammers and nails, chunks of rock, bullets, and a few candy bars. "Hyydra, locate any object with live gun powder," Freddy commanded.

Hyydra quickly scanned the pile and, using her dexterous fingers, carefully picked out several bullets that had been hidden in the heap. "Dangerous objects detected!" Hyydra said. "Dangerous objects detected," she repeated. Holding them, Hyydra moved toward a locked bin in the corner of the lab. She scanned the lock, opened it, and carefully set the bullets down. Then she resealed the bin and made her way back toward a smiling Jacqueline.

A second later, Jacqueline's computer dinged with a notification from Hyydra indicating that she had placed five objects containing gun powder in Safe 4130, complete with a photograph of the bullets and a list of their dimensions.

"Well done!" she said to the robot. She turned to Freddy. "I know we've got a lot more tests to run, but it's looking more and more like she's in good shape!"

Freddy offered his colleague a half-smile. Sure, the fact that Hyydra had likely not been compromised was good news, but there was still the matter of ISAC and the ire of KiTov and the Israeli military.

"What are you and Camille planning to do?" Jacqueline asked as she inspected Hyydra's appendages, her back to Freddy.

The night before, as they had refreshed their phones for

updates on Vincenzo's trajectory and force, Freddy and Camille had decided they would evacuate and stay with Freddy's mom in New York. She was expressing a lot of fear and anxiety on the family chat, and had practically commanded that they come.

"I'm going to drive to Philly to be with my family, too," Jacqueline said. "I can't imagine dealing with this alone."

A forceful bang abruptly sounded through the room. It was coming from the door of the lab. Startled, Freddy jumped up from his seat just as the door swung open.

Three people charged in. Two in police uniforms and one in a suit.

The one in the suit immediately approached Freddy, getting close enough for Freddy to see his printed Leviathan Labs visitor badge. *Gavin Gladstone*, it read.

"Freddy Fuentes?" he asked. Freddy froze. Out of the corner of his eye, he saw Gordy, who must have slipped in after the cops.

"After an extensive investigation," Gladstone said, "we have found additional logic in both Hyydra's and ISAC's control systems with your digital fingerprint on them, plus a clear record of your attempt to hide the incursion. Our team has concluded that you endowed the robots with the ability to defy orders and intentionally programmed ISAC to escape, which is tantamount to stealing the property of KiTov Robotics."

Freddy's own control system was setting off alarms in his head. He had been worrying for the past week that something like this might happen. And frankly, he did not know if he was in fact the one that had set this disaster in motion.

He knew, at least, what to do to make the best possible case for himself. Sound as smart as possible. Don't reject their story or put them on the defensive. Find ways for his narrative and theirs to be cohesive. As someone who had felt like an outsider in so many worlds, Freddy had developed plenty of survival strategies to activate in any given situation. Though in this one, things were moving so fast. Too fast. He pleaded with Gordy with his eyes, but Gordy avoided eye contact. Where the hell was Sal? How could he just let this happen? Sal, who Freddy had trusted. Sal, who—more than that—Freddy had *believed* in.

"We have a warrant for your arrest," one of the cops said. "You have the right to remain silent. Anything you say can and will be used against you in a court of law. You have a right to an attorney...." Everything around him turned into a blur, besides the sharp pain of cuffs being forced onto him too tightly.

Freddy had done his best to avoid any encounters with law enforcement, by following rules, building up structures of success and protection to make sure it never happened—another file of instructions stored away inside his ACS. And yet somehow, here he was: an employee of a renowned robotics company flush with investment cash, cold handcuffs tightening around his wrists.

CHAPTER TWENTY-SEVEN

VIVIAN PACED AROUND her office practicing what she would
say to the board, to all the stakeholders, to convince them
to keep Beth Abraham open as a storm shelter. She racked her
brain for a verse of Torah, a line from Psalms, something that
would make it clear. But everything she came up with just seemed
like a distraction, because the point was already clear: It was the
right thing to do.

When you are part of a community, Vivian thought, *when you
are within the eruv, you say, I'm here. We're here. You say yes without hesitation. Na'aseh v'nishmah*—"we will do and then we will
listen." To the details. To the requirements. To the risk of insurance liability.

As she continued her laps around the office, Raymond walked by and stopped for a moment. "Hey, Rabbi," he said, leaning against the entrance. "You preparing a sermon or something?"

"Not exactly," Vivian said. She had paused, but her body was still rocking from side to side, as if she was praying. "The city asked if we would keep the building open as a shelter during the storm."

Raymond stood up straighter and walked into the room. "Hmm, interesting. Alton and I were just talking the other day about how this building is definitely safer than anywhere else we would hole up."

"Exactly. And I believe that we have a responsibility to share it with the broader community. But getting the board to approve that is a tall order." She started pacing again.

"What are you and Karla planning to do?" Raymond asked. "Evacuate or stay?"

"Karla has to stay because of her job, and I'm not going to leave without her. And I'd like to be of use, I'd like the whole community to be of use, if there is a way to be." She looked at Raymond. "What about you? You going down to be with Sheila and Mac?"

"It's too tricky to get to Georgia right now," Raymond said. "I'm glad Sheila and Mac are together, though." He paused and then laughed. "Mac used to be so scared of storms." Vivian tried to imagine what he must be remembering.

"If the board says yes to the shelter plan, the City Hall folks will need to create a team to run it," Vivian said. She waited a beat. "Of course, you'd be the perfect person to oversee it rather than them hiring someone else. Would you be interested in staying and doing that?"

Raymond folded his arms and cocked his head. "Hmm," he

said, straightening his back. "Yeah, I'd do that. Could Alton be a part of the team too? We'd need more hands on deck to do everything. Cook, clean, manage inventory."

"I'm sure the city leadership coordinating this would be relieved that we could figure the staffing out on our own, especially given the time crunch," Vivian said, knowing that when she said *city leadership*, she was mostly talking about her wife.

"Okay then. Sounds like a plan," Raymond said. "*Almost* a plan, at least. Good luck with the board."

After he left the office, Vivian, still swaying, looked at her bookshelf. The tractates of Talmud caught her attention. Jews have always been doing this work, she thought—negotiating and renegotiating ways of being in community. *What does it mean to be safe? What boundaries do we enforce? Do we stay or do we retreat?*

She pictured a few new volumes next to the older ones, asking and answering today's questions and dilemmas. An expansion of the writings on eruv. A whole new tractate on natural disasters. Maybe even one about robots.

After exhausting her list of modern Talmudic titles, Vivian noticed that her body had finally stilled.

· · ·

The Beth Abraham board gathered in the multipurpose room for an emergency planning meeting. Hurricane Vincenzo was just a few days away from its arrival in Providence, and half of those attending arrived via video chat, having already evacuated to safer places. Another few were too busy executing their own safety plans to attend at all.

Tamar Benayoun got right to business. "Okay, let's lay out our options here," she said. "One obvious choice—"

"Wait...no go-around?" Barry Katz interjected from the screen.

"Not tonight, Barry," Tamar said.

Vivian giggled to herself. Perhaps the habit of the board-meeting icebreaker had successfully crystalized into a *minhag*. Perhaps the members couldn't even remember a time without it, as if it could be traced all the way back to the thirteenth century. *Another W for the win column*, she thought, watching analogue Vivian do a touchdown dance in her head.

"One obvious choice," Tamar continued, "is to close up the building, and make sure to communicate the possible forms of support that congregants who plan to stay in Providence can access from the city."

"Do we know how many people are planning to stay?" asked Joel Fishman, who was there in the flesh.

"Judging by the fact that there is still time to get out and half of us are already gone," said Vera Cohen, also physically present, "I'm guessing that the majority of members will leave."

"I think many will," Vivian interjected, "but I've been in touch with a lot of the older folks in the community, and it's just not possible for many of them to evacuate, so most of that demographic is planning on staying put."

"Okay, so that's one option," Tamar said, "to lock everything up and connect members who stay to the city's resources."

"What are the others?" someone asked.

Tamar looked at Vivian. "Rabbi, would you like to share?"

Vivian dug her feet into the floor and straightened her back. "Representatives from City Hall have asked to use our building as a shelter for residents who don't want to or can't evacuate and don't feel safe waiting out the storm in their homes." It all came rushing out more quickly than she had intended.

"Can you repeat that?" asked Shlomo Seidel, from the computer screen. Vivian repeated the proposal. Twice.

"Someone would have to stay and manage everything and take care of the building. We wouldn't just leave that to the city officials, right?" Joel Fishman asked.

"I would stay," Vivian said. "And Raymond has said that he would. And Alton, who works for Raymond on building upkeep, might also."

"I would stay," Flora chimed in from across the table.

"Me too," Vera said. "And you can count on Charlie as well."

"Don't you need to ask him first?" Barry Katz said.

"No," Vera said dryly. Vivian tried to hold in her laugh.

"What does Rabbi Glass think about this?" Shlomo asked from onscreen.

Vivian clenched her fists under the table and let little Vivian give a shout. "Rabbi Glass is in Israel, and has had spotty phone and internet service," Vivian said. "I've tried to fill him in but have not heard back from him. And now it's two a.m. there."

"Should we wait?" Barry asked.

"It sounds like we need to make this decision now if we are going to have time to prepare," Vera responded. "Waiting for Rabbi Glass to respond is basically defaulting to closing up the building."

Shlomo spoke up again. "Then I vote—"

His sound cut in and out, and no one could decipher the rest of his comment. Or no one tried to. Everyone probably felt they could guess well enough.

"I have to ask," Tamar broke in. "Doesn't this open us up to insurance liability? Having all kinds of strangers in our building, and leaving it more vulnerable during a hurricane?"

"You know," Flora responded, "I think hurricanes in general lead to insurance concerns."

"Though it is true that there are a lot of other things that could go wrong here," Joel said. "Someone who wants to harm us could gain access to the building…I'm sure we're all aware of the attacks on synagogues that have happened in recent years. Or someone could get injured for a totally unrelated reason."

"Could we hire security?" someone asked.

"Should we have people sign waivers?" asked someone else from onscreen. "Or check with the insurance company?"

"I did try that today," Vivian said. "I was on hold for an hour and a half and then hung up. Seems like a busy time for them." She folded her hands and laid them on the table. "The fact is that we aren't going to know every answer or every possible thing we might be liable for. We will do what we can to try to mitigate that, but there are going to be a lot of unknowns. So, if we chose to do this, we would do our best to prepare, and then we would have to be ready to take a risk." Vivian paused. No one filled in the silence. "To be innovative once again," she added uncertainly, attempting to channel how the white-sneaker-wearing robot guy would sell something to his crowd.

"Maybe...*too* innovative?" Barry Katz said.

Vivian's miniature self screamed once again in her mind's eye.

"Like Abraham...parsha...ooz...odd," Shlomo said, most of his words too garbled by the bad connection to decipher.

This time, Vivian was intrigued enough to ask him to repeat himself, though she wasn't even sure she had heard those few words correctly.

"Like when Abraham took a risk in this week's parsha, in choosing to follow God," he said, the connection perfectly clear for a moment.

"That's right," Vivian said. "Exactly, Shlomo."

"Hmm, well. I may reconsider then," he said.

"What do others think?" Tamar asked. Vivian could hear several chairs adjusting.

Finally, Vera spoke. "I think we should do it."

"I agree," Joel said, more firmly than Vivian would have expected given his previous line of inquiry. "It sounds like there is a team willing to take this on. I'm heading out of town, but I trust that group and will try to help however I can from a distance."

"I'm a yes," Flora declared.

"Me too," another said.

"Same," one more voice spoke up.

Vivian nodded silently as she looked on, grateful.

"Hold on, hold on," Tamar said. "Sorry, I got a bit distracted. We need someone to make a motion for a vote."

"I make a motion that we vote to keep the building open as a storm shelter," Vera said.

"Second!" Joel said.

"All in favor?" Tamar asked.

Everyone, around the table and onscreen, raised their hand. Even Shlomo Seidel.

Tamar followed up with the requisite "All opposed?" and "Abstentions?" but there were no more hands to go up.

"The motion passes!" she said with gusto. "Looks like we've got work to do."

As the meeting broke up, Vivian thought about Abraham accepting God's challenge to leave what he had known and go forth toward the possibility of a new home and a new people. Vivian was appreciative of—and not a little surprised by—Shlomo's analogy. But she also realized a key difference: Abraham was alone when he took that risk. The board of directors of Congregation Beth Abraham—and their soon-to-be senior rabbi, Vivian Green—certainly were not.

CHAPTER TWENTY-EIGHT

KARLA SIPPED HER second coffee of the day as she found a spot amid the reporters and city employees. Mayor Margaret Heath stood at a lectern framed by the grand marble staircase in the City Hall lobby.

"We have been preparing for this storm for a long time," she began. "The question was never, '*If* a destructive storm came, what would we do?' but '*When* it comes, will we be ready?'

"For years, we have been working across multiple departments to ensure that our new buildings are resilient and to prepare public infrastructure as central repositories for resources and support." Mayor Heath paused. "I believe that we are ready."

Karla, who had left the building the previous evening around midnight and was back at work by seven a.m., kept her exhaustion at bay with another swig of caffeine.

"We do strongly encourage those who can to evacuate the area," Heath continued. "and if you and your family need transportation to get out of the city, free public busses will continue to travel to safer locations through tomorrow evening. But for those who cannot, or who feel as if staying is their best or only option, know that our administration is offering a variety of resources to help keep you as safe as possible. We have put so much into planning for this storm. We are as ready as we can be today to face this uncertainty.

"I would now like to call up Providence's secretary of climate adaptation and resiliency, Winona MacLean, followed by the secretary of budget management, Clarissa Fox, to explain more about what will be available to residents during—and after—the storm."

Heath stepped back into the line of city officials behind the lectern, and Nona stepped forward.

"Good morning," she said. "I want to thank our partners for being here today. It is with your support that we have been able to assemble a network of thirty shelters—which include libraries, rec centers, houses of worship, and, of course, City Hall—all ready to open their doors to anywhere between 50 and 500 people each."

Standing on tiptoe and looking across the room, Karla made eye contact with Vivian and Heather, who were there representing their congregations. She dipped her head and winked in their direction.

"Residents seeking a place to go can call the city's information hotline to secure spots," Nona continued. "We've also been coordinating with utility companies, local municipalities, and the state in order to reinforce the electrical grid with more inputs from our renewables, and to increase workforce capacity to respond after the storm. While we anticipate major power outages across the area, we will do everything we can to restore power as quickly as possible."

Nona ended there and stepped away from the lectern. As she was about to reclaim her spot in the line of city officials, she abruptly turned back and took the mic again. "We are as ready as we can be to face this uncertainty," she muttered, more quietly than Mayor Heath had said it.

Karla chuckled to herself. This was the refrain that each speaker was supposed to end with, and Winona MacLean had almost missed it. But she'd recovered, albeit not particularly gracefully.

Secretary Fox approached the lectern next. "For those who do lose power for significant periods of time, the city has stores of food, rainwater, and backup generators ready to go—both for those who seek shelter and for those who stay home—that will be accessible after the storm.

"There will be clear routes assigned to each mobile rapid-response unit, bringing those and other supplies and aid through each neighborhood of the city. All the information about the routes and shelters operating in your neighborhood is available on the city's website or by calling 311.

"Some may ask where the money is coming from," Fox continued. "In addition to state and federal grants, some is a direct result of the redistribution of funds from the Providence Police Department. Because of this shift, the city is now able to employ a corps of several hundred emergency responders." Fox took a deep breath, which was audible through the microphone, and concluded with the same chorus as the others.

Mayor Heath returned to the lectern as Clarissa Fox shimmied her way back into the row of government officials.

"Lastly," the mayor said, "we are working on a plan to evacuate the city jail, which is not a safe place to be during the storm."

"Or ever!" someone in the back yelled. A few others hollered with approval. Heath went on. "Our policies represent the belief that every resident of this city deserves the best shot to make it through this storm with support." It seemed to Karla that most of the crowd applauded.

After Heath took several questions from reporters—which mostly focused on the decision to release people from jail—Karla glided through the crowd toward Vivian and Heather.

"This is really something," Vivian said.

"Seriously!" Heather added. "Listening to all these visionary women leading the way, I can't tell if we are living in a dystopia or a utopia."

Karla scanned the room. "It's definitely a mix," she said.

"I mean, evacuating the jail? How'd they pull that off?" Heather asked.

"Actually, the mayor is still working on it," Karla said. "The sheriff hasn't budged, so she said that to force his hand."

"What a badass!" Heather said.

"Right?"

Vivian's phone started buzzing. "Shit," she said when she looked down at it. "Shit, shit, SHIT."

"What happened, baby?" Karla tried to stop herself from imagining the long list of things that could have gone wrong and just wait patiently to find out, but Vivian's silence was not helping. "Vivian?"

Finally she spoke. "It's Camille," she said. "Leviathan Labs had Freddy arrested." She looked up from her phone. "He's in jail."

"What the hell?! How is that possible? I mean, I could imagine them suddenly firing him, maybe—given what he's told us—but an arrest?! *Now?*" Karla's heart was beating what felt like 100 times a second.

Vivian covered her face with one hand. "I should have tried harder to get through to Gordy when I had the chance," she said. "He was standing right in front of me!"

"I…I don't get it," Karla said. "Why didn't Freddy tell me things were this bad? Oh, God. If I hadn't given him so much shit for his job, he would have told us!" She and Vivian stared at each other. Vivian looked as sick as Karla felt.

"Umm," Heather chimed in. "I'm not totally sure what's going on. I mean, it's obviously horrible, but I'm pretty sure that this is neither of your faults. So, let's just bypass this whole part and think of how we can help Freddy."

Vivian's phone buzzed again and she read from it aloud. "Camille says, 'Only lawyers and ministers are allowed to visit jail right now, and I can't get a single Providence lawyer on the phone. Because of storm, I think. Could you go?'" One more text came in. "'Like, as his rabbi?'"

"Bingo," Heather said. "So. Viv, you go do that." Vivian bobbed her head. "And Karla, you try to get back to, umm"—Heather stuck out one hand, palm forward, and motioned toward the city officials at the center of the room—"all of *that*, so we can survive this storm. And if either of you needs anything, let me know."

"Okay, okay, yeah," Vivian said. "That sounds like a good plan."

"Thanks, Heather," Karla and Vivian said simultaneously. Vivian hugged her, and Karla did next, and then Heather said goodbye and left. Karla watched quietly as Vivian texted Camille back. "Of…course," Vivian narrated as she typed. "On…my…way."

Vivian looked up, and her eyes met Karla's. "Good luck with the planning," she said. She leaned into Karla's arms and squeezed her tightly. "I'm so proud of you."

"You too," Karla said, resting her chin on Vivian's shoulder.

Vivian let go of her and stood up straight. "Okay, I'm off."

"And you are as ready as you can be to face the uncertainty," Karla said to her, catching hold of her just as Vivian turned to leave. Vivian looked back at her and repeated it.

"As ready as I can be to face the uncertainty."

CHAPTER TWENTY-NINE

VINCENZO WAS SET to hit in two days. More than half of the desks in Flora's classroom were empty. The absence of so many students felt like a different kind of presence, Flora thought.

The remaining kids, along with their families, would be riding out the storm in Providence, while everyone else had evacuated to who knows where. Flora looked out the window and noticed how blue the sky was.

Like many of her students and some of the other teachers, Flora and her husband, Ben, were planning to stay. Right after the Beth Abraham board meeting, Vivian had asked Flora if they would be on a team of coordinators at the synagogue, carrying out the plan to transform it into a storm shelter and then remaining onsite during the storm. The building was safe, they would have plenty of supplies, and they would not be alone. Seemed as good of a place as any to ride out Vincenzo.

Rather than stick to her planned economics lesson in the supply-and-demand unit, Flora reviewed the resources that the city was making available and asked each of her students what they and their families were planning to do.

"We're heading to one of the shelters," one said.

"Us too," another chimed in.

"We're sticking around the apartment. We're on the third floor, so...I guess that will help?"

A few of those who had plans to stay home had scheduled deliveries with the mobile rapid-response units to ensure they'd have supplies before and after the rain came. But a few hadn't been able to yet. Flora encouraged them to keep calling, and told them that if they needed any help, they could call her.

Not everyone had shared their plan by the end of class, and Flora caught Didi Guerrero, one of the silent ones, as they were walking, slumped, toward the door. "How about you, Didi?" she asked. "What's your family planning to do?"

Didi's shoulders sagged even more as they dodged Flora's gaze. "My sister is immunocompromised," they finally said. "She has a lot of medical equipment that she needs, so my parents thought we should just stay in our house. But it's not in the best shape...I don't know."

"Do you want help calling around to see if any of the shelters could accommodate her?" Flora asked.

Didi kept looking past Flora. "I don't think so," they said. "See...." Flora waited.

Didi finally turned their body toward her. "My parents are undocumented, so they're scared to get involved with the government," they said. "I know that the message has been that we should seek out shelter too…but they just don't trust that."

"I hear you, Didi," Flora said, reminding herself to proceed carefully after her student had trusted her with this information. "If it makes any difference, you can tell your parents that the shelters are not checking IDs." Flora thought back to the webinar training for shelter volunteers that she had sat through the night before, grasping for details that might comfort Didi. "And none of the data beyond aggregate numbers are being shared with city government." Flora paused, waiting for a response. None came. Didi's eyes wandered around the room.

"I'm going to be working at one, and if you wanted, I could probably get you and your family in there," Flora said. "I can't ease all your parents' fears, but I can tell you that there will be doctors there to provide medical care. And I would also be there to support you all." She paused. "But it's your choice."

"Great. Another bad choice," Didi said. "That's all we get."

Flora felt like she had swallowed a peach pit and it was stuck in her throat. "I'm sorry this is so hard, Didi." Her student kept looking away. "I'll tell you what. I'm going to go ahead and put your family on the list, without your names for now—I'll just add you as members of my family—so you know you can go there if you need to, okay?" Flora grabbed a piece of scrap paper from her desk and scribbled down Beth Abraham's address and her cell phone number.

Didi took the paper and crumpled it into their pocket. "Thank you, Ms. Moore," Didi whispered, and walked out of the classroom.

CHAPTER THIRTY

VIVIAN FOUND HERSELF stuck at a red light amid a bustle of traffic. Apparently the pace of pre-storm evacuations was picking up. Google Maps had predicted that the drive to the outskirts of town, where the jail was located, would take twenty minutes, but it had already been fifteen and she had barely moved.

How could Gordy do that? she kept repeating in her mind, her thoughts oscillating between horror at Freddy's arrest and fear of what was coming.

Offering pastoral care in times of need was one of Vivian's primary responsibilities in her job. And that meant being present, it meant listening to her congregants, it meant not judging them. For her newest congregant, Freddy, that seemed like an easy charge. But for others, it was a tall order. Sometimes it even felt impossible.

Like when Vivian made a hospital visit to Sanford Kaplan after his emergency hernia surgery, and he could not stop saying bigoted things to the Haitian nurse trying to care for him.

Or when Bess Kahn told Vivian how stressful it was to plan a simple bar mitzvah these days and showed her the budget for the event, which included a $20,000 catering bill and a $180 donation to a soup kitchen. What was the pastoral response to that?

And she was definitely judging Gordy Silver for throwing Freddy in jail. She thought of all the possible things she would say to him if they were face to face. Perhaps rabbis should institute a new tradition: calling-congregants-out-on-their-shit visits.

As Vivian imagined confronting Gordy, her phone rang. It was Joseph. She didn't have time for Joseph. "Ugh," she said out loud.

"Hello?" she answered.

"Hi, Vivian," Joseph said.

"Yes?"

"I saw the update email you sent to the congregation," Joseph said, his voice crackling from across the world. "About keeping the shul open as a storm shelter."

Vivian rolled her eyes. "I'm sorry that we didn't wait for your response, but we had to move ahead quickly on the decision and—"

Joseph jumped in. "Do you think this is such a good idea? What about the insurance? We—we have to think about the future. Although I appreciate how much you—"

Oh, if she could have a word for every time Joseph patronized her, she could quill a whole *sefer Torah*.

"Listen, Joseph," Vivian interrupted. "You left! You left us and you escaped this storm. And you're leaving for good in a few months. Frankly, this isn't your decision to make."

Joseph tried to respond. "That is not—"

"And don't talk to me about the future. This whole effort is about the future. It's about a good and just future for our community, and our neighborhood." She sucked in some air. "And our children," she added.

"And that future doesn't include supporting Israel?" Joseph huffed.

Vivian shook her head. "What does any of this have to do with Israel?"

"I just met with a friend who was telling me all he does to ensure a strong connection between his synagogue in the diaspora and our country…. When there are emergencies *here*, you don't act with the same kind of urgency, you don't think about ways for our community to stand by our own homeland. You just wait for it to pass. But we need Israel. Don't you see that?" Joseph's voice was getting louder. "Given everything going on? There is nothing wrong with directing our care and resources here, there is nothing wrong with—"

Vivian could feel hot air in her ears. *How was this the conversation they were having right now?* But if Joseph wanted to go there, Vivian would go there, albeit with fewer tools of calm at her disposal than she might have had otherwise.

"What's wrong with it, Joseph," Vivian interrupted again, "is that you don't seem too invested in moral progress in either Providence *or* Israel. If Providence and Beth Abraham are your home, then maybe you can go pick up the baby formula order I still need to get from across town before the storm hits. And if

Israel is your home, then stand with *everyone* who lives there and go protest the horrific settler violence against Palestinians in the West Bank enabled by this atrocious Israeli government."

"Vivian," Joseph said, "Slow down. Let's have a rational conversation about this."

Oh my God. Two sefer Torahs. "Joseph, there is so much to do," Vivian said. "My friend was thrown into jail by one of your beloved congregants. And a Category 4 hurricane is about to hit our city. This is not the time. Please just…just stay out of the way. I have to go."

Joseph tried to get in a few more words, but Vivian could not process them. She thought back to the text she had recently studied with Flora. In Vivian's estimation, Joseph was so far outside of the eruv at this moment that there was no chance of a human partition, or any other hack, closing the gap.

So she hung up.

But somehow, amid the argument with Joseph, she had arrived in the parking lot of the Rhode Island Department of Corrections. Time to tackle the next challenge. She sat in the car for a moment and closed her eyes. Taking a few deep breaths, she worked to center herself so she could shift gears and do her part to help her friend.

As she walked in the door of the jail, she was confronted by a series of metal detectors and three armed police officers. "Who are you here to see?" one of them asked.

"Mr. Freddy Fuentes," Vivian said, noticing how quiet and sterile the lobby was, imagining how different it must be from the rest of the building.

"Ma'am, given the commotion, only lawyers can visit today," another one of them said. "Are you an attorney?"

"Actually—" Vivian began, hoping to will an answer out of her mouth that would get her through. "I'm...Mr. Fuentes's rabbi," she finally said.

The guard stared Vivian down. She figured it was a lot to take in.

"Do you have clergy ID?"

She pulled out her Rabbinical Assembly membership card, plus her driver's license. The guard took the RA card and studied it. His eyes traveled between the two IDs and Vivian. "Uh. Okay. Fine." He picked up a phone and made a call, typing into a computer at the same time. With the phone wedged in his ear, he told someone to bring Freddy down to the visitation room.

Vivian was led to a short flight of stairs and through a windowless white hall lit by flickering fluorescent bulbs. It was ominously quiet. Inside her mind, though, it was busy. With every step, anger—at Joseph, at Gordy, at Leviathan Labs, at fossil-fuel companies, at the Israeli government, at sexism—churned through her.

Vivian and the guard entered another white room with bad lighting. It contained ten or so booths, all cut in half by a plexiglass pane running the length of the room, with phones hanging at each one. There was only one other visitor there, already talking to a prisoner. The briefcase seemed to indicate a lawyer.

The guard instructed her to sit down in one of the booths. As she waited, she studied the wooden desktop in front of her, which was covered with words carved into its cheap wood. "Fuck the police" had been engraved particularly nicely, almost calligraphically.

Freddy was soon led in, wearing a dark blue jumpsuit and looking ten years older than he usually did. He sat down on the other side of the glass, and they both picked up their phones.

"Thanks for coming," Freddy started. "It's good to see a friend. Though it did take me a minute to process when they told me my rabbi was here."

Vivian smiled. "How are you holding up?"

"Um…it's not the best place I've ever been trans," Freddy said, almost in a whisper, his eyes darting to the guard leaning against a wall behind him, like he wondered if he was being listened to. "And everyone is so on edge because of the storm. I need to get out and figure out what to do with Cam and Xo, but how on earth…I mean, there are rumors of us being released, but that seems hard to believe." Freddy's voice trailed off. He looked down at his hands. "I'll never forgive Gordy and Sal—*especially* Sal—for this."

Vivian could almost feel the storm clouds rolling in above and around them. "Freddy, how can we convince them that you don't belong in jail?"

"I don't know," Freddy said. "They haven't made any progress with any of the other possible suspects. I'm the most obvious fall guy they've got at this point. And they want to pin this on someone, fix things with our partner companies and move on."

"You know the, umm, brains of these robots better than anyone," Vivian said. "There have to be clues."

Freddy looked down again. After a long silence, he said, "It is strange that there haven't been any signals back at the lab, given that ISAC was outfitted with an emergency tracking device."

"Okay, okay," Vivian said. "And what might explain that?"

Freddy looked away and squeezed his eyes shut. "Toward the

end of the development stage," he finally said, "our lab—well, *I*, really—added an additional goal to the control system, a clear threshold, so that neither Hyydra nor ISAC could aim to kill. It was a rational extension of everything else we'd done."

"How is that possible for a robotic soldier to obey?"

"It may not have been," Freddy said. "If two conflicting goals are built into the same system, that could lead to, um, malfunctions."

Just then, the other prisoner and his lawyer stood up to leave. Freddy and Vivian both looked on as they left the room. They were now the only ones left in the visitation room, except for the lone guard watching Freddy.

"Malfunctions?" Vivian asked, cutting through the distraction.

"Yeah, malfunctions," Freddy said. "Like ISAC destroying his own safety features, including the tracking device. Like disabling the building's alarm system. Maybe shutting himself down or even...."

"Or even what?" Vivian asked.

"Complete self-destruction." Freddy rubbed his temple. "I keep burying that possibility in my mind. Still, though, it's the only one I can think of, because if a human tried anything with ISAC, they would lose every time...but, I mean, that would be... it seems so implausible."

"Freddy," Vivian said, shifting the phone to her other ear, "you are building machines to settle Mars and manage an occupied population. It's all implausible."

"I included the extra subroutine because Sal and Gordy were forcing us to move so quickly. The KiTov partnership came out of nowhere, and there was no chance to figure out if that project even fit with the systems we had already built." He shifted around in his plastic chair. "But the integration with ISAC had only happened the day before…I suppose it's possible the system clashed right off the bat, or maybe it was that damn bird. Or maybe the ACS was advanced enough for him to detect his entire existence as crossing the threshold. I don't know how, but maybe. I mean, I crossed that threshold a while ago, and these machines have the most advanced *brains* out there," he said, using Vivian's word. "So…."

"Freddy, where do you think ISAC could be?" Vivian asked. "Think about it."

"The area around the lab was searched multiple times. And the police were on the lookout…."

He was tapping his fingers on the desk, looking pensive, when the loudspeaker started to crackle. "Attention." Freddy and Vivian both turned toward the speakers protruding from the ceiling. "All prisoners will be released in one hour." The message was repeated.

Freddy sat frozen, continuing to stare at the now-silent speaker. The guard in the visitation room repeated the message. "Visitation hours are over. Go pack your things and get ready for release," he said. Freddy looked at him, presumably waiting for more information, but he was not given any.

"Wow, that's—I mean, I heard that the mayor was working on it, but it seemed like such a long shot," Vivian said to Freddy. "I'll wait for you to be released and bring you home."

He was quiet, his face unmoving, but through the glass, Vivian detected a tear rolling down his cheek.

"Thanks, Rabbi." He looked down at his hands again, then sighed and slumped over. "What is it, Freddy?" It was a silly question, she realized as she asked it.

"I—I know this will sound crazy, given everything going on," he said, wiping his eyes. "But I'm—I'm sad for ISAC, thinking about the possibility of him choosing to…you know."

"That makes plenty of sense. You created a part of him." *Creators love their creations, no matter how flawed they are*, Vivian thought.

"Hey!" the guard said to Freddy. "Time to go."

Freddy exhaled. "Okay, let's get out of here." He stood up, still holding the phone. "And never come back," he added.

"Amen," Vivian said, hanging up the phone and rising from her chair.

. . .

When Freddy opened the door, Camille ran over from the kitchen and hugged him. Hard. Freddy coughed. He could feel her tears wetting his sleeve. He had held it together during the ride back with Vivian. Mostly. A few silent tears here and there, but he was stoic, watching the people of Providence out the window, going about their day and presumably preparing. Vivian was quiet too, aside from her invitation to ride out the storm at the synagogue.

But now, in Camille's arms, everything came flooding out, his own hurricane of emotions. The fear for himself, for his family, for the city, for the whole fucking galaxy. The anger toward Gordy, Sal, capitalism, militaries. Freddy wrapped his arms around Camille. He tried to hold it in, but his body wouldn't let him. He didn't say anything. And neither did Camille. But, despite the clouds of doom hovering over them, despite his sobbing, in this moment, he could at least breathe. For what felt like the first time in a while.

At some point, Freddy felt something squeeze his leg. He looked down and saw Xo, gazing up at him, holding her beloved Cuckoo. "Daddy ho! Daddy ho!" she yelled, jumping up and down. Over and over again. And this time, Freddy knew exactly what she meant.

CHAPTER THIRTY-ONE

Gordy LISTENED TO the echoes of footsteps reverberating through the lab's wide halls. He and Jack Phillips were conducting one more tour for the new security team they had hired to protect headquarters during the storm. The windows were boarded up. The most valuable projects were locked into sections of the building so secure that not even the team would be able to access them. Sal had somehow gotten his hands on a few extra generators, which were ready to go if the built-in power sources got knocked out.

Another thing Sal had done was evacuate to a vacation home in Costa Rica. Gordy, meanwhile, was planning to ride out the storm with his wife and daughter at his in-laws' house in upstate

New York. The two of them had evacuated a few days earlier and were already settled in.

Every now and then, Gordy pulled up his text chain with his daughter to look at her strings of nonsensical emojis. *Baseball, storm cloud, sad face, ice cream cone.* The riddles, which he imagined had no definitive meaning, made Gordy feel calm for a fleeting moment.

He would be getting on the road in the next hour or so to meet up with them; the Tesla was packed and ready to go. He was pushing it, though. The storm would make landfall in less than twenty-four hours, and he certainly couldn't be the only one planning to leave at the last minute. The traffic might be intense. But Gordy Silver could always figure out plan B in the face of a challenge.

Three security guards followed him and Jack up and down the hallways, in and out of laboratories and offices. The boarded-up windows made the vast building feel small and fragile. As the group rounded an echoey corner and faced the triple-padlocked main lab, Jack said, "And in here is where we are securing our most valuable machines. You won't have access to it, and for all I know, Gordy's so careful that he took away mine too." Jack winked at the guards.

Gordy did not laugh. "This is the heart of the lab," he said, trying to convey the appropriate level of seriousness, "the part that needs to be monitored with utmost attention from its perimeter."

"So these are the robots that are going to put us out of business someday, huh?" one of the security guards said. Indeed, Gordy wished that a whole corps of ISACs was ready so that they could secure the building through the coming storm. Someday their capabilities would certainly outweigh those of SG Security Solutions. Gordy was counting on it.

Three managerial offices had been turned into makeshift bedrooms for the security team. As they walked through, each guard dropped an identical black-and-gray duffel bag into one of them.

Gordy and Jack led the group to the control room. "Someone should be stationed here at all times tracking the network waves. If anyone tries any monkey business, it's going to come from tampering with our code," Jack said. "So keep an eye out here." SG specialized in "hybrid security"—on the ground and in the cloud.

"Roger that, boss," one of the guards said, munching on a potato chip. Gordy watched his crumbs fall onto one of the keyboard below.

He could not shake his anxiety about leaving the security of Leviathan Labs' most valuable machines—at least the ones that remained—to others. He did not know these people. Or trust them. Sure, Jack Phillips knew someone who had vouched for SG, but something about Jack's matter-of-fact tone, not to mention the mess of the ISAC investigation, made Gordy wonder if he truly understood the gravity of the situation. The stakes. Yes, Freddy was in jail and no longer posed a threat. But Gordy was not sure that identifying and arresting him had accounted for all that had gone wrong. Or still *could* go wrong.

He returned to his office to gather his computer; he would definitely be keeping an eye on things from a distance. It hardly felt like enough, even with the pile of money Leviathan was paying for SG's team. *Storm surge prices*, the company had said a few days earlier when Gordy called them up, worried that Leviathan's typical reinforcements could not handle the job during the storm.

A storm which all kinds of hackers could take advantage of. And what if ISAC found his way back to the building? Gordy still held out hope.

As he trudged through the employee parking lot—to get on the road, to reunite with his family—Gordy stopped midway to his car. His eyes fixed on a cloud moving slowly above him.

Suddenly, he turned back toward the building. *Someone* needed to stay, to ensure the survival of the Hyydras and Leviathan's other work, to safeguard the future of the company. Someone who understood what they stood to lose if anything else were to go wrong. Sal was long gone. Jacqueline, a trustworthy department head, was too. And Freddy…Freddy was in jail, which, as far as Gordy was concerned, did not do enough to neutralize the possible threats.

And so, plan C. He would do it himself. He would wait out the storm in his office. If needed, he could move to the basement, which had been outfitted like a bomb shelter. There was plenty of food, a few comfortable beds, an extra generator, and a magic USB stick loaded with any movie one could want.

After he informed his wife that he would be staying, which she was not too pleased to hear, he let Jack and the security team know. He sent emojis back to his daughter in addition to his apology. *Flowers, red heart, spaceship, sleeping Z's, purple heart.* To which she replied: *Angry face, pizza, construction hat, red heart.*

As Gordy paced through the silent building, texting back and forth, he focused again on the sound of his footsteps echoing through the halls.

CHAPTER THIRTY-TWO

HURRICANE VINCENZO WAS set to hit the following day, and there was still so much to do. Karla sat in her cubicle in City Hall calling up the shelter site coordinators, ensuring that the plans were coming together. Deliveries of food, water and medical supplies. Extra generators for the bigger sites. Extra spots for residents who would, inevitably, decide to come at the very last second.

She looked over the list on her whiteboard. She had done her job, but that did not seem sufficient in the face of the storm. No matter how good the coordination was, no matter how many graduate-school seminars had prepared her for exactly what she was charged with…they were fighting something that was so much bigger. She *was* glad that her boxes were checked. And she was *extremely* relieved that Freddy was out of jail. But there was no way to contain and prepare for all the possible variables.

Nevertheless, she would go home, and come back the next day to face the inevitable, knowing they had done everything they could—both in the short-term lead-up to this moment, and over the years preceding it.

She stopped by Winona MacLean's office before heading out, but her boss wasn't there. Karla found her down the hall in the meeting room. MacLean was facing the huge map of Providence on the back wall, which was now covered with even more pushpins and color-coded Post-it notes than there had been just a few hours earlier.

Without turning around, MacLean started speaking. "We could use more generators. Clarissa was just giving me a rundown on our inventory. Some of the big companies in town snatched up a lot of them, even though most of their buildings already have at least one built in. Maybe, if we need more after the storm, we can convince them to donate their extras to meet actual people's needs." MacLean turned around and faced Karla. "Something to keep our eyes on after the storm passes."

"It's unfathomable how they could be so invested in their own property at the expense of real humans," Karla said.

Her boss laughed dryly. "It's pretty easy to fathom, actually."

Karla's cheeks reddened. "Right. Of course." She adjusted the strap of her messenger bag. "Well, all the shelter sites seem as ready as they can be at this point. Tomorrow, the key will be making sure their capacities match the people seeking them."

MacLean turned back to the map. "And responding to whatever other last-minute challenges arise," she said.

"Roger that." Karla tapped her foot lightly, waiting to see if Nona had anything to add. When nothing came, Karla spoke to her back again. "Good night, boss."

"There's a story I heard at a conference once," Nona said suddenly, "from a Penobscot woman I met there." She turned, slowly, to face Karla. "Her people tell about a cannibal giant that Mother Earth summons because she fears that humankind's propensity for consumption will lead to her destruction. And the giant entices all the people to dance and dance and dance, and consume and consume and consume, until they dance so fast and consume so fast that they hasten their own demise. And then Mother Earth can replenish herself without the presence of such a destructive species."

Nona paused, and all Karla could hear was the wind outside.

"The storyteller said that the elders believe we are living in a time when this giant is awake." Nona's face fell into her hands, muffling her voice, but Karla could still hear her. "Sometimes I wonder if it's even worth standing in the way."

Karla took a few steps toward her.

"This whole city is going to be grateful that you did. That we did," she said.

Nona lifted her head, and their eyes met for a moment. One corner of her mouth rose upward. "Go get some sleep," she said.

"Aye aye," Karla replied. "Good night, boss."

CHAPTER THIRTY-THREE

"**N**OW THAT IS a whole lot of toilet paper," Vivian said, pointing toward the open back doors of a rapid-response van that had just arrived. She was standing outside of the synagogue, hours before Vincenzo was set to hit Providence. Raymond and Alton, whom the city had contracted to manage Beth Abraham's makeshift shelter, stood beside her, taking stock of the supplies piling up. When they were finished, Alton piled all that toilet paper, plus bread, peanut butter and canned beans, onto a cart and pushed it toward a rear entrance of the synagogue.

Vivian glanced at Raymond's clipboard. Diapers and toiletries: check. Food: check. Medicine and doctors: check. Boarded windows: check. Cleared sewers: check.

"We are as ready as can be," Raymond said. Vivian thought back to Joseph's sermon the previous Shabbat. While she did not know if she fully trusted God to protect the ark, she certainly trusted Raymond and the competent and visionary planners in their city government. After all, poor Noah had had to build his own ark to survive.

"Hey, Viv," a voice shouted behind her, interrupting her thoughts. It was Camille, accompanied by Freddy and Xo, who had changed their plans again and decided to stay in town. They walked up with several duffel bags and a babbling Xo slung onto Freddy's back.

After they hugged and checked in on each other, Vivian led them into the building and up to the registration table, which Vera Cohen was managing. Vera greeted them warmly, and then, fulfilling her administrative duties, she took their names and handed them a pouch of snacks and toiletries.

Freddy and Camille followed Vivian into the social hall, which had been transformed into a shelter. Six lines of ten beds each were spread out across half the room. Most were air mattresses that had been collected by the congregation, but a few metal frames had been sent over by a City Hall team. A play corner, with toys from the Hebrew school, was set up in the back of the room.

Several Beth Abraham congregants traversed the room, still spreading sheets and blankets onto beds. None of the blankets or linens matched; Vivian noticed a few printed with characters from old Pixar movies. She had no idea where they all had come from, but she didn't need to know. She thought of the manna the Israelites were given in the desert. These supplies—they all seemed like manna, several portions over.

Freddy and Camille spotted two open beds next to a crib and plopped their stuff onto one of the mattresses.

"Take all the time you need to settle in," Vivian said. "I'm glad you're here." She offered one more set of hugs and left them.

As she moved through the space, she recognized a few of the families from Two Rivers. *What a beautiful assembly*, she thought.

Then she remembered that a Category 4 hurricane was coming for them.

A few families with younger children had just arrived, and Vivian watched from a distance as Flora and Ben helped them find beds to claim. The people who had signed up to come to the shelter were a mix of those from the neighborhood—families from Two Rivers, some older folks who couldn't evacuate—and people from all over the city who had just needed an open spot at the last minute. Flora and a woman Vivian did not recognize were addressing a group of families in Spanish, giving them the lay of the land. From across the room, Vivian deciphered a single word: *baño*.

As Vivian looked on, she saw Flora excuse herself from the group and run straight over to a newly arrived family. It looked like two parents and two teenagers, one in a motorized scooter. Once she reached them, Flora gave one of the teens a hug.

Curious, Vivian walked over.

"Rabbi Vivian, this is Didi Guerrero, one of my favorite students, and their family," Flora said. She quickly slapped a hand over her mouth, catching herself. "Don't tell anyone I said that." Flora winked at Didi, who offered a half-smile.

When they had all introduced themselves, Flora walked the family over to a far corner of the room where Vera's husband,

Charlie, was fussing with what looked like some medical equipment. He was one of the two doctors on duty. Vivian did not fully understand what was happening, but was heartened by the alliance being formed.

Next, Vivian made her way to the kitchen, where a sizeable group was packing the extra freezers and preparing food. A few volunteers, including Tamar, were working on a massive pot of chili, which looked almost as large as some of the children helping chop vegetables to go into it. Vivian had the instinct to inspect the food and make sure it was all *hechshered*, but she reminded herself how much else there was to do. They could always clean and re-*kasher* the kitchen after.

Her phone buzzed with a text. The message, from Heather, was a picture of St. Paul's shelter. It looked quite like Beth Abraham's—lots of unmatched beds of different sizes, lots of people scattered throughout. The only discernable difference was the presence of crosses on the wall.

Vivian took a picture of the social hall and sent it back. *Nice ark*, she wrote. *Here is ours. Sending you all love and strength. We will make it through.*

She went into her email briefly to check for messages from the city's shelter coordinator. Instead, she found that her inbox was full of notes from other rabbis active in Tekiyah, responding to the listserv message she'd sent about Beth Abraham acting as a storm shelter, offering prayers and encouragement, and warmly asking for updates when the storm was over. Vivian held her phone to her heart.

The preparation continued. Guests who had registered to stay in the shelter kept trickling in, and by early evening, there were just over seventy people in Beth Abraham's social hall. A group of small kids played together in the children's corner, and off to the right, a few volunteers set up tables for a buffet-style dinner.

Amid the continued buzz of activity, dinner began. Vivian was helping to serve portions from the big pot of chili when two kids whose names she didn't know ran into the center of the social hall. "It's starting to rain," they shouted.

Everyone in the room grew quiet. So quiet that they could hear the wind howl and the soft tap-tap of a drizzle giving way to the steadier beat of a rainfall. A nigun came into her head, a melody she often used for a few lines of the Hallel prayers. *Please God, save us. Please God, redeem us.* She hummed it to herself a few times.

She surveyed the room. Only a few handfuls of those present were her congregants; most of the group was made up of people who had found their way to this storm shelter without any attention paid to what this building was and what usually happened inside it. But still, in the silence, Vivian could hear a need for *something*.

She set down her ladle and moved toward an open area between the tables and the beds. She raised her arm, and a number of people turned to look in her direction. "For anyone interested in a prayer, please come join me," she shouted. She repeated herself a few times until she noticed others begin to pass the message out toward the far edges of the social hall.

A few people weaved in and out of the lines of inflatable mattresses, backpacks, and duffel bags to join her in the open space. And once the early adopters had started moving, some of the seemingly more hesitant guests followed suit. Others, who had been off in the bathroom and the kitchen and other parts of the building, migrated toward the gathering crowd too. A spontaneous circle was starting to form.

Vivian closed her eyes and took a deep breath.

"God, whom we call by many names," she began, "spread over us a canopy of peace. Please protect us from these waters. Protect our families, protect our city. Be a fortress for us and allow us to be fortresses for one another. And please, remember your promise never to destroy the world again."

The room was silent. No one moved. She heard a few quiet and disparate amens, but Vivian did not feel fully satisfied with her own prayer. "If anyone else would like to pray," she said, looking around, "the floor is open."

No one said anything. Vivian wondered if anyone would.

And then Flora did. "Blessed are you, God. Thank you for bringing us all here, for bringing us all together, inside these four walls," she said. "Please bless all of us within this storm's path, taking refuge in homes and in shelters, with the food and supplies and care that we need."

"Amen," said a choir of scattered voices, a few more than before.

Flora's prayer was followed by several more seconds of silence. Then Didi's father spoke up, sharing a short prayer in Spanish that went untranslated. The responsive amens continued to grow louder.

A woman carrying a baby while holding the hand of a bigger child spoke next. Vivian remembered from registration that her name was Demi, and her kids were Curtis and Bella. "Lord, take care of my babies. Take care of our house. Take care of my family down in Florida still recovering from the last storm."

"Amen," the group said, now settled into a rhythm.

Next, an older woman whom Vivian didn't know started to hum. Vivian swayed back and forth, matching the cadence. The woman began to sing. "Be still, my soul, the Lord is on thy side…."

Her voice got stronger with each word. "Leave to thy God to order and provide. In every change, He faithful will remain."

Those who knew the hymn started joining in. Vivian could pick up the tune; it sounded to her like so many nigunim she had heard before. She and others hummed along. She let her eyes close again.

"Thy hope, thy confidence let nothing shake. All now mysterious shall be bright at last."

Vivian opened her eyes. From across the room, she could see Raymond singing the words, as he too rocked his body back and forth.

"Be still, my soul: the waves and winds still know. His voice who ruled them while He dwelt below."

It was one of the more Christian-y prayers that had been sung in the building, Vivian thought. But at this moment, as the rain and the wind were getting louder and no one knew what was to come, in this ragged circle where at some point they had all reached out for each other's hands, it became clear that they were all talking about, praying about, the same thing…as their ancestors had done for millennia. Since before the thirteenth century. Hoping—believing—that in the midst of a community, in the midst of a city, there was a great source of help and protection at a time like this.

CHAPTER THIRTY-FOUR

VINCENZO WAS HITTING his stride in the early hours of the morning. Gordy remained awake, listening to the rain pounding onto the building and onto Providence. The howling wind sounded like planes flying right above him.

SG's security guards stood watch over the control room, ensuring that no one was using this opportunity to tamper with Leviathan's technology. Gordy had stayed with them for several hours. "Nothing's happening," he kept saying. "Nothing is good," one of the security guards would respond.

He was not used to waiting around, doing nothing, and so he paced in the hallways for a while and then decided to try to sleep in his office. But he couldn't. He was thinking about his family, about his wife and daughter, about how scared and worried they must be, about how he should be spending this time with them.

And he thought about Freddy. He had heard that the jail was cleared just before the storm, but he didn't know for sure if that meant Freddy had been released. He hoped it did. The hurricane raging around him felt like a manifestation of his own guilt. Freddy, he was sure, was to blame for ISAC going missing, and some punishment, some justice, was in order. But alone in a city jail was no place to wait out Vincenzo. Days ago, Sal had made that exact point, but he had let it go in the face of Gordy and Jack's certainty that holding Freddy accountable was the right move.

The regret was uncomfortable. The doing nothing was uncomfortable. The being in a cold office at three in the morning during a Category 4 hurricane away from his family while tormented by the prospect of being sued by the Israeli army was uncomfortable.

He started some emails that had been on his to-do list, but quickly realized that very few of his colleagues were likely to be checking their email. He returned to the control room, where a security guard had fallen asleep leaning on one of the master computers. When Gordy walked in, the guard jolted awake.

They both sat in the room for a while, where it was much quieter.

"So, what do these robots that you all make do?" the guard asked.

Didn't you read the brief for this job? Gordy thought. "Someday," he said, hoping his voice conveyed the rebuke, "they are going to explore and build up Mars."

"Mars, huh?" the guard said. "How long is that going to take?"

In the dim lighting of the control room, Gordy tried to read his nametag, but it was too hard to make out the letters. "Just a few years to build up a full fleet, and then we begin our onsite experimentation phase."

"I wonder what *this* planet will be like by then."

A sadness overtook Gordy, who had no response. At first the feeling was difficult to pinpoint. But then he realized it was longing. He missed the security that Leviathan's and KiTov's creations had once made him feel about his own future. About his kid's future.

He thought of Freddy again. He wondered: If ISAC had been in Gordy's position, would he have made the same choice—to arrest Freddy so fast? Maybe not. *And that's why we invest in—trust in—technology*, he thought. *To compensate for our human shortcomings.*

He took out his phone and looked at a picture of his family. It was from a trip to a farm the previous summer; they were holding buckets of fresh strawberries. He wished that he could break through the screen and be with them, wait out the storm together. But he couldn't. All he could do was continue to stare at his device powered by Leviathan's extra generator. Gordy closed his eyes and pretended he was inside that picture, with his family, tasting the fresh summer strawberries.

CHAPTER THIRTY-FIVE

THE WINDS OUTSIDE were relentless. But inside, the newly assembled community of Congregation Beth Abraham was making it through. Some children played while others cried, roused by this strange place and these strange people. Many guests prayed. And some even seemed to fall asleep.

Freddy, Camille, and Xo were not among the last category. Xo wailed for much of the night, and Freddy and Camille took turns sitting with her outside of the main room, hoping to minimize the number of people she woke up. Midnight found Freddy rocking her in a hallway, singing an old Noise Machine song.

Whenever she was quiet enough, his mind shot back to the

puzzle he couldn't stop thinking about. *What am I missing? Where could ISAC be?*

It was still hard for Freddy to imagine him disabling all the safety and surveillance measures without leaving a trace, much less outsmarting the whole security force that had been sent out to find him. Where would he have gone? Was he hiding on purpose? And whatever his location…was it vulnerable to the storm, would any part of him be salvageable after tonight?

"Wada!" Xo cried. "Wada!" Freddy tried to shush her, but she kept screaming for water, so he just paused and looked her in the eye. And then it hit him: *water!*

Freddy marveled at his child for a moment. He had not even considered this. Hyydra's control system, which he knew inside and out, trained her to be cautious in the face of danger, to avoid situations in which she would have little control—or at least to have a clear plan of action that would ensure success, and certainly survival, before purposely engaging risk. She would never, for example, walk into a river without a strategy for getting out of it.

But perhaps ISAC was different. Perhaps the danger he assessed was different. Perhaps the irreconcilable goals contained in his ACS opened up possibilities that were different. It would certainly explain how a six-foot intelligent robot who seemingly hunted birds and did acrobatics for fun went undetected in a city full of people.

The lightbulbs above Freddy and Xo began to flicker.

Then the electricity went out altogether, and the sudden darkness raised Xo's howls to a fever pitch.

Two men whom Freddy recognized as building managers walked swiftly by him with flashlights, ducking into a nearby storage closet. He could hear them futzing around with what he assumed was a generator, seemingly without any progress.

A few minutes later, after more rocking and gulps of water from her sippy cup, Xo had finally fallen asleep. Perhaps the darkness helped after all. Or maybe his mini mind-reader was responding to Freddy's increased sense of internal calm in light of their collective revelation. Or maybe she had really just been thirsty. Whatever it was, Freddy was now free to go explore other people's problems. He walked carefully toward the closet and peeked in. The two men, their silhouettes visible in the glow of the flashlights, were pressing different buttons on the control panel, but nothing was happening. After several more attempts, they just stood still and stared at the machine.

"Need a hand?" Freddy asked in a whisper.

The older man nodded. Freddy tried to maneuver into the small area, but it was a difficult task given the sleeping child whom he was trying very hard not to agitate. As he was angling unsuccessfully for a better look, another person appeared in the entrance of the increasingly cramped closet.

The newest helper, who was just a shadow in the dark, slipped past Freddy and sank down into a baseball catcher's stance to get a better look at the generator. The rest of them watched. "You have to turn the voltage to 2.33. It's currently set too low to function," the newcomer said. "These new models can take time to learn, but once you know, you know."

One of the men did as they said and the generator turned on—along with the rest of the building's electricity. With the lights on, Freddy saw that the person who had solved the puzzle appeared to be a genderqueer teenager.

"You seem to know your way around a generator," he said in a whisper, lightly rocking Xo and praying the lights wouldn't rouse her. "Are you an engineer or something?"

"An aspiring one, I guess," they said, matching Freddy's whisper. The two walked in lockstep back through the door of the social hall. "I learned everything from my dad, who's practically an engineer. He can build or fix anything." They pointed to a man who was pacing around in a corner of the room. "I'm Didi, by the way."

"Cool. I'm Freddy," he said. "And an engineer," he added.

Didi pursed their lips. "What do you build?"

Freddy closed his eyes, immediately regretting that he had opened up this line of conversation.

"Autonomous robotic control systems," he finally said.

Didi's eyebrows lifted. "That sounds rad."

Freddy wondered if Didi would, in fact, think what he did was *rad* if they knew the whole story. "I can tell you more about it if you'd like," Freddy heard himself say. Apparently he was that eager for a distraction from his own thoughts.

"Yes, please," Didi said, sounding rather awake given the time. "I can't sleep anyway."

"Alright," Freddy said, maneuvering Xo to his other arm, now only half-regretting putting himself in this situation. "First, I'm going to put this little monster down now that she's finally asleep. And then how about we meet back in the hall?" Didi agreed.

Freddy walked through the dark to his family's stretch of beds and placed Xo down in her crib. He tucked the green-and-orange striped blanket they had brought from home around her. Sighing with relief, he set back out to traverse the obstacles in the dark room and meet up with Didi. He managed not to trip over a crib or a bed or a duffel bag, and found them sitting with their legs crossed by the storage closet.

Freddy sat down next to them. He went on to explain Hyydra's advanced mobility, and the technology Leviathan worked on to equip her with moral differentiation abilities. He didn't mention ISAC.

"So where will Hyydra be deployed once she's ready?" Didi asked.

He couldn't avoid this part any longer. "Mars," he whispered.

"Hold up, hold up!" Didi said. "Did you just say Mars?"

Freddy bashfully bowed his head. Didi laughed, and Freddy could hear the judgment. He often detected it in people's reactions to his work, but he had built up defenses in response...they just were not automatically activating right now. Freddy wasn't even sure if the judgment was coming from Didi or himself.

"It seems like you could apply that technology for this kind of thing, too," Didi said. "You know, storms. Here on earth."

"Go on."

"Well, Hyydra sounds so resilient and mobile—maybe even enough to function *during* hurricanes," Didi said, shifting to face Freddy. "And because of the ACS you built, she could independently solve any problems she encountered. You know, in the storm chaos!"

"Hmm." Freddy was impressed with the teen's thinking—and a little abashed, to be honest. His mind jumped into imagining the possibilities.

"My dad, his name is Hector, he would probably have good ideas about all of this. And it would be good for him to have something to distract him since he's just anxiously pacing right now." Before Freddy could respond, Didi jumped up and disappeared into the social hall.

A few minutes later they returned, bringing along an older, seemingly exhausted man. Hector Guerrero introduced himself in Spanish and the conversation continued that way.

Didi described how they and Hector were always tinkering with things at home after their dad's construction shifts: old radios, broken air conditioners, computer parts. And they were right; Hector had plenty of ideas. The city seemed to have an effective plan to deliver supplies to Providence's residents, but the whole thing was dependent on coordination before and after the storms. But what if Hyydra had a thick layer of weatherized protection, and more agile feet, and another machine learning regimen? She had the potential to tread through heavy rains, swirling winds and growing floodwaters. She could transport supplies before it was safe to send out humans, and reach hard-hit areas before floodwaters had receded enough to permit vehicles.

To Freddy, it all made so much sense. By morning, it was as if they had a whole business plan. Forget Mars. Screw armies across the ocean.

Sometime around then, a woman walked over to them. "How are things going over here?" she asked, shifting the conversation back to English. "You look too energized to be living through a Category 4 hurricane right now," she said directly to Didi.

"Ms. Moore," Didi said. "We've basically just developed the perfect plan for localized storm resilience technology!"

"Now that's something!" she said. Freddy still couldn't place her, but she clearly knew Didi. "I could probably connect you to my friend Karla, who works on stuff like that down at City Hall," she continued.

"Oh, you don't have to worry about that," Freddy said. "We've practically already set up the meeting."

CHAPTER THIRTY-SIX

IN THE EARLY morning, as the worst of the storm continued to bombard Providence in the dark, Karla fiddled with her walkie-talkie. She finally found channel three. Amir was on the other end. There was a lot of static, but she got the gist. A library on the north side of the city, which lost power and had sixty people sheltering in it, had never received their extra generator.

"As soon as it's safe, we'll send an extra one from City Hall," Karla replied. She had to repeat herself several times so Amir could make out what she was saying. Meanwhile, she seethed at the companies that had acquired extra generators for no good reason but to power their empty offices. She was relieved when

Amir confirmed that, in the meantime, the library had the supplies they needed to get through another several hours of downpour.

Karla and her coworkers were standing by for any important overnight communications from the shelter sites. Her office had distributed long-range walkie-talkies to all the coordinators, which allowed the whole group to communicate throughout the storm, no matter what went wrong.

Karla listened as a few messages came in. Just downstairs, in the City Hall shelter, someone had passed out from dehydration. Someone else had a panic attack at a church on the south side. Several sites were running low on water, and one on baby food. But mostly, it seemed like everyone—a whole corps, or an army even, of people—was finding some way to make do.

She took out the map of all the shelter sites scattered through Providence to review the numbers one more time. Eighteen percent of residents sheltered in place; that was more than 30,000 people. About a fifth of those went to shelters. And all the shelters had medical personnel in case of emergency.

She had done the best she could. They all had. And the systems they had set up were mostly working, as well as they could. But still, there was no way to avoid oversights given the scale of the challenge. As her eyes grew heavy, Karla marveled at how the threshold for what constituted success kept moving, with each year, with each disaster.

"Come in Karla, this is Amir."

Karla found herself jolting awake. At some point she must have fallen asleep on her makeshift bed.

"Roger that. This is Karla." She tried her best to sound fully alert.

"Let's start planning the deployment of the rapid response units in a few hours," Amir said. "Once we know who's been hit the hardest."

"Okay, I'll come down first thing. But first I'm going to try to get a little sleep. You should too, Amir." A few others chimed in on the channel and said they would join the 7:30 a.m. meeting. For now, though, they would all rest, on their inflatable mattresses in offices scattered around the building.

Karla had set up camp in the Department of Immigrant Advancement on the third floor. She scanned the room's countless posters in a variety of languages. There was a time in her life when having this kind of access to City Hall would have been so exciting, almost like a nerdy fantasy. But there was a hurricane raging outside and Karla wished that Vivian was with her...even if she knew that the tasks they both had to do, the roles they had to play, were probably the best way to pass the time anyhow.

She tried to quiet her thoughts, but she couldn't stop mentally tracking the status of each shelter site and the route of each mobile unit that would be implemented when things settled down. Finally, to distract herself, she started to think about another kind of tracking: her ovulation cycle.

Since the fertility clinic visit, she had been inputting her body temperature, along with other data that could help predict the times when she would be able to get pregnant, into a cheery pink tracking app. Opening the app, she realized it was possible that she was ovulating at this very moment, as Vincenzo raged on. She didn't know if she'd get a response, but she texted Vivian about her discovery.

And then Karla closed her eyes.

A few hours of sleep later, she woke up to see Vivian's message, sent at 6:14 a.m., that she would spext around and get back to her if she found any promising leads. Karla giggled, hugged her phone and stood up. She stretched out her back, which was feeling the effects of such an uncomfortable mattress, put on a new shirt, and went to check in with Nona.

Her boss's outfit, Karla noticed, had *not* changed from the previous day. Had she stayed awake the whole night? That would be on brand, Karla thought.

Nona greeted her with the usual number of pleasantries: none. "It sounds like a few other towns in the area won't have the supplies they need once the rain stops," she said. "We'll have to figure out how to share our leftovers."

Karla thought about all the Providence residents who were still in their homes and would likely need food and medical supplies and electricity on the other side of all of this. "Is that really our responsibility?" she asked.

Nona was silent for a few seconds. "Yes," she said. "People should not be punished because they do or don't live within the imagined border of a city or state. We share. That is the ethos of this office."

Karla hunched her shoulders and hid her face, ashamed of her own selfish instincts. "Of course."

She left the room, grateful for the fact that Winona MacLean was her boss and Margaret Heath was mayor. She thought back to Mike McCann, Heath's competitor in the mayoral race, whose campaign she had worked on way back when. He certainly would not have been able to handle these challenges the way that Heath could. And he probably would never have put Winona MacLean in charge of such an important office. *Thank God he lost*, Karla said to herself.

CHAPTER THIRTY-SEVEN

V IVIAN OPENED HER eyes. The first thing she noticed was a digital clock blinking the numbers 1:17, which must have been when the power went out. She had finally gotten a few hours of sleep on a rickety cot set up in one of the Hebrew school classrooms.

Sitting up, she put her hand on her heart and, in the darkness of an early morning overtaken by storm clouds, silently thanked God for returning her soul. Then she spotted a text from Karla on her phone. She hugged the phone close, as if it were a stand-in for her wife, and replied.

The rain continued to fall hard, bolstered by loud, gusting winds. Judging by the traffic over the walkie-talkie airwaves, it seemed as though most of the other shelter sites had also lost their power, and had subsequently restored it through generators. Vivian found comfort in hearing a report from Heather across town.

She left the classroom, following distant echoes of chatter. It was much like the sounds that spilled over from kiddush after a Shabbat morning service. She stumbled into the main hall not having bothered to change out of her sweatpants and flannel shirt. The thought crossed Vivian's mind that this was her first time wearing pajamas at Beth Abraham. She liked the feeling: informal comfort in a holy place.

At the far end of the social hall, a crowd of people scrounged for breakfast around a table piled with cereals and fruits. Others were still sleeping. The heat was working, and the lights, where they were on, were too. The refrigerated food seemed to have lasted through the night as well.

She made her way over to the breakfast area and got herself a drink. She brought the paper cup close to her lips and paused. "*Baruch atah…shehakol nehiyeh bidvaro,*" she whispered. *Thank You, God, by whose word all came to be.* She took a sip.

"Good morning, Rabbi," said a quiet voice behind her. Vivian turned around and smiled at Raymond, who gave her a few updates. Water had entered the basement, but so far, the new pump system was absorbing it. And one of the kids spiked a high fever in the middle of the night, but Charlie had taken care of him and said he was doing fine.

"Well then. It sounds like things are under control."

"It does, doesn't it?" Raymond said, scanning the room. "I'm going to wrangle the coordination team for a meeting to review today's plan. Be in the preschool classroom down the hall in a few minutes, okay?"

"You got it, boss," Vivian said. "I love it when someone else plans the meetings. I can definitely do the showing up part."

Vivian popped a piece of sesame bagel in her mouth and walked through the rows of beds toward the meeting location. Eventually, Raymond, Alton, Vera, Charlie, Tamar, Flora, Ben, and a few others, including some residents from Two Rivers, had gathered around the low table. One of them turned out to be the woman Vivian was accustomed to seeing with romance novels on a bench in Two Rivers' playground. After years of noticing her from afar, Vivian finally learned her name: Millie.

"The storm reports predict heavy wind and rainfall for a few more hours, followed by some residual showers," Raymond said to the group. "When the worst of it passes, we can make rounds to see how the rest of the neighborhood is holding up and help get supplies to anyone that may need them.

"Meanwhile, the folks at City Hall are saying that people might need to stay in shelters for another few days, until the power is restored and it's safe to go out." He turned to Vera, who was in charge of inventory. "How are we doing with supplies?"

"The food and water will last us another day at least," Vera said. "I'll make up a list of what we'd need to request from the mobile units if we stay past tomorrow."

The team went on to divvy up which neighborhood streets each of them would check on later. As they were staking out sections of the map, a corner of the classroom brightened up. Vivian turned toward the window. The storm had quieted down for a moment, and the sun was peeking through.

They continued to strategize. Another patch of the room began to glow.

"Someone should go update the community," Raymond said. "People might want to leave, but it's not the right time yet."

Vivian wondered if she should volunteer. "I can do it," Ben said, beating her to it.

Vivian looked on as he left the room, moving swiftly, and wondered what blessing might match this particular moment.

. . .

After the worst of the storm had subsided, after they'd double-checked their routes and recruited more people to join them, and after Raymond had briefed them on staying vigilant, avoiding areas with the deepest water, and looking out for fallen electrical wires, the group set out beyond Beth Abraham to check on their neighbors.

Vivian opened the front door and stepped outside. She descended the short flight of stairs at the building's entrance and walked into a pool of water that reached above her ankles. A drizzle continued to fall, and now and again the winds whipped up. Vivian inhaled the crisp air. She wanted to pray, she wanted to wrangle up a minyan of ten people to say *shacharit*, but she knew there were other things to attend to. And so a moment of silence, of gratitude, of fear and hope for the future, would have to suffice.

Raymond walked up beside her, and they continued together, sloshing through the water toward the Two Rivers housing complex.

The area was very quiet and mostly dark. The apartment

building's front door, which was up a ramp that elevated it above the flooding waters, was locked. Vivian wondered what to do.

"No need to be polite," Raymond said. "You can just yell."

She squinted upward. "This is Rabbi Vivian Green from the synagogue next door," Vivian hollered. "Does anyone need any help or supplies? If you do, we have extras in our building. We have electricity, too. You are welcome to come any time."

The building remained silent. Then one head peered out of a third-floor window that was only partially boarded up. The woman seemed to study Vivian and Raymond. "I could use more formula for my baby," she said finally. "There was none left at the supermarket a few days ago. I tried three different stores." Raymond wrote down the request and asked the woman for her name and apartment number. "Charlene, 303," she told him.

By now, someone had opened the main door and a few people had gathered at the entrance. An older man asked for water; the building's system was shut down. Someone else shouted out that their food had spoiled when the electricity went out, and Vivian said she could bring over beans and bread and powdered milk. An older woman told them that she was running low on insulin.

After they took down the requests, Vivian and Raymond returned to Beth Abraham through the floodwaters. Raymond went to alert Charlie about the woman who needed insulin, while Vivian scrounged up the rest of what they'd need.

When they returned to Two Rivers, they found the residents waiting by the front door. "There's a better way for you all to do this," said Charlene from 303 when she received the two canisters of formula for her baby. "How about I collect the next round of orders in the building, and someone walks them over to you all at once?" Raymond agreed, and he stepped to the side to make plans with Charlene, the new supplies coordinator of Two Rivers.

When they had finished their rounds, Vivian paused instead of turning back toward the synagogue. "I think I'm going to walk around for a while, Raymond. Just check on things and clear my head a little."

"Okay, but be careful, Rabbi."

"I will," she assured him.

As she set out on her own, a beam of sunlight glimmered through a cloud and shone on her face. She walked down streets on higher ground, where the water was shallower, dodging the fallen tree branches that were everywhere—on the street, on side-walks, on a few parked cars. "*Ashrei yoshvei veitecha*," she sang to herself, alternating between singing the words of the prayer and humming a tune her community often used. *Happy is the one who dwells in God's house.*

Vivian noticed that most of the houses here were boarded up... and very quiet. The cars were nearly all gone. In this wealthier part of town, most people seemed to have evacuated. She continued to walk and hum, enjoying the way her prayer bounced through the silence.

Suddenly, she heard yelling behind her.

"Help!" a voice shouted. Turning around quickly, she spotted a teenager running through the water on Myrtle Road, clearly headed for Vivian. "My grandmother needs help! Please, can you help?" She nodded and he gestured for her to follow as he turned back the way he'd come. He headed down a side street, and two blocks later, they stopped in front of a house that was smaller than most of the others surrounding it.

There were no front stairs, just a walkway. When they entered through the front door, she saw that the floodwaters had flowed directly into the living room and kitchen. The first floor was quiet, and it seemed clean, except for the several inches of water and a distracting smell.

Vivian followed the teen through the water and up the stairs to a bedroom. An older woman lay in bed underneath a pile of blankets, the top one patterned with pink and yellow flowers. "She's very cold and thirsty," he said, "and the water's no good." Thankful that she still had supplies in her backpack from the morning's rounds, Vivian pulled out a bottle of water and handed it to the teen. He opened it and brought it to the woman's mouth. She took a few sips.

"Thank you, honey!" she said. She took a few more sips and sighed, deeply. "You're an angel." Vivian's instinct was to refute that, but she held her tongue. Knowing that members of her makeshift community were spread out across the neighborhood looking for where they could be helpful, and that so many others in Providence must be doing the same, made her wonder if perhaps this woman was not entirely wrong.

Vivian took down the address and told them that she would send a doctor from Beth Abraham to check in on them later in the day. Then she left a few more bottles of water, said goodbye, and continued on her way.

She turned onto Carleton Street, splashing with each step. A handful of boarded-up stores dotted the corner ahead of her. Walking into the intersection, she remembered from the eruv map of Providence that she should be close to its edge, to the twine that was visible only if you knew where to look and what to look for. With a light rain misting her face, she gazed upward, trying to spot the thin twine above the electrical wires. Vivian found herself hoping for a little miracle; that, against all odds, the eruv had survived the storm. She tilted her head and squinted, hoping that slightly better vision would do the trick, and—

"Ouch!" A sharp, sudden pain in her ankle. Her yelp echoed in the empty expanse. Leaning on a telephone pole, she lifted her leg out of the water and eased off her rainboot so she could examine herself. The cut was deep, and blood was pooling fast. She set her leg down again. What the hell? Was it a tree branch? A fallen street sign?

Some part of her brain tried to recall the date of her last tetanus shot. As she peered into the waters around her, afraid of getting hit again, something bobbed up and bumped into the telephone pole. Yanking off her backpack, she used it to trap the thing against the pole, and then, very carefully, she dragged it upward so she could see it. It was a piece of metal, about a foot across, triangular. And there—a piece of it had been twisted off, leaving a sort of claw that was sharp enough to have inflicted the damage on her ankle. Several wires poked out of it, too. It looked like a car part had detached from one of the few left on the street.

Being alone in the floodwaters with a gash in her leg caused by an unidentifiable sharp object with exposed wiring did not seem like a good idea. Out of all the threats swirling around, she hoped that this would not be the one to vanquish her. Working carefully, she got the maybe–car part into her backpack without cutting herself. As she wrapped her scarf around the wound, she prayed that she would make it back to Beth Abraham—and

Karla—unscathed. She turned around and limped as fast as she could back toward the synagogue.

The hymn that the shelter community had sung together the previous day came back to her. She couldn't recall the words, but the melody was certainly imprinted in her mind. She hummed it over and over, trying to rush and stay calm at the same time.

When she returned to the building, Vivian made a beeline for Charlie in the social hall. Without speaking, she lifted her leg to show him the bloody scarf. "Let's get that cleaned up," he said, and led her to the administrative office that had been turned in to a makeshift infirmary.

"We'll need to clean out the wound," he said as Vivian sat down, "especially given all the bacteria in the water." He crouched down to inspect the ankle more closely. "But first we'll control the bleeding." He pressed a handful of gauze onto the wound, then showed Vivian how to hold it with the right amount of pressure while he arranged a chair to keep her leg elevated. "What caused the cut?"

With her free hand, Vivian pulled the culprit out of her bag to show Charlie, pointing to the sharp end. He took it from her to examine it.

"It doesn't look rusted over or anything, so that's a good sign, right?" she said.

Charlie rotated it several times.

"Whoa," he said. He looked up at Vivian.

"What?" she asked. "Did you find tetanus on it or something?"

Charlie let out a little laugh. "That's not how tetanus works." He handed the part back to her and pointed to some engraved lettering on the bottom. Vivian looked closer.

"Is that...could that be Hebrew?" he asked. She stared at it. "That looks like the letter—"

"Yup," another voice said. Vivian twisted around. It was Freddy, standing in the open doorway. "I came to check on you, after you tracked blood through the social hall." He gulped. "Seems like you were just injured by a piece of ISAC's foot."

"Whoa." Vivian looked back down at the object. "But I don't understand. How could...it... so he's just floating around in the storm waters?" she asked, finally formulating a question. "How?!"

Freddy walked toward Vivian and took the foot from her. "I think," he started, "that ISAC knew the best way to ensure he would not execute any immoral orders was to systematically disconnect different parts of himself. Starting with his tracking device."

"And this ISAC," Charlie asked. "He speaks Hebrew?"

"Yeah," Vivian said, looking back at the doctor. "He's Israeli." Charlie's brow wrinkled. "I can explain more later," she added. She turned back to Freddy. "But how could he systematically disconnect parts of his *own* body?"

"Pretty easily," Freddy said, still studying the object. "His fingers are very dexterous. He also knows how to use tools, and his body parts are designed to come apart for repairs and upgrades and all that."

"How has no one found his parts until now?" Vivian asked.

"He might have figured out how to hide. Blend in."

"This ISAC character sounds very impressive," Charlie chimed in.

"To some," Freddy said.

"But where would he have hidden?" Vivian asked.

"My money is on the river," Freddy said. "And then the force and direction of the storm scattered the pieces."

Freddy placed the foot on the table. He folded his arms and frowned. And then...he laughed.

"What's so funny?" Vivian said.

"I mean, I knew that the control system I built would give ISAC the capacity to make his own decisions, but the fact that he actually did it, it's just.... It sort of confirms that robots are better equipped to make important decisions than us."

Vivian caught Freddy's eye and raised an eyebrow. "Excuse me!" she said, gesturing toward Charlie and through the door to the buzz of activity in the social hall. "Than *some* of us, perhaps."

"Yes," Freddy conceded. "But still, I—"

"Look outside! Look outside," a child running down the hall yelled.

That was hard to do with the windows boarded up, but by angling her head, Vivian got a glimpse through the crack between two slabs of wood. She noticed it right away. Amid the swiftly moving clouds, a rainbow had appeared above them.

CHAPTER THIRTY-EIGHT

VIVIAN OPENED THE door and ran over to Karla, who was sitting on the couch wrapped in a towel.

"Baby, I just got all the grime off! Now I'm going to have to shower again."

"I don't care," Vivian said, embracing her wife for the first time in days.

Karla's body softened into the hug, her arms collapsing against Vivian's green raincoat. Vivian squeezed her tight.

"When did you get home?"

"About an hour ago," Karla said, into the curls of Vivian's hair. "The shower was cold, but it felt good. No electricity, obviously, but everything else seems okay. I hope the first-floor apartments were as lucky as us."

She pulled out of the hug and looked at Vivian. "I don't think we have much edible food at this point, but I did bring a few bagels back from City Hall. I was too scared to open the refrigerator."

Vivian rolled her eyes. "She fearlessly coordinates a hurricane safety plan for hundreds of thousands of people, only to be done in by one stinky refrigerator. Well, we're in luck. I snagged this from Beth Abraham." She pulled a half-jar of peanut butter from her bag.

"Oh, I almost forgot," Karla said. "My office gifted us the dregs of some bottles of cold brew. That's the big treat."

"Looks like we've got a respectable brunch!" Vivian said.

"Then you better get cleaned up."

Vivian made her way to the bathroom. Ten minutes later she reappeared, shivering, in sweatpants and a sweatshirt from rabbinical school. Karla had set out plates and placemats for the bagels, and poured the black and pulpy cold brew into the nicest glasses they had.

"It's beautiful," Vivian said through chattering teeth. She sat down and took a sip of coffee. "Hmm. More like warm brew." Karla scowled. "But nonetheless, the most delicious brew I've ever had," Vivian said, recovering.

They both turned their focus to their bagels. "So, what now?' Vivian asked.

"We spent last night activating the storm recovery plan," Karla replied. She took a bite and continued. "So now the mobile units—the same ones that delivered supplies initially—go back out. They make some stops, bring water and food, check for medical needs.

Public Works will pump the flood water into the river, but that'll move a little more slowly since restoring power everywhere is their first priority."

"How long will the power part take?"

"About a week. So our office will fill the gaps. Right now we have a twenty-four-hour help line that people can call from anywhere to request a visit from a mobile unit."

"And how far out are people calling from?"

"All over the state," Karla said. "We've started coordinating with other municipalities."

"I'm so proud of you, baby," Vivian said, her voice muffled by a mouthful of peanut butter and bagel.

Karla reached over and rubbed Vivian's knee. "I'm proud of you, too." They finally kissed each other, taking a few moments to linger in the embrace.

"And I'm proud of this whole city," Karla said after a while. "This is how we are going to survive, by setting up local systems of support."

"May it be so," Vivian said, raising her glass.

"Amen!"

Vivian smiled and kissed her wife again.

"You know, someone should write a prayer for these kinds of things," Karla said.

"That's a great idea." Vivian thought about all the different prayers they had been saying in the face of the storm. "A prayer for the city."

CHAPTER THIRTY-NINE

"I T'S ALMOST AS if a Category 4 hurricane never hit this place," Vivian said, as she and Freddy walked through the doors of Leviathan Labs. The company had clearly spent the days after the storm cleaning up their grounds and ensuring that their building was quickly returned to its usual glory.

Recovery continued around the city. As water was pumped back into the river, more vestiges of ISAC had turned up. Some were small, unexceptional pieces: rods, bolts, coils. But in a few instances, there were more detectable robotic body parts—a finger, a forearm, a shin. Upon the filing of a perplexingly swift court order, the city's cleanup crew had been required to collect and save anything stamped with the KiTov logo that they found.

Leviathan had also acted swiftly in moving forward the case against Freddy, and his lawyer, Ariana Vance, had suggested mediation, saying it could often resolve a conflict and bring about closure much more quickly. Gordy and Sal were surprisingly open to it, as long as it happened immediately. Vivian got involved when, a day earlier, Freddy had asked her to come with him as moral support. "Given that you're my rabbi and all," he joked.

Now Freddy was quiet as they made their way toward the conference room. When they walked in, Gordy and several lawyers, in what looked to Vivian like matching suits, were all there waiting. Sal appeared on a large screen, and Avner Ben Ami was right beside him from Tel Aviv.

A mediator named Grace introduced herself. Vivian found the very fact of her name encouraging. She hoped Freddy felt the same.

Within a few minutes, Grace was explaining how it would work. "Each side will have the opportunity to tell their story and state the problem in their own words, *uninterrupted*," she instructed. "And then we will work to identify a resolution that addresses all grievances."

Right from the start, it was clear that Leviathan's and KiTov's position, primarily communicated through Gordy, was that Freddy was responsible for ISAC's demise since it was Freddy who endowed him with the capacity to self-destruct. His obvious hesitation and his requests to stall the hastening timeline before the press conference, they maintained, basically amounted to evidence that he had intentionally arranged to destroy ISAC during that time.

Freddy, led by his lawyer, admitted to adding an extra subroutine right before the handoff with KiTov so that ISAC could make the best decisions in the face of morally questionable orders. But, he stressed, Freddy did not direct ISAC to disable the alarms and electricity in the building with impressive stealth. And he did not direct ISAC to escape from Leviathan Labs and walk into the Seekonk River. And he certainly did not direct ISAC to shut down for good. Those were all things ISAC *chose* to do—and many of them were things Freddy hadn't even known ISAC *could* do. Those choices were the result of an autonomous control system that Freddy and his team had originally built for a different purpose altogether, for a different robot altogether. And which KiTov had *chosen* to buy.

Vivian looked on, trying to avoid Gordy's accusing glares. She did not quite know if accompanying Freddy was worth the inevitable rift between her and Gordy, maybe even between Gordy and Beth Abraham. Nor was she quite sure what her role was supposed to be. But given what she—what they all—had just been through, the risk was an appropriate one, by her calculations.

As Freddy continued to speak, Gordy suddenly and loudly interrupted. "Let's cut the crap here, Freddy. You did this! You murdered ISAC!"

"ISAC did this on his own, Gordy," Freddy responded. "You say this yourself every time you make the pitch for Leviathan's work. We are training robots to make better decisions than humans would. That's what happened here."

Under the table, Vivian saw Freddy squeezing his hands into fists, perhaps willing himself to sound calm, which he somehow was managing to do.

"But the IDF is the most moral army in the world," Avner said. "Always trying to reduce casualties in an impossible geopolitical situation. So this argument you keep making...." Avner waved his arms in the air. "It makes no sense." Vivian glared.

"Right. There is that," Gordy said. "And then there is the fact that *you were the one whose actions led to this.*"

"I didn't know this would—I didn't intend for this to happen!" Freddy retorted.

"Wasn't it you who explained to me that the difference between intent and impact doesn't matter? Remember—at that DEI training?" Gordy shouted. "If a negative impact occurs, then the *impact* is the focus, not the intention behind it!"

"That's different, Gordy," Freddy said, with a very strange facial expression that Vivian eventually realized was him trying to stop an eyeroll he had already begun.

"How so?" Gordy demanded.

"It just is," Freddy said, elongating his words. Vivian thought she noticed Freddy looking toward Sal, even as he was responding to Gordy.

The mediator, Grace, lifted her arms. "Let's all take a deep breath," she said.

Vivian could already hear Gordy's breathing from across the table. It certainly didn't sound like the calming kind.

And then it came to her, like a fastball right in the middle of the plate.

"Gordy," she piped up, "if you want to use that line of reasoning, Freddy's actions were not the first to determine the impact."

Gordy huffed, and Vivian continued before the mediator or anyone else could disrupt her disruption. "The rabbis of the Talmud argued a great deal about how to assign responsibility for damages in the face of ambiguity—when who to blame was not always clear. Intention matters, sure. But if that's the case, then even though Freddy and his team were the ones who built the control system and trained Hyydra and ISAC to run on it, we have to take into account that the directive to do so—to create the most morally sophisticated actors—came from the visionary executives."

Vivian's gaze now went back and forth between Gordy in person and Sal on the screen.

"Many rabbis would thus deem you responsible," she said.

"But the rabbis could not be expected to be fully self-governing actors," Gordy said. The others looked at him blankly. "I mean, the *robots*," he said.

"Right, right!" Avner said excitedly. "That's why we needed a new control system in the first place."

The room went quiet. Vivian couldn't tell if Avner's screen froze, or if it was just his face.

"What do you mean by that?" asked Freddy's lawyer, Ariana.

Avner played with the pen on his desk. "We…em…needed a new system because the original was…em…too unpredictable."

"Unpredictable?" Ariana said. "Can you elaborate on that, please?"

"You know…em…erratic."

"I'm sorry, I still don't understand what you mean," Ariana pressed on. "Can you be more specif—"

"Violent!" Avner shouted. "ISAC was too violent! And we needed a better system. Okay?"

Ariana asked him for more of the story, and Avner seemed to have no more energy—or euphemisms—to circle around what he meant. He groaned.

"In the first few months of ISAC's testing phase, he badly injured a few members of the KiTov team," Avner said, pinching the top of his nose. "Our training, which focused on ISAC assessing the appropriate amount of force in complex security scenarios, was not leading to the desired outcome. ISAC had become dangerous and we needed a new plan. A new control system."

Gordy was pressing all his fingers against his face. Vivian got the sense that he had not heard *that* part of the story before.

Ariana jumped in. "The rabbi's original point is a good one," she said. "This is clearly a torte case. Intention *does* matter. It seems clear that neither Mr. Fuentes, in the programming of the robots, nor Mr. Maraj nor Mr. Silver, in creating the vision of Leviathan Labs, intended for ISAC's implementation of Leviathan's ACS to bring about its self-destruction. And they did not pull the proverbial trigger here that immediately led to the outcome in question, an outcome that Mr. Ben Ami has now given us more reason to believe was not entirely unexpected, given that the robot had serious issues with its first control system as well.

"Therefore, it could be argued that ISAC's destruction, while unfortunate, is the responsibility of no one in particular. And that it is the job of the insurance company, rather, to decide the damages KiTov and Leviathan are entitled to." Ariana surveyed the office, eventually settling on Gordy. "You must have good insurance coverage, right?"

Vivian wondered how discussions of damages in the Talmud might have been different if there had been an insurance industry in Babylonia.

"Sure," Gordy said, "but I don't think we are done here." He looked down. "I concede that having Freddy arrested when we did may have been a, um, miscalculation. But"—he shifted his body to look at Freddy directly—"you still defied orders without any of us knowing, so—"

"Gordy," Sal said, from onscreen. "Stop!" He ran his fingers through his hair. "Just stop." Vivian was pretty sure those were Sal's first words of the whole meeting.

Everyone stared at the screen.

"I knew," Sal said quietly.

"What do you mean, you knew?" Gordy asked.

"I saw the logic Freddy added to the ACS. The instructions intended to prevent ISAC from killing."

Freddy's jaw dropped open and he leaned forward, toward the screen. "What? When?" he asked.

The room was still. "Right before the simulation," Sal said.

"And you didn't get rid of the instructions or confront Freddy about it?" Gordy asked.

"I thought…." Sal sighed. "I thought it made sense," he said, looking away from his screen. "I thought it aligned with our work."

Vivian turned to look at Freddy, whose fists seemed to be digging into his knees.

"Are you serious?" Freddy said. "You knew?" His volume was rising with each question. "You agreed with me? And you *still* had me *arrested*?"

Sal continued staring to the side, and Vivian again wondered if the connection had frozen. Then he dipped a hand into his shirt pocket. He pulled out something circular, like an old-fashioned pocket watch…or perhaps a compass? He ran his fingers over and over it.

"What can I say?" he said finally, almost whispering. "I made a bad decision. Everything was so chaotic after ISAC went missing. I believed you caused it and I thought…I thought that if you left the team, the company could get back on track."

"Sal," Freddy said. "Do you have any idea what you…. You had me thrown in jail! Before a hurricane!" He gasped for air. "I have a toddler!"

Sal turned toward the camera. "I'm sorry, Freddy," he said. "I really am."

Vivian put her hand on Freddy's back and held it there. She thought about the few rabbis who, in the Jewish texts about repentance, say it's never too late to apologize, and that that's why Yom Kippur comes around each year. To offer a chance at repair, even if delayed. *Not this time*, she thought.

"I'd like to ask everyone to take a deep breath," Grace said, trying to regain control of the room. The group complied. Even Gordy seemed too stunned to resist, and Vivian thought he might even have appreciated the moment of quiet.

"Now, a lot has come to light today," Grace continued, after the round of audible sighs had died out. "It's important that we get back to the heart of things: the desired resolution for each party. So, let's restate each of our goals here today." Grace turned toward the screen. "Mr. Maraj, what do you need from this process?"

Sal looked down. "To continue to fulfill our original mission," he said. "It's clear now, more than ever, that we need to keep our eyes on Mars exploration."

Vivian let out a small laugh. Self-conscious, she tried her best to follow it up with a convincing cough.

"And you, Mr. Ben Ami," Grace said. "What is it that you and KiTov Robotics need?"

"To recover the Israeli government's money," Avner said without hesitation.

Grace shifted her attention to Freddy. "And you, Mr. Fuentes?"

Freddy dropped his face in his hands. "I need this to be over," Freddy said, the sound a bit muffled. "And to move on with my life."

Vivian's attention shifted from Freddy to Gordy. She thought she noticed Gordy's body soften, maybe even surrender.

"Can we take a moment to discuss the insurance route as a team?" Sal asked.

"Yes, Mr. Maraj," Grace said. "Now would be a good time for each side to gather and discuss on their own."

Freddy, Ariana, Vivian, and Grace left the room, and Grace excused herself down a hallway. The others arranged themselves on a few green couches in a waiting area.

"Freddy," Ariana said, turning to her client. "I know that was a lot. But we are in good shape. The goal was to get them invested in pursuing the insurance route, which will allow them to recoup the money much faster than taking you to court, and it looks like we are almost there."

Freddy bowed his head and reached his hands into his pockets.

"It does," he said. He bit his bottom lip. Vivian wondered if that gesture meant the same for him as it did for her: an attempt to hold back tears. "But somehow," Freddy continued, "knowing everything…I feel worse."

Vivian listened to the heat circulating through the vents. "That's understandable," she said softly. "You were betrayed, Freddy. And by someone who you trusted. And you just found out the full extent of it."

Her eyes caught Freddy's. He kept gnawing at his bottom lip. "I think I need to be alone for a minute."

"Sure," Ariana said. "Take the time you need."

Freddy rose from the couch and made his way down the hall, moving slowly. Vivian watched as he walked out of sight, still imagining her hand on his back, trying to offer comfort.

"So," Ariana said, interrupting Vivian's thoughts. "It sounds like you work with very smart people."

"Huh?" Vivian was confused.

"Uh, the colleagues you mentioned…."

Vivian scrunched up her face quizzically. "I'm sorry," she said. "I'm not following."

"The other rabbis from the, um, Tal-something group?"

"*Oh!*" Vivian chuckled. This would make an excellent anecdote for the next Tekiyah meeting. "Yeah, they are, um, sort of colleagues. But they lived in Babylonia about 2,000 years ago."

Ariana nodded politely. Unflappability was probably a learned trait of most lawyers.

Vivian continued. "After the Jews were exiled from Jerusalem, with their temple having been destroyed, this group of rabbis created a totally different focal point for their community: a new legal system, which became the foundation of new communities and practices. A whole new way of life. And that's more or less what we're referring to when we say Talmud. To varying degrees, Jews today still use that system, as it has evolved over the millennia, to guide our own practices and lives."

"Sounds interesting," Ariana said, leaning back into the couch.

Vivian went on to give Freddy's lawyer a history lesson in the trajectory of halacha. As she was describing a seminal code of law from the seventeenth century, Freddy returned, carrying snacks.

"From the fancy vending machine," he said, placing a few bags of artisanal potato chips and a package of molasses cookies onto the side table. They snacked in comfortable silence until Grace appeared and summoned them back in.

When Freddy, Vivian, and Ariana had returned to their seats, she began.

"Mr. Maraj, I believe you have something to say."

"Right. Okay." On the screen, Sal was framing his face with his pointer fingers, his thumbs touching under his chin. "We would like to seek resolution through an insurance claim. KiTov will hopefully get money back both from our insurance policy and their own. And Freddy, you'll be done with all of this, as long as you cooperate with us through that investigation."

Freddy clasped his hands together and slightly dipped his head in Sal's direction.

"And again," he continued. "I'm sorry." Freddy was expressionless except for biting his lip again. He offered no response. No resolution.

Vivian scanned the room. On the big screen, she noticed that Sal's hair had become more disheveled than she remembered. In the video box next to Sal, Avner was looking at his watch, seeming beyond ready for his next meeting.

Next, Vivian's gaze fell on Gordy. She noticed the dark lines around his eyes, and tried to summon empathy for him. It did not seem as though the partnership between these two companies would survive all of this. She spent a moment wishing Gordy well in her mind. Then, Vivian let the relief set in. And she hoped that Freddy was able to feel some of it too.

The consolation was both great and minimal. Humanoid robots would still someday be used by the Israel Defense Forces and other formidable armies across the world. Humans with more power would still find ways to oppress those with less of it. Hurricanes would continue to hit the coasts with growing force and frequency. And tech companies would keep building their escape hatches to Mars for when, they believed, the chaos was no longer controllable.

And yet. Today was a win. Vivian would take it.

Sal officially dropped the charges. Freddy officially quit.

On the way out of Leviathan Labs, Vivian felt the heat of the sun cut through the cool air. "What do you think you'll do next?" she asked Freddy.

"I think it's time to do work that means something *here*," he said. "On planet Earth."

CHAPTER FORTY

THE SOCIAL HALL of Beth Abraham was speckled with hundreds of used paper cups, Legos, other mismatched toys, and mostly deflated air mattresses. After the floodwaters had receded and power had been returned to most neighborhoods of the city, and after residents were able to get back into their homes and assess the damage—basements needing repair, trees fallen in dangerous spots—a crew of volunteers had returned to the synagogue to clean up the mess.

The usual suspects, Vivian thought to herself. Tamar was leading a deep clean of the kitchen, Vera was running around moving piles of supplies into the storage closet. But several people who had stayed at Beth Abraham during the storm and were not members, including Millie from Two Rivers, had also returned to assist. They were spread out across the synagogue doing whatever Raymond directed them to do.

Flora and Ben were next to arrive. Vivian put Ben on Lego collection and assigned Flora the task of gathering the air mattresses and piling them in a corner of the social hall. In the same corner, Vivian was stacking up the laundered bedsheets, none of which seemed to match.

"Where will it all go?" Flora asked, hoisting a mattress onto the growing mountain of deflated beds.

Vivian wiped her hands. "Karla said the city is going to send people to put them into storage. You know, for next time."

"Next time, huh?"

"Yeah," Vivian said. "But the city did a good job preparing for it, and at least we'll be as ready as we can in the future." She bent over, shaping the sheets into more orderly stacks.

"I don't know how we can all keep making it through," Flora said. "Sure, Beth Abraham is still standing, and my house downtown is mostly fine. But my students who live in the areas that got the worst of it are telling me that their places are in bad shape. I still haven't even heard from some of them. I don't know how their families will be able to survive another one of these."

Vivian stood still. What Flora said was true. Beth Abraham was okay. Her house was okay, besides for the plants that she and Karla had put in their window boxes, which had been destroyed by the water and winds. But so many other people in Providence—in the surrounding towns—did not have the same kind of luck or resources. Or insurance.

"I guess we continue to work for better support…and policies too," Vivian said.

"And expand the eruv whenever we can."

"Amen to that. We certainly expanded ours during this storm. And we'll keep doing that. We'll keep figuring out ways to take care of each other and share what we've got."

"Easier said than done," Flora said with a raised eyebrow. "But I do know students whose families are getting help from the city to fix up their houses. So that's something."

Vivian felt a confusing expression cross her face, like a smile and frown all at once. They both continued their tasks.

"Vivian?" Flora said.

She turned around.

"I was thinking about the future during the storm." Flora paused and sat on an air mattress that still had a little air left. "I think I want to be a rabbi."

Vivian's smile-frown quickly reshaped into a wide grin. "Wow! *Flora*," she said. "That's amazing! You'd be such a phenomenal rabbi."

"Thanks for saying that," Flora said. "I like teaching; sometimes I'd even say I love it. But I want to be able to support and challenge people and be there for them in the fullness of their lives. And during the storm, I could see glimmers of that." Flora paused. She rubbed her forehead. "I'm just scared that I'll never know enough."

Vivian sat down next to her, finding her balance on the slowly sinking pile of mattresses. "I still feel that way all the time," she said. "But Flora, you know far more than a lot of rabbis. There are so many kinds of wisdom that spiritual leaders need. Especially these days. I mean, the rabbis of the Talmud weren't dealing with a climate emergency, or the destruction and inequality wrought by late-stage capitalism, or a robot takeover. And this storm made it clear that you have phenomenal pastoral skills. You don't need me to tell you this, but you have so much to offer." She put her hand on Flora's shoulder. "Let me know if you need a recommendation for rabbinical school, okay?"

"Oh, you're on my list," Flora said.

"Whatever community you end up in would be so lucky to have you." Vivian planted one hand on the ground, heaving herself up from the squishy mattress stack. "If only you were already ordained, you could be Beth Abraham's second rabbi."

"That's so sweet," Flora said. "I don't know if I could lead this kind of community, though." She examined the room. "Don't get me wrong—I love Beth Abraham, as you know. But there's got to be others out there where the rabbi doesn't need to spend so much time reworking the existing patriarchal systems. And where Jews who aren't white could feel more at home—even build the community from the ground up."

Vivian tried to picture the community Flora was describing.

"I hear about such awesome projects on the Jews of Color listserv I belong to," Flora continued, "so I know it's possible."

Vivian couldn't help but grin at that. Another win for the list-servs. Flora unplugged a large mattress, which let out a burst of air. "And being here during the storm was a strange taste of what could be. I just want that to be available beyond when disaster strikes."

To Vivian, Flora's hazy vision sounded like exactly what was needed. In fact, it sounded like what the rabbis sought to do in the aftermath of the destruction of the second temple. "*Ken yehi ratzon,* may it be so," Vivian said. "If we're in the same city, maybe I'll secretly come to your community on my weekends off."

Flora heaved the last air mattress onto the pile. They both surveyed the social hall, now mostly empty save for a number of pesky Legos that Ben was still chasing down.

"Let's not get too ahead of ourselves here," Flora said.

Vivian noticed Tamar and Raymond heading her way. She hugged Flora and walked toward them, still dreaming about what the future might hold.

Tamar's eyes were glued to her clipboard. "Okay, let's review!" she said, jolting Vivian back to reality. "Kitchen? Check!" Tamar drew a checkmark on her list. "City supplies ready for collection?"

"Check," Vivian said, pointing to two separate corners of the hall.

"I've talked with our contact at City Hall." Raymond said, winking at Vivian. "Someone should be coming to pick it all up tomorrow."

They reviewed the rest of their list. Check, check, check. Tamar exhaled. "We did it!" She looked back and forth between Raymond and Vivian and then reached out both hands for high-fives. They indulged her. "Thank you for all you each did," Vivian added. "It was an honor to be a part of it."

"You know," Raymond said. "Between being here nonstop last week and spending every free moment this week doing cleanup for my house and helping my neighbors with theirs, I could use an extended vacation." He massaged his lower back with one hand. "I was talking to Mac last night, and he said his team on the farm could use extra hands getting ready for winter."

"Are you sure that counts as a vacation?" Vivian asked.

Raymond chuckled. "Enough of one, at least."

"You should take the time you need," Vivian said. She turned toward Tamar. "As board president, how does that sound to you?"

"That sounds right," Tamar said. "And if you both agree to do a go-around with me right now of the most meaningful moment of the storm for you, I'll email the staff and board as soon as we're done."

CHAPTER FORTY-ONE

KARLA POINTED TO an open bench under an oak tree in the park outside City Hall. Carrying their takeaway boxes of Tibetan food, she and Nona headed toward it and sat down. Most of the leaves had already fallen off the tree branches, but enough remained to create a panorama of fall colors.

A few weeks after Vincenzo's hit, much of the newer or renovated construction was in adequate shape, but there were patches of the city that required substantial repair. In response, with support from newly received FEMA funds, the Heath administration had kept open a few of the shelter sites for those who were still awaiting the necessary fixes, and subsidized hotel stays for those with longer delays.

Recovery was going to take much more work than preparation had. But the two could also go hand in hand. Karla was now heading an effort to secure private money to be invested in Providence's future resiliency. She was spending a lot of time consulting with her ICAN colleagues, many of whom had, over the years, succeeded in raising sizeable capital for climate adaptation projects.

Another idea straight from the ICAN listserv was to buy up old delivery trucks and offer them to local restaurant owners for cheap, allowing affected businesses to stay afloat while their brick-and-mortar locations awaited repairs. Luckily for the staff that worked at City Hall, a handful of delicious food trucks had set up shop just outside their offices.

Karla's boss had never invited her to lunch before, but surviving Vincenzo—and helping so many others to survive it—seemed to have ushered in a new era in their work together.

"I got a call last week from a contact in D.C. who works at FEMA," Nona said after settling into her seat. "They offered me a job directing federal storm preparedness."

"Wow," Karla said. "Congratulations!" Nona took several sips from her sparkly mug and didn't reply. "Um…are you going to take it?"

Still nothing. Karla listened to the chirping of a few very loud birds hidden in a nearby tree.

"I think I'm going to say no," Nona finally said. Another pause. More chirping. "We've figured out a lot here. And Rhode Island is my home. The home of my ancestors, too. I feel responsible to it."

Karla bobbed her head slowly up and down, trying to summon an appropriate response. Just then, she heard her name.

"Nona, Karla. Hi!" said a voice behind them, interrupting

nothing. Karla turned around and saw Clarissa Fox approaching. "Mind if I join you?" Nona smiled and shifted toward one side of the bench to make room, motioning Karla to follow suit.

"Still wavering on your decision, Nona?" Fox asked as she sat down.

MacLean choked on a bite. "Um, I was just, uh…starting to update Karla on the situation."

"Oops." Fox shrugged her shoulders, seemingly unconcerned. "Well, Karla," she continued, fixing her with a steady gaze. "Maybe you can help me convince Nona that this is an amazing opportunity. Not just for her, but for the whole country, which would benefit from her incredible leadership and wisdom."

Karla—wedged onto a small bench between two of her biggest role models—looked back and forth from one to the other. She had no clue about the right answer to this trick question.

Fox sighed. "Nona, these chances don't come around all the time," she said, leaning over Karla to address her. "I respect your decision to stay if it's the right thing. But we all know that you'd have a huge impact on so many parts of this country if you took the job.

"Think of what you could do with that role. Think about climate resiliency—in Indigenous communities, in Black and Brown communities, in poor communities. We still have time to shape a better future, and you can help us do that. You know you can. You already do."

"I agree with Secretary Fox," Karla blurted out. Nona turned to her. "And I, uh, I also respect whatever you decide to do," she added.

Clarissa Fox—a likely next mayor of Providence, according

to many—elbowed Karla. She was officially trapped. Perhaps it was best to say nothing more.

Nona shook her head. She looked almost—could it be?—confused. Karla had certainly never seen *that* before.

"You make some good points, Clarissa," she said finally. "You know, my daughter has been saying the same things."

Allowing herself a smile, Karla wondered what Winona MacLean's daughter must be like.

CHAPTER FORTY-TWO

FREDDY STEPPED TOWARD the wall to get a better view. He was standing in the lobby of a company called Kaleidoscope Solutions, in a town just west of Boston, peering at a display of photographs hung closely together.

In each picture, there were people, *real* people, standing knee-deep in water next to a large piece of machinery with what looked like tanks of liquid on both sides. These pictures had not been captured by a privately hired PR firm, or formed with stock figures on a fancy graphic design program. They accompanied a newspaper article on the wake of a recent hurricane in Florida, where one of Kaleidoscope's products, which could sufficiently filter storm water and then store and distribute it to residents, was being put to use.

Freddy nodded slowly. *Yes. This.* He stepped back and looked around, surveying the rest of the scene. Like Leviathan's head-quarters, the building was a renovated warehouse, but this one was smaller, with less fancy lighting and softer paint colors. Heavy concrete beams crisscrossed the ceiling and walls.

"Freddy Fuentes!" shouted an enthusiastic voice. He smiled as Aisha Mitchell, an old friend from graduate school, came into view.

Aisha was on the team that had birthed Kaleidoscope, with the goal of building robotic technologies to address climate change. Back in school, Freddy and Aisha had been a part of a crew of engi-neers that were sure they wanted to build and program machines that would make things better—like *actually* better. They took on pro bono projects to do just that, building assistive technologies to help under-resourced kids with disabilities learn at home better, and widening the access to broadband internet in several rural towns a few hours from their school.

After graduation, it had been easy for Freddy and other engi-neering friends to get swept up into jobs promising amazing sala-ries and benefits at places where the leadership seemed to say the right words, even if they never quite matched those words with their actions and work.

But Aisha was different. Even before graduating, she had cul-tivated several investors through an HBCU alumni network and lined up funding for a start-up focusing on climate adaptation and resilience in vulnerable communities.

Freddy grinned and hugged her.

They caught up a bit, sharing updates on their families and

on how they had fared during Vincenzo. It turned out that the current storm season was a big one for Kaleidoscope, which was beta-testing new projects in several southern cities.

"Let me give you the grand tour!" Aisha led them swiftly toward the labs, introducing Freddy to several people along the way.

They soon landed in a sprawling room with vestiges of old machines strewn about on desks and all over the floor, and a bunch of electrical cords running across the ceiling. "This is the project I was telling you about on the phone," Aisha said, stretching out her arms to showcase what appeared to be a pile of used train parts. "It doesn't look like much—"

"Yet!" Aisha and Freddy said simultaneously. Aisha wagged her finger at her friend gleefully.

They walked over to a table on which an enormous set of plans was splayed out. "Our current vision for this project is to utilize the infrastructure from electrical bus lines to host a network of emergency-response vehicles that could function during a storm and outlast the losses in power." Freddy leaned closer to Aisha as she continued to explain.

"The hope is to partner with municipal and state governments, given that sharing public infrastructure would make things a lot easier for us. And it would mean that we could leverage our investments to improve the city's key assets, too. Like public transportation."

"That's *genius*," Freddy said, folding his arms, taking it all in.

"We have a government affairs team that focuses on building those partnerships," Aisha continued. "Cambridge and Boston are in, and we're working on Miami and Austin."

"I know folks in Providence who might be interested!"

"Wonderful! I'll connect you with the people to talk to about that." Aisha paused. "I should probably say: We move quickly around here. Our internal motto is 'just the right amount of fast to fix things.'" Freddy chuckled. "We're growing a lot, and we need people with the skills but also with the vision, and, frankly, the right priorities. And I think you would be a great fit, Freddy."

"Thank you, Aisha," Freddy said, bringing his hand to his heart. It would be easier to work fast, he thought, when a part of him wasn't afraid of the mission. "And it sounds like you are looking to hire more than just one engineer?"

"Definitely. If you've got more people who fit the bill and are committed to doing good work, send them our way!"

Freddy thought of Jacqueline, who had also recently quit Leviathan Labs. And then he thought of Didi, who had practically dreamed up a Kaleidoscope invention in a few sleepless hours in a storm shelter.

"What about high school internships?" he asked. "Is that something we—I mean Kaleidoscope—could do?"

"Yes! We just started taking on interns this year. Young people have learned the tricks of the trade so fast, and we want to take advantage of that."

Freddy turned in a slow circle, taking in the scene. He could feel a different energy in this building, around these people doing such important work to make things better on the planet where humans already lived.

He thought about the moment when he, Camille, and Xiomara had returned to their home after the storm. Freddy and Camille had stopped in their tracks as they walked in the door, faces dropping as they took in the inches of water on the floor. The cleanup would require a lot of time and money.

But Xo had continued toddling through the water, unfazed, and too fast for her parents to stop her. She was the first one who made it to the living room sofa, which she managed to climb up and sit down on. "Ussy! Ussy!" she had said, patting the empty spots next to her.

"Is she calling us wussies?" Freddy asked Camille.

Camille had laughed, wiping tears away. "No, Fred. You're so freaking paranoid. She's saying 'tushy, tushy,' you know, just like what we say to get her to sit down."

Xo had pounded on the cushions again, repeating her demand. "Ussy!" Freddy had reached for Camille's hand.

Now, standing in the headquarters of Kaleidoscope Solutions, Freddy felt far less dread for his child's future, and for his own, than he had been feeling—even if he wouldn't have admitted it—for quite some time.

CHAPTER FORTY-THREE

A S VIVIAN WALKED up the pathway, Congregation Beth Abraham looked almost as it had before Vincenzo, except for a damaged spot on the roof on which a small tree had fallen. A permanent fix would take a while, but Alton could keep an eye on it while Raymond was on vacation in Georgia. And the building had certainly been through worse, she thought, remembering the sight of smoke billowing from the sanctuary on a spring Shabbat evening six years earlier.

The synagogue's interior was back to normal, too—although when Vivian looked closely, there were vestiges of the shelter operation in a corner here, on a shelf there. One time, when she needed a book from the very back of the library, she'd stumbled on a sleeping bag and a half-drunk plastic cup of water tucked beyond the final row of books. Her heart warmed, thinking back to the temporary community that sought refuge during the hurricane, and imagining who might have grabbed a nap in this nook of the building.

While she was watching her congregation, and the whole city, put itself back together again, Vivian had kept wondering about the idea that she and Karla had come up with together: *a prayer for the city*. Words of petition to tether her and her community and offer them a well of strength when the moment called for it.

And then, a few days after the waters had receded, it came to her. A prayer—a plea—that gave voice to what they all feared, hoped and needed. Stopped still in the depleted produce section at the grocery store, Vivian had typed furiously into her phone. *"May residents of all races and creeds forge a common bond to banish all selfishness and bigotry…. Protect us from storms of all types in whose path we may be, now and in the future…. Remember your promise to Noah never to destroy the world again."*

The words poured out.

She had read the whole thing several times over, swaying side to side, as she stood in the checkout line. When she got home, she had dropped her grocery bags by the front door and immediately transferred the file to her computer, reading it again on a screen that was slightly more capable of containing all the meaning the words held.

She had emailed it to Beth Abraham's ritual team. They loved it. Tamar had been the first to propose that they incorporate it into the Shabbat service over the next few weeks, try it out, and then decide on next steps.

And so, in the aftermath of so much disaster, Vivian was feeling strangely hopeful—a feeling she had carried with her into the board meeting at which she now found herself.

Most of Beth Abraham's board members had returned to Providence, and they were gathered around a few tables pushed together in the multi-purpose room. Joseph, back from Israel, was present too.

"It's been a while since we've all been together, and a lot has happened," Tamar said. "Let's do a straightforward go-round prompt: How's everyone doing?"

"It was all just...a lot," Joel Fishman started off. "We left in such a hurry to get to my daughter and her family in Chicago." He pulled at his hair. "And there's some damage at our house. But we'll, uh, we'll manage."

A few people who had also evacuated followed Joel, and they shared similar experiences.

Next up was Flora. "A family I know through my work ended up staying here during the hurricane, and they wanted me to pass along their thanks to the community for the support." She presented a card and passed it around the table. Vivian sighed happily, her shoulders loose. Flora continued, "I'm proud of what Beth Abraham was able to do for the city."

"Me too!" Tamar broke in, disrupting the usual go-round procedures in her excitement. "I never realized how much a shul could be a resource for the whole community."

As more people shared and Vivian's attention shifted to each speaker, she spotted a pile of Band-Aids, water and aspirin on a high shelf. A smile spread across her face.

"So, there is still some rebuilding to do," Tamar said, jumping into the agenda of the meeting, her tone a bit more somber. "And we don't know yet what insurance will cover. And Raymond is going to be out for a few weeks, and—"

Joseph spoke up. "I could put in a call to our former president, Harry Mermelstein, who negotiated our insurance policy once upon a time. He might be up for liaising with them."

Vivian thought back to the years she had spent sparring with Harry when he held the board presidency. But she also remembered all the ways that his business sense had benefited the community. Rather than let her criticisms of him take hold in her mind, she summoned gratitude, gratitude for those moments when just the right person could step up into the role they were suited to play.

"I think that's a great idea, Rabbi," Shlomo Seidel said. Tamar nodded, Vivian nodded, and others around the table followed suit. Tamar exhaled deeply.

"You know, this was really something," Joel Fishman said, "the way the community came together and acted so fast. But do we think this was a one-time thing, or are we are going to have to do this again?"

For a moment, the room was quiet.

"We can't know for sure," answered Vera, who had stayed in touch with various coordinators at City Hall. "But now that we have transformed this place into a shelter once, I think we'd be ready to do that again if we're needed."

"And there is more to do in the aftermath, too," Tamar said. "Rabbi Vivian shared with me that a church closer to the river has asked us to use our space while they make repairs. Their building absorbed much more damage than ours."

"There is nothing new under the sun, huh?" said Joel. In the wake of the fire, Beth Abraham had had its own experience of needing to borrow space, and the Unitarian Universalist congregation down the street had provided it.

As Vivian refolded her legs under the tablecloth, her left foot collided with something. She peered under the wide table and discovered three empty juice boxes, some granola-bar wrappers, a deck of cards, and a tiny Mickey Mouse blanket. She made a mental note to clean up what appeared to be a kids' storm fort later.

"That sounds good to me," Shlomo Seidel said. "It's important for us to open our doors to those in need." Everyone turned to Shlomo. "Like Abraham in Parshat Vayera!"

Vivian wondered if he was about to make a joke, but he didn't. Maybe the Torah portions at the beginning of the cycle were of particular inspiration to Shlomo—something she should remember for the times in the future when she'd be searching for a common language with him. Or maybe he was just changing, becoming more open, like so many in this time of crisis.

Shlomo scowled. "Why is everyone looking at me like that?" Vivian quickly relaxed her facial muscles as several others also reconfigured their faces in an attempt to cover up their astonishment.

Tamar gracefully moved the conversation forward, initiating a plan to find out more details about the church's needs. Hebrew school happened on Sunday mornings, but not in the sanctuary. If other communities were searching for a temporary home, the Beth Abraham leadership could work it out.

"Next agenda item," Tamar said. "Let's revisit the job description for our second rabbi." She passed around a stack of sheets and gave everyone a few moments to revisit them. "Personally, I think that if storms aren't going away," she continued, "and if we'll need to continue to respond to these challenges, then it does seem like we could benefit from someone who is committed to the vision of, in Shlomo's words, 'opening our doors to those in need.'"

"I agree," Vera said, "though I don't know if that's something that can be adequately conveyed in a job description."

"We may just need to find the *right* person," said Joel. "And work out the details later."

"Exactly," Tamar said. "Like when we met with Rabbi Vivian in the interview process."

"Right—we just knew," Joel responded, offering Vivian a warm grin.

Vivian saw Joseph nodding too. She hadn't heard any of this before.

"What do you think, Rabbi?" someone asked Joseph.

This was usually a moment when Vivian would activate her internal defense strategy, but she noticed that in place of it was curiosity. This time, she wanted to know what he would say.

"I think that in this ever-changing world"—Joseph spoke slowly, as if he was deliberately choosing each word—"we need to be open and flexible. Change can take time in our community. In our tradition. But ultimately, we do what we need to survive."

Vivian breathed deeply, taking in Joseph's words.

A memory came to her. Soon after the hurricane, she had gone to visit Gert Fineman, one of the oldest members of Beth Abraham, to make sure that she was okay and had what she needed.

Gert had mentioned to Vivian that Joseph had paid her a visit every month for the last several years, ever since her husband passed away. He had even called to check in on her right after the storm, in what was the middle of the night in Jerusalem. And Gert told Vivian a story she had never heard before.

In the early '90s, Gert's son, Henry, had come out as gay. She had mostly been understanding, though it took getting used to. But her husband, Leo, had a very hard time accepting it; there were years in which he did not say a word to Henry. Gert turned to Joseph, and Joseph talked to Leo. And to Henry. Gert didn't remember the specifics of what he said to whom, but after that, Leo warmed up to his son. And for the rest of his life, he made moves to accept Henry and the family he later built.

Joseph is a good rabbi, Vivian thought. *He means a lot to a lot of people.* To her, too. He had also checked in on her after the storm, apologizing for his initial skepticism about the shelter plan and letting her know that he was grateful for her leadership. The tension remained, but it was certainly loosening a little.

Perhaps it was easier to think and feel such things now that the two of them had crossed some threshold and his retirement felt so close. But Vivian knew that what she was able to do at Beth Abraham—and what others would do after her—had been set in motion because of Joseph. From generation to generation.

As the board moved on with plans to start the hiring process, she basked in a feeling that was rare at these meetings: satisfaction. She felt the energy of agreement—maybe even of a shared vision—in the room. From Vera. From Flora. From Shlomo. From Joseph. From her team.

. . .

On the way out of the meeting, Vera pulled Vivian and Flora aside.

"I've been thinking a lot about the next stage of the bonds campaign," she said.

"Oh my gosh, right," Vivian said. "To be honest, given everything else going on, I'd almost forgotten. What are you thinking?"

"Well," Vera started, clasping her hands together. "I've been learning about an amazing organization that invests in community projects in Israel *and* Palestine. They work on improving environmental conditions and water access in both, and then they help to promote collaboration between all the different leaders."

"Hmm," Vivian said.

"What I'm thinking is, what if we proposed alternating the Rosh Hashanah pitch each year between something local, like Rainbow Capital, *and* something like that, in Israel/Palestine?" Vera asked.

Vivian thought about it for a moment. She had been so set on shifting the focus of investment from Israel, turning her heart—and her community's—to their own neighborhood. But maybe this was exactly what they needed. She could also be flexible and open to the ideas of others…right?

"I love it," Flora said.

Vivian grinned. "Let's get that on a future agenda!" she said, feeling full of love and appreciation for these amazing teammates who pushed change forward.

"A lot seems possible around here these days," Vera said.

"It does, doesn't it?" said Flora.

And, to Vivian's surprise, she agreed with them.

CHAPTER FORTY-FOUR

VIVIAN SHIFTED AROUND her Bananagrams tiles. Glancing up from her own board for a moment, she saw that poor Karla had a whole lot of letters she hadn't placed yet: four I's, a few J's and P's, and a Z. Heather, on the other hand, was on top of her game. But then she was probably a lot less distracted.

"Peel!" Heather said, grabbing a new tile from the pile.

"Aha!" Vivian shouted. She had finally gotten the L she was waiting for. She swiftly reassembled her whole board, exiling many of the tiles to a pile of extras she would need to deal with later. But it was worth it: Right in the middle of her Bananagrams configuration was the word "ovulate."

Karla looked up from her board and over to Vivian's. She burst out cackling.

"You can't fluster me!" Heather said, remaining determinedly focused on her own tiles.

They kept playing until the door opened and Paul stepped gingerly onto the porch.

"Well, that was, uh, weird," he said. "I left it on the bathroom counter."

"Damn! I was doing so well." Heather rose hastily. "I guess we'll have to finish this game another day." She grabbed her tote bag from the chair's handle. "We're going to head out now, so you can, uh, you know...." She made an inscrutable gesture with her hands.

Paul, Heather, and Addie had come over for dinner. And then, afterwards, Paul had left them some of his genetic material, so that Karla and Vivian could try, for the first time, to get pregnant.

At many points during this day, Vivian had found herself laughing unprompted. About living in a world where robots could make complex decisions. And where a mustard jar and syringe could be vital parts of the reproductive process. What a strange time this was turning out to be. She had worried for her potential children, and then she had calmed down, reminding herself that there were so many good and wise people in the world planning for the future and for their survival.

"Yes...we know, Heather," Vivian said. Karla looked up as she quickly collected the game pieces. "Thank you, Paul," she said, meeting his eyes with a smile.

"Anytime!"

They all chuckled. "Come on now, honey," Paul continued. "Let's retrieve our sleeping child and leave them to...." No one seemed to be able to identify the right words.

Heather saved them from trying, her face softening.

"Good luck," she said. "Or—what does one say at this occasion?"

"Actually," Vivian said, "I'm not sure what *one* says, but I know what I'd like to hear. Sometimes we say 'in a good time'—like, may it happen when it happens, whenever is right. In Hebrew, it's *b'sha'a tova*."

"Shana tova!" Paul and Heather said simultaneously. "Oh, we totally already knew that one," Paul added, looking pleased with himself.

"No, it's...well, I'll accept that," said Vivian. "Thanks, guys."

After Heather and Paul had carried a groggy Addie to their car, Karla and Vivian hurried to the bathroom and peered into the jar on the counter.

"So, um, we should get to it, huh?" Karla said.

"Wait," Vivian said. "One more thing before we do." She closed her eyes. She remembered learning from their internet research that there could be as many as 100 million potential sperm in each batch, and she brought her focus to the contents of the jar, wanting to bless it in her mind.

Beside her, Karla didn't miss a beat. "Oh right, of course," she said, squeezing Vivian's free hand. "Thank you, O Creator, for this gift of potential life."

CHAPTER FORTY-FIVE

WINTER WAS ON its way—hopefully free of unexpected storms, but who could really know. After all, disasters could come in so many forms. But for now, it was Shabbat, and Vivian and her community were together and safe.

After the Torah reading, Vivian stood up to recite the new Prayer for the City. It was the third time she had said it, and she was starting to anticipate the rhythm in the sanctuary, as if the recitation was already becoming commonplace. Each time the community prayed it, it got louder, the sound more cohesive.

Vivian had also sent it around to the Tekiyah listserv. Several rabbis had written back asking if they might use it, so she pictured the same process—of a new *minhag* forming—taking place in communities beyond Providence, too.

She took a deep breath and began, her congregants joining in.

"God and God of our ancestors, bless all the inhabitants of this city. May residents of all races and creeds forge a common bond to banish all selfishness and bigotry, to safeguard this land—the ancestral home of the Narragansett people—and our institutions, our homes, and the lives of all who live here, in this holy place. Protect us from storms of all types in whose path we may be, now and in the future. Endow us with the resolve to face any disaster that may come and to do our part to keep one another safe. And remember your promise to Noah never to destroy the world again. Grant us the foresight and wisdom to make the same promise with our own actions."

Vivian glanced up, finding that the words were already imprinted on her memory. In the seats in front of her, she saw Tamar, and Shlomo, and Vera, and Flora, and Gert Fineman.

"May we find comfort in You," they continued, "in our neighbors, and in one another. May we commit to the well-being of all who live in our city, now and in times of crisis. For as it is written in Jeremiah, 'Seek the welfare of the city to which I have exiled you and pray to God on its behalf; for in its prosperity, you shall prosper.'"

As she recited this new prayer, which might someday feel just as old as some others—even as old as the thirteenth century—Vivian looked over at Joseph. "May you grant us strength so that all may survive and all may prosper," they chanted in unison. "And let us say: Amen."

Echoes of amen reverberated through the sanctuary. Perhaps well outside of it, too.

ACKNOWLEDGMENTS

N OW THAT THIS second book has come to fruition, my cup is truly overflowing with gratitude. It has been a gift to return to such a supportive and wise community of friends and readers. To those who offered valuable and honest feedback on earlier drafts: Helen Bennett, Shahar Colt, Talie Lewis, Sunnie Rosenstein, Becca Thal and Ora Weiss. I am particularly grateful to Rachel Jacobson for generously sharing her knowledge and insight into the world of climate adaptation. And to Matt Goldfield for helping the robot storyline make any sense, given that it's a somewhat ridiculous undertaking to forefront robots when one doesn't know anything—like *anything* at all—about them.

To Anna Schnur-Fishman, whose editing and guidance has made the world of Rabbi Vivian Green one hundred times more vivid than it would have otherwise been. And certainly funnier. (If *spexting* ever becomes a thing, the record should show that it was Anna's *chiddush*/innovation!) To Brian Phillips, for the beautiful design and cover, which I hope people judge this book by.

To Harry Kemelman once again, whose Rabbi Small series remains my inspiration and invitation to write.

To Liz Aeschlimann, whose love language of astute feedback has come in handy on this project and made this book so much better. And to Raya Lev, who slept just enough in her first few months so that I could get this book to the finish line: Whatever the future holds, I am so grateful to be facing it with you.

This book is not an op-ed. It's not a policy proposal. It's fiction. An exploration and intersection of different experiences and points of view, some of which feel like mine and some of which don't; some of which seem righteous—or circling around it at least—and some of which don't; some of which I've known in my bones for years, and some of which took a while to crystallize. This imagining, this grappling, this practice of writing and rewriting and rewriting again daily, has been a balm in a time of constant change and upheaval and feeling like I should have it all figured out. And so, last but not least, to fiction, to storytelling, to building (sort of) alternate realities, I extend my abiding love and appreciation.

Printed in the USA
CPSIA information can be obtained
at www.ICGtesting.com
LVHW040535220823
755857LV00004B/688